Kinky Companions

Kinky Companions

Kinky Companions 4

Alex Markson

This paperback edition 2020

First published by Parignon Press 2020

Copyright © Alex Markson 2020

Alex Markson asserts the moral right to be identified as the author of this work in accordance with the Copyright, Designs and Patents Act 1988

ISBN: 979 8 58 007126 8

Chapter 1 – Lucy

As I arrived at my counsellor's house, I was more relaxed than I had been for the last few sessions. Jenny welcomed me, and when we'd settled ourselves, I told her what had happened. How Sally and I had revealed our love for each other; how we'd both been scared to voice our feelings, fearful about what it would mean.

"How do you feel now?" Jenny asked.

"It's such a weight off my mind. At least it's out in the open; there are no secrets anymore, but I'm still a bit confused."

"About what?"

"Well, it's not a common situation, is it? I know it happens but how does it work? The more I think about it, the more questions I have."

"Have the three of you sat and talked?"

"No. Sally suggested it, but I suspect they're waiting for me, letting me think things through. Marcus is always so conscious of other people's feelings."

"Isn't that a good thing?"

"Yes. But sometimes I need someone to give me a nudge. Someone to guide me, like you."

Jenny smiled and shook her head.

"I don't see my role as guiding you," she said, "but I know what you mean. Perhaps you need to take the plunge and sit them down."

She was right and I knew it. Things had been so much better since Sally and I had opened to each other; Marcus was the last piece of the puzzle. I was staying with them the following weekend and I'd have to bite the bullet.

I was staying at their place because I'd agreed to take a stall at the 'kinky market', as we were calling it. Marcus and Sally spent Saturday afternoon helping me get everything ready for the following day. I hadn't been sure about taking my pictures to the play party, but they'd persuaded me to try. I was originally going to take fifteen or twenty items, but I'd ended up taking fifty to my framer to get them mounted. It was a good thing I knew him well, given the subject matter he was forced to look at for hours while he worked on them.

Marcus had sat with me the week before and helped me produce notices to go on the stand, with my name and an email address we created for my artwork. We made little fliers with one of my pictures and contact information. He'd even got me a card reader and helped me set up an online account to take payments on my phone. I thought we were wasting our time.

We had a long debate about pricing. When I'd put my work into a gallery, I'd gone with the prices the owner had suggested. I found it difficult to value my own creations. I'd been pleasantly surprised, but they'd been more completed works and less controversial subjects.

The items I was taking here were mixed: some mere sketches, some washed, and some more complete. But they all shared a common subject, the human body. From sensuous outlines to explicit action. I had no idea how much to charge. In the end, Marcus and Sally helped me divide them by size and complexity into three ranges and we priced them accordingly. We loaded everything into one of their cars and sat down, exhausted.

"Takeaway?" Sally suggested. "I don't feel like cooking."

As we ate, we chatted about the play parties and whether the kinky market idea would prove successful. I listened more than I talked.

"Tense?" Marcus asked me suddenly. I frowned, frustrated he'd spotted my nervousness.

"Yes. You know how scared I get when people look at my work. This is a whole different level."

"Because of the subjects?"

"Yea, absolutely."

"Luce, I doubt anyone there will bat an eyelid at any of these. Think about it; these are some of the most open-minded, genuine people you'll ever meet."

That was true. The members of the group I'd met had been unfailingly welcoming and friendly. But I was still scared.

"Anything else on your mind?" Sally asked flatly, watching my reaction closely. I saw a look of concern on her face and took a deep breath.

"Yes," I replied. "I need to talk to you; both of you."

"Shall we move from the table?"

We moved to the sitting room, and it was only later I realised Sally and Marcus didn't sit together, risking me feeling like the odd one out. We ended up on a sofa each.

"Want to start?" Sally asked quietly.

"I … I don't know what I want to say, really. I'm still trying to understand how this is going to work. What the rules are."

"Why have rules?" Marcus asked.

"Well, perhaps rules is too strong. But I don't want to say or do the wrong thing."

"Luce," he said, sitting forward. "Have you said or done the wrong thing up to now?"

"No, I don't think so."

"Exactly. Just carry on being yourself. That's why Sally loves you." It was the first time I'd heard him say it, and it made me shiver. "It's why I love playing with you. If you start changing, we might not fancy you anymore." He was smiling, and I returned the smile, relaxing a little. "All I ask is we use our common sense. Let's be open with each other. If any of us is unhappy about something we owe it to the other two to talk about it."

"Agreed," I replied.

"Anything else?" he asked Sally.

"Well," she said. "We've already agreed the practical stuff, so that won't change. We're bound to come across little bumps in the road and we'll have to deal with them when they occur."

"Okay," I said, accepting they were dealing with the situation better than I was. "I still can't work out how calmly you're both taking this. Particularly you, Marcus."

"I love Sally and she loves me. I'm happy to share that love with you. I don't know what that says about me, but frankly, I don't care what anyone outside thinks. We both make her happy, and you and I seem to be enjoying the situation as well."

"I know," I replied. "It almost seems too … perfect."

"Oh, it's a relationship," he replied. "We'll hit problems; you can count on it. But with three such clever people, how can we fail to resolve them?"

We spent some time opening about any fears we had, things that might go wrong. But in the end, Marcus was right; they were issues which any relationship might face. Very few were the result of there being three people in this setup. I realised I was simply afraid of the unknown. I also found out they'd been thinking the same things I had. I wasn't alone.

When we finished talking, we took comfort breaks and Sally opened another bottle of wine. Filling my glass, she winked at me.

"Right, Luce. Let's get drunk and see if Marcus can handle both of us."

Marcus was already dressed and waiting upstairs. We'd sent him away because we were getting into our new corsets. We'd collected them during the week, and I had to admit falling in love with mine. It was sumptuous. We already knew how well they fitted, but when Helen, our corsetiere friend, showed us the final product with the finishing touches, it blew us away.

Mine was deep red, with tiny roses embroidered all over it, all joined by light green trailing foliage. Sal's was green with an overlay of intricately embroidered black lace. They gave us both a beautiful cleavage in an old-fashioned way, without being overly revealing. Helen had even supplied two pairs of knickers each, in different cuts and embroidered to match. All we had to do was go out and treat ourselves to new shoes and stockings.

We didn't tighten the corsets fully, as we had to get all my artwork into the venue and set it up. We'd adjust each other when we'd sorted that out. We threw on dresses and joined Marcus, who was clearly disappointed not to get a preview.

"Patience, darling," Sal said. "It'll be worth the wait."

We arrived early and lugged all my stuff inside. Matt, Yas and Dave were there, organising everything. They'd opened an area which normally wasn't used, so there was plenty of room. I was surprised how many people were already setting up; it seemed a popular idea. But I did wonder; if everyone had a stand, who would there be to look around and buy?

We each got a table and a display stand to hang things from. It was more than enough. I'd brought half a dozen framed works to hang as finished examples, which we arranged on the display. We laid some of the mounted pictures on the table, alongside boxes containing the rest. Leaving Marcus as security guard, we went to finish our attire.

When we entered the ladies changing area, we came across Helen adjusting Penny's outfit. She looked fabulous, and a little exposed.

"Hello, you two," Penny said, as Helen carried on tightening the lacing on her corset. It was blue satin, but it ended under her breasts, which were only covered by black lace, and this had also been used to fashion a short frill around the bottom edge. Helen greeted us and gave a last satisfied tug on Penny's lacing.

"You'll do," she said. "Now, let's sort you two out."

We removed our dresses, and Helen and Penny fussed around us, getting everything exactly as they wanted it. The result was tight, and I felt a little uncomfortable, but when we looked in the mirror, we had to admit we looked good.

Helen herself outshone us all. She was wearing a corset dress. It was a deep russet colour and complimented her hair, flowing loose over her shoulders, to perfection. The tight bodice gave way to a long, loose skirt, hanging perfectly to her ankles, and the whole thing was covered in intricate lace and embroidery.

She took a final look at us, a faint smile on her lips. I remembered Marcus's comments and wondered if she was looking at more than our clothes.

"Right," she said. "Try not to trip up, drop food on yourselves or generally mess things up."

With that, she sailed out of the room.

"Don't mind her," Penny said, giving us a hug and a kiss. "She's enjoying it really."

"You could have fooled me," Sal said.

"She's nervous."

"Does she get nervous?" I asked.

"Oh, yes. She's not always as confident as she appears." I'd wondered if that was the case. "She's not done anything like this for years. Her business is normally word of mouth and promoting herself – even to people she knows – doesn't come naturally."

We left the changing room and returned to the hall. It was already busy; it seemed people liked this new feature of the day.

"Did you take a stand?" Penny asked me.

"Yes, and I'm more nervous than Helen."

"It'll be brilliant; I'll come and see you later."

I headed for my stand and Sally went with Penny. When I arrived, Marcus was talking to a couple.

"Here's the artist," he said. "Lucy, two admirers." I saw his eyes taking in what I was wearing, and his expression told me he liked it.

We'd agreed I would use just my real first name. I still wasn't comfortable putting my full name to these subjects publicly. The couple said some positive things about my work and said they'd return later, but I wasn't confident.

Sally came back and handed me a wad of business cards.

"They're Helen's," she said. "If anyone admires our corsets, give them one and point them to her stand. How's it going?"

"A few people have stopped and looked."

"Plenty of time yet." She turned to Marcus. "Have you seen Penny?"

"No, not yet. I'm still admiring you two."

"Like them?" We did a synchronised twirl. His face was a picture.

"Breath-taking," he said. "You both look … mmm."

"Yup, I think he likes them," Sal said.

"How do they feel?" he asked.

"Tight," I said. "They certainly reduce your flexibility."

"That might be interesting," he replied.

"Don't go getting ideas, darling," Sal said. "Helen's warned us it's difficult to get stains out of all this embroidery."

"Then I'll be forced to watch you take them off."

"Or help us," I said, grinning as they both turned to look at me.

I made my first sale ten minutes later. I thought we were asking far too much and was prepared to haggle. A steady stream of people came to browse, and I relaxed as I got more and more positive reactions. Marcus and Sally made sure one of them stayed with me and were able to make introductions to lots of people, none of whom I knew. After a couple of hours, I'd made a few sales and not one person had tried to haggle.

Sally was with me on the stall when Marcus returned.

"Why don't you two go and have a look around? I'll mind the shop."

I needed the loo anyway, and we left him in charge. In the rest of the venue, things were proceeding as they had the first time I came. People milling around and events going on in the display area. Sally stopped and chatted to several people and introduced me to those I hadn't met before. Several admired what we were wearing, and we gave out a few of Helen's cards.

"Come on," she said. "Let's have a look around the other stands."

We wandered from stall to stall, Sally casting an interested eye over many of the items. I was intrigued, sometimes not even sure what I was looking at. She had a long conversation with the guy who had done the demonstration about clamps and came away with several items. My mind boggled while one or two other bits of me did their best to hide.

We ended up at Helen's stand. She was talking to a couple I'd noticed before. Around our age and dressed in a style reminiscent of burlesque. Helen saw us approaching.

"Ah," she said. "Perfect timing. My two models. I've completed these in the last few weeks."

She introduced us to the couple – Charlie and Moira - and we self-consciously let them take a closer look at our corsets. Moira was entranced; the dress she was wearing had a shaped bodice, but it was quite plain and didn't fit well. She asked if she could touch the material, the embroidery, the lace. Charlie was standing back, an amused smile on his face. Close up, we could see he was a fair bit older than Moira.

"These are beautiful, Charlie," she said. "Look how well they fit."

She asked us what they were like to wear, how they made us feel. I overheard Charlie talking to Helen about the process and eventually, the cost.

"Those are the most elaborate I've made for a while," I heard Helen say. "But I can work to most requirements."

"How much were these?" he asked. "If you don't mind me asking."

"Sally," Helen said. "Are you happy for me to reveal the price?"

"Of course," she replied.

I was as well. Sally hadn't told me, insisting mine was a birthday present. I had to stop myself gasping when she told Charlie they were over two thousand each. He didn't bat an eyelid, just got together with Moira and Helen to arrange an initial appointment. I glowered at Sally.

"Don't start," was all she said and gave me a quick kiss.

Penny returned from parading around handing out cards. She'd clearly enjoyed the attention she'd got. She was smiling broadly, and I could see her erect nipples peeking through the lace.

"Enjoying yourself?" Sally asked, staring straight at Penny's breasts. Penny looked down and blushed slightly.

"I don't know," Helen said behind us, having finished with Charlie and Moira. "Can't take her anywhere." But the look she shared with Penny was one of mutual affection.

"Have you seen Marcus?" Sally asked Penny.

"Only from a distance, earlier on."

"He's on Lucy's stand. Go and show him what you're wearing."

Penny looked at Helen, who nodded, and Penny strode off.

"I don't know what you three did to her," Helen said, looking down at her diary. "But since she got back from holiday, she's been something of a handful."

"Oh," Sal replied. "Sorry."

Helen stood and turned to us, a glorious smile on her face.

"I wasn't complaining."

She went to talk to someone looking at the pictures on her display stand as we shared a grin and headed back.

Chapter 2 – Marcus

"I'm not sure if Lucy has priced the framed pictures," I said. "They were designed as examples of the finished product."

"Pity, I love that one."

I spotted Sally and Lucy returning.

"Ah, we can find out, here's the artist now."

The girls slid in behind the table.

"Sal," I said. "You remember Sophia?"

"Of course, hello."

"And this is Lucy. Luce, Sophia gave the whip demo we told you about." They greeted one another. "Sophia has fallen in love with this picture and would like to know the price."

It was our picture of Sally's bum with cane welts. Lucy looked at me in panic.

"Well …" she stammered. "I …"

I looked at Sal and she gave a brief nod of assent.

"Lucy's unsure, Sophia, because Sally and I have had the picture on loan. But we're happy to let it go to another appreciative home."

Sophia looked at the picture again, then at Sally.

"Are you the subject?" she asked.

Sally flushed slightly.

"Possibly."

"Mmm, interesting," Sophia said. "Do you take commissions, Lucy?"

"Er, yes."

"Good. I may have one or two for you. In the meantime, how much for Sally's beautifully marked rear?"

Lucy looked at me; we hadn't thought about it.

"Make us an offer," I said.

Sophia took a long look at the picture and checked on the table to see what we were asking for those which were simply mounted. A lot more work had gone into the one we were discussing.

"Two hundred and fifty."

"Did you mind selling it?" Lucy asked when Sophia had taken her purchase away.

"No," I replied. "On the condition you do something to replace it."

"It'll be a pleasure. But two hundred and fifty? I couldn't believe it."

"Told you there'd be a market," Sal said.

"Have you sold many?" Lucy asked. I looked at the tally I'd been keeping.

"Sixteen."

"What?"

"And I've given your details to quite a few people."

She looked genuinely shocked.

Over the next couple of hours, we sold well over half the items Lucy had brought. By that time, we were tired and decided to call it a day. We packed up, said our goodbyes, and set off for home. On the way, Lucy tried to work out how much she'd taken. She counted the cash and recounted it. She checked the payment app and double-checked it. Then let out a little shriek. Sally winked at me.

"Well?"

"I don't believe it," Lucy said.

"How much?"

"Two thousand three hundred."

We were silent for a while, Sally and I leaving Lucy to let it sink in.

"Sal ..." Lucy eventually drawled.

"No," Sal replied. I didn't know what she meant.

"Half?"

"No."

Lucy tutted in the back; I was still at a loss and looked at Sal.

"She wants to pay for the corset," she said.

"Ah."

"All we want are a couple of pictures to fill the gaps we now have in the playroom."

There was a happier chuckle from the back.

"Know any willing models?"

***

My hand was aching. I'd been signing books for over an hour. Eva's secretary was smoothly laying down an open book, then removing it when I'd signed it. I was sure my signature was different in every one, and now it looked like an ageing spider falling down a flight of stairs.

I'd never understood signed books. Why did people want them? I'd been a reader all my life, and never once sought out a book signed by the author. But it was part of the plan we'd agreed, and Eva had had to work hard to persuade me to do anything at all.

Tonight was the official launch. 'A quiet little affair', she assured me. It was being held in a bookshop and I was making a short speech followed by a reading, before meeting and greeting … who? I wasn't sure.

I'd spent the morning being interviewed by a couple of book bloggers and two other people whose exact role I never did work out. It was the sort of thing I hated, answering the same questions four times. Utterly pointless.

We finally got to the end of the boxes, and I could put my pen down. I held my hand out and flexed my fingers, trying to feel them again without pain.

"All done?" Eva asked, coming into the spare office she'd commandeered for the exercise.

"If you find another box," I replied, "you can sign them."

"I hope you're going to be on your best behaviour this evening," she said. We'd worked each other out now and weren't tiptoeing around. Over the last few months, we'd called each other several impolite things, but we'd got to launch day unscathed.

"Don't bank on it," I replied.

"You'll enjoy it."

We glared at each other until she faltered.

"Well," she said. "At least pretend to enjoy it. Have you decided which passages you're going to read?"

"How about the copyright notice?"

She rolled her eyes and sat by the desk.

"I had a couple of ideas," she said.

I let her choose, she was used to these events. I'd never been to a book launch and had no idea what to expect. The passages she showed me seemed a good choice. They were short and dramatic and gave a true flavour of the book.

To be fair to Eva, she had impressed me. Once she got to work, I'd been provided with editing and proofing resources and all the admin had been taken care of. She'd done a lot of publicity and sent advance copies out. The feedback had been positive; at least, that's what she told me.

When I got back to the hotel to get ready for the evening, Sally had arrived. She gave me a big hug.

"Been busy?" she asked.

"Having the same conversation four times and signing a million books that'll end up getting pulped."

"Oh, dear. Someone's not a happy bunny."

"Sorry. I'm nervous, that's all."

"How long have we got?"

"A couple of hours. We need to be there at six."

"Right, let's see if I can find a way to relax you."

I did feel better as we made our way to the bookshop. When we arrived, Eva was waiting and introduced us to the manager. She led us upstairs to an area largely cleared of displays, with chairs dotted around and a low dais in the corner. There were two tables at the entrance. One had glasses lined up, with wine bottles and jugs of juice. The other had two stacks of Shadows of Gold on it.

"One pile you've signed," Eva said. "The others you can sign if people want them dedicated."

I groaned; she shook her head and went off to do whatever it was she did at these events. As the time neared, people started wandering in. I didn't know any of them and they didn't know me. Peter, my agent, appeared in something of a panic.

"I'm sorry I'm late, Marcus. I had an accident this afternoon and I've been sorting a few things out."

"Are you hurt?"

"No, no. No-one was injured. But my car's in a bit of a state. Come to think of it, so am I."

I introduced Sally and went to get him a drink; he looked as if he needed it. We kept him company and he gradually relaxed. From what he said, it didn't sound as if the accident was anything serious, but he was clearly shaken.

The room was quite full by this time, and my gut was beginning to remind me of the reality of the situation. In a few minutes, I was going to stand in front of this group of strangers and try to tell them how wonderful my book was. To be on the safe side, I went off to the loo.

I wasn't sure if the sight I returned to made me feel better or worse. Sally was still with Peter, but they'd been joined by Lucy, Mary, Ken, and Penny. They all greeted me rather formally, given the setting. I didn't have time to be astonished by their presence, as Eva came and ushered me towards the dais.

Getting everyone's attention, she thanked them for coming, outlined what was going to happen, and introduced me. I had my copy of the book in my hand, as well as a sheet of prompts. But as I walked forward, the hand was shaking, and I had to put it behind my back.

"Good evening," I began. Even I knew I sounded like a speak your weight machine. "I'm pleased to see you all here tonight, although those of you who write will know this is every author's nightmare. Talking to real people." I heard one or two laughs which were welcome. "I've been an author for some time, though you won't know my name because until now, I've been self-published."

A couple of whoops from the back made me smile. "And as we all know," I said, turning to Eva, "self-publishers don't exist as far as some people are concerned." She shook her head, smiling. "But I've been lucky enough to find someone who thought this book was worth a bigger audience, so here I am."

I gave them a brief outline of how the idea had come to me and how the story had developed into its final form. I kept it brief; they seemed interested, but I didn't want to overdo it. I read the passages we'd selected. My voice had recovered, and I hoped I did my writing justice. When I finished, I got a polite round of applause and Eva pointed out the signing area.

The shop had placed a till by the table; near enough to be seen, but far enough not to look too predatory. In the initial surge, many people picked up signed copies and a few bought blank ones, asking me to dedicate them to friends and family. Two or three surprised me by telling me they'd read some of my earlier work.

I wasn't sure how to react as the room emptied rapidly; was that a bad sign? Eva hovered nearby; whether to support me or to step in if I committed some faux pas, I wasn't sure. I turned to ask her how it had gone, only to see my support group standing by her. They were all smiling, and Sally blew me a kiss.

There were only a few people left now and I dealt with their requests and questions. One hovered at the back and when he reached the table, he introduced himself. I knew the name immediately; a man I'd known online for years. We'd occasionally shared our work and given each other moral support. He promised to send me a detailed review of Shadows of Gold.

I leaned back in my chair; it was all over. The bookshop staff started to clear things away. Penny came over and put two copies of my book in front of me.

"Can you dedicate them?" she asked. "One to Helen and one for me."

I thought about what to write. In one I wrote, 'Helen, this should make a nice sound if you catch her bum exactly right, Marcus', and in the other, 'Penny, don't ever change, Marcus'.

She read them, blushed a little and put them in her bag. I stood up, ready to leave. I'd had enough. Sally came over, put her arm around me and gave me a kiss.

"Proud of you," she said.

"Was it all right?"

"Yes. You were great."

"Not bad," Eva said, joining us. "I've seen a lot worse."

"Ready?" I asked.

"We're not finished yet," Sal replied. I looked at her and recognised her scheming face. She was up to something. We gave our thanks to the bookshop staff and followed Eva out of the building. She went a little way down the street and headed into a restaurant; I gave Sally a stern look.

"What have you two been up to?"

"I asked Eva to arrange a little get together so you could say thank you to everyone."

I hadn't even thought of it. I'd have thanked them in some way but had to admit this was a good idea. We were shown to a room with a buffet laid out and bottles of wine and beer. My gut had settled, and I was famished. There were a dozen of us, and I realised they were all waiting for me.

"This part of the evening has come as a surprise to me, though not," I said, narrowing my eyes at Eva, "to all of you. But I'd like to say thank you to everyone in this room for making my book real. You've all helped in your special way. It's a bit surreal now, and I've no idea what will happen. But right now, I need to eat, so help yourselves."

I wasn't the only hungry person present; we descended on the food and not much was said for a while. When I'd eaten, I forced myself to do the rounds. I spoke to Eleanor, the editor who'd picked my book to pieces and helped me put it back together. She had improved both it and my opinion of editors. I thanked Eva's secretary, who's name I could never remember, and had a chat with Peter. He'd calmed down but made his excuses early and left us.

I took Eva to one side and asked her how it had gone.

"You did well," she said. "A bit of humour got them onside, you read well and did the glad-handing. That's all there is to it. Now we wait and see."

"I'm glad it's over."

"We'll see."

That phrase filled me with dread. After a pause, she leaned closer.

"Tell me something," she said. "Your friend, Penny ..."

"Mmm."

"Is she wearing a collar?"

I looked at her warily; she'd put me on the spot.

"It ... might be a necklace," I replied.

She gave me a challenging look.

"Come on, Marcus. I'm not that naïve."

I saw no reason to lie, Penny was proud of her status.

"Yes, she is."

"Is she yours?"

"No."

"Belong to a friend of yours?"

"Not my place to say, Eva. You could always ask her."

"I might do that."

She gave me a long appraising stare.

"Are you part of that scene?" she finally asked.

"We have … one foot in it."

"I see."

"Do you have an interest?" I asked.

She studied me hard before answering.

"More in a parallel one, now." I gave her an expectant look and she yielded. "I'm more into ink and piercing these days."

We looked at each other for a moment, aware we'd shared mutual secrets.

"And is Lucy the artist who did the pictures I saw when I stayed?" she asked.

"Yes."

"That's two people I need to speak to before you all go. I'll keep you up to date with the sales figures, and you should start seeing reviews in the next few days. I probably don't need to tell you, but don't take poor ones too seriously, and don't respond to any. Ever."

"I know, I've seen one or two authors do it. It's not a good look."

She went to get a drink and managed to intercept Lucy as she came back from the loo. Lucy could handle herself, but I decided to warn Penny she might get a few personal questions.

"Don't worry, Marcus," she said. "I don't shout about it, but I'm happy to talk if I'm asked."

Eva's team drifted off one by one. By ten-thirty, it was just our party and Eva, who was, inevitably, chatting to Penny in a corner. They were quite animated, but Penny seemed perfectly happy, so I left them to it.

"They seem to be getting on," Sally said, coming up to me.

"A bit of common ground," I replied. She gave me a questioning look. "Tell you later."

Chapter 3 – Sally

Marcus wasn't quite his usual self after the launch. The books he'd self-published in the past had sold well for an author with little marketing muscle, but Shadows of Gold was a whole different matter. A publisher had thrown its weight behind the book and I could tell he was on edge. Little things: missing something I said, a restless night or two and a distracted air.

The early reviews were positive, and the initial sales figures exceeded Eva's predictions. She dropped in one evening after she'd visited one of her more prominent authors who lived nearby, and we made a quick meal to share with her.

"It's going well," she said. "Of course, I knew it would."

"Of course," Marcus replied.

"Seriously, it's selling well. I'm hoping it'll make the bestseller charts this weekend."

"Does that make a difference?" I asked.

"Bookshops will display it more prominently; often, just inside the door. Readers are lazy, they'll buy something from the top seller shelves."

"You cynic," Marcus said.

"You know what I mean. And with Christmas coming, people buy books as gifts. If we get your book in front of them …"

"They'll simply fly off the shelves," he said, with more than a hint of sarcasm.

"Hopefully," she replied, turning to him with a look I recognised. "Which means I'd love you to do something for me."

"Which is?"

"A few appearances, some signings."

He visibly deflated and let out a long sigh.

"I know," she said. "But if we arrange a few things in the run-up to Christmas, it could make all the difference."

"You saw how I was at the launch; I'm not cut out for these things."

"You were great."

"Eva, cut the bullshit."

"I mean it. I've had authors who were gibbering wrecks, and one or two who nearly started fights. You handled it like a pro. Anyway, authors aren't expected to have charisma."

"Thanks."

"You'll do it?" she asked, glancing at me. "If the book continues selling as it is, I'm going to need a follow-up."

I knew he hated the publicity stuff, but I understood the need, and the mention of another book was an obvious lure.

"What did you have in mind?" he asked.

"Well …"

She took a sheet out of her bag; I wasn't surprised she'd prepared. They spent a few minutes going through her suggestions. He immediately refused a few of them, but after some discussion, he agreed to four book signings and a handful of interviews.

"I'll get to work on it and let you know. And in the new year, you'd better get to work on the sequel."

"I can send it to you tomorrow if you like."

She turned sharply to look at him, before letting her face relax into a grin.

"Written?" she asked.

"Yup. Only second draft, but it's clean. I'm sure the vulture can pick the bones out of it."

"The vulture?"

"For some reason, I can never remember the editor's name."

"So, she's the vulture."

"Sorry."

"No, Eleanor might like that. I expect she's been called worse."

"I don't doubt it."

***

"… happy birthday to you."

The singing – if you could call it that – came to an end, and everyone around the table was smiling at me. Our birthday group had grown; first Ken last year, and this year Helen and Penny joined us. Helen was thawing; she still had the look of the ice queen at times, but cracks were appearing more often.

Lucy reached beside her and lifted a bow-covered bag onto the table.

"Right," she said. "Present time."

She slid the bag towards me, and I felt myself flush.

"Don't worry," Lucy continued. "Nothing embarrassing, we're in company. One from each of us, only little things. You've got to wait until Monday for anything else."

They were silly things, sweet things, loving things, fun things. When I'd unwrapped them all, we resumed our meal. As we parted at the end of the evening, I thanked everyone and gave them each a big hug. Even Helen relented, though it was clear she wasn't used to it.

This time, Lucy wasn't sharing a taxi with Mary. Mary now had Ken to escort her safely home and Lucy came to the car with us. Last year, I'd spent a night at Lucy's then spent my actual birthday with Marcus. This year, our relationship had changed. When we got home, they pulled me to them and put their arms around me.

"It's your weekend," Marcus said. "We've got a few things planned, but there are no big surprises. We're going to pamper you."

"I'm here 'til Monday morning," Lucy said. "Then I'm leaving you to it."

They started by taking me downstairs and slowly stripping me; and themselves. For the next two hours, they focussed solely on me. It was one of the most sensuous nights of my life. Everything was in slow motion, our bodies flowing around one another, their fingers and mouths working together to take me up and up and keep me there.

By the time I came down, I was almost numb, and I cuddled against them as they gently satisfied each other. We hardly moved before falling asleep in one happy heap.

The next day, I wasn't allowed to do a thing. They gave me a bath in the morning, dressed me and made me breakfast. Lucy took me shopping. She insisted on buying me things; I knew she still felt the need to give me something back. After lunch, she took me for a spa afternoon before we went home.

In the evening, they took me for dinner to the restaurant where Marcus and I had first revealed our fantasies to each other. We told Lucy the story; interrupting each other as we remembered little snippets the other had forgotten or perhaps, not even known. About the pictures, the texts, and the teasing.

That led to some outrageous flirting. By the time we got home, we were ready to rip each other's clothes off. The result was like the night before, but the route there was considerably more vigorous.

Sunday was a lazy day. I still wasn't allowed to do anything, but we lounged about the house, enjoying one another's company. We went for a long walk in the afternoon and stopped off for a couple of drinks before returning home.

"Lucy and I are going to cook dinner," Marcus said.

"Do I need to dress?" I asked.

"You will, but not yet."

They wouldn't elaborate and I didn't push. We chatted while they prepared everything, but when they were ready to cook, they stopped.

"Right," Marcus said. "Time to change. I'm showering up here, Lucy's using her room, and our room is yours."

I looked at him, puzzled.

"What shall I wear?"

"Whatever you find on the bed. Take as long as you need. We'll be waiting here."

Lucy and I went downstairs, and she disappeared into the spare room she'd previously used. When I entered our bedroom, there were four wrapped presents on the bed. I went to unwrap them but decided to have my shower first. After I'd dried myself off, I sat on the bed, not sure what to expect.

In the first box was a short, flared PVC skirt with a heavy belt at the waist. Then came a PVC crop top with full arms and a zip front. In the third box was a short riding crop, and when I opened the last, all I could see at first was a heap of PVC. But as I lifted it out, a pair of thigh-length boots were revealed.

I put the skirt and top on, then spent some time struggling into the boots. They were a tight fit, but after a lot of pulling and smoothing, they were in place. They felt wonderful and when I stood in front of the mirror, I looked quite intimidating.

The next question was knickers or no knickers. If this was how the evening was starting, I'd need some; to protect the furniture, if nothing else. I popped on a pair of high cut PVC briefs and spent a few minutes applying some makeup and tying my hair in a ponytail.

After one last look in the mirror, I picked up the crop and went upstairs. The boots had high heels and the material didn't support your ankles like normal boots, and I had to walk slowly.

When I entered the dining room, the table had been beautifully set. Candles were the only light; several on the table, and others around the room. But that wasn't what I was staring at. Marcus was standing waiting for me, in a tight pair of black boxers with a similar top. He smiled at me, looking me up and down, clearly liking what he saw.

Lucy came out of the kitchen in my most revealing maid's outfit. It was tight on her and she looked incredibly cute. Marcus came and gave me a kiss.

"Like it?"

"Yes, it all fits perfectly," I said.

"It sure does," Lucy said with a chuckle.

"You're in charge, tonight," he said. "We're your playthings."

This was going to be fun. I walked slowly around them, enjoying the view, and running the end of the crop over their bodies. As I was dressing, I'd guessed I was going to be playing the dominant role and I was ready for it. The sight in front of me only increased the desire and my mind was running through the possibilities. I used the crop to lift Lucy's tiny skirt revealing little white shorts, stretched tight over that gorgeous bum.

"Well," I said, allowing common sense to lead for the moment. "I think we'll have dinner first."

They'd prepared some of my favourites and dinner was a relaxed affair. Although they always served me first, and I made a point of running my hand or the crop over them when they were standing by me. The whole thing was intoxicating. The meal, the candlelight, the scene we were setting up. The anticipation was affecting all of us along with the wine. By the end of the meal, I wanted some fun with my new toys.

"I want you downstairs in the playroom," I said. "Wait for me."

I decided to take a leaf out of Marcus's book and kept them waiting for fifteen minutes. When I arrived, they were both standing in the middle of the room. A wave of panic overtook me. I took charge with Marcus quite often, but I'd never done it to any extent with Lucy, and never with both together. Where to start?

I did what Marcus sometimes did; I walked around them slowly and began to touch and stroke them. It gave me thinking time. I'd spent the time I'd kept them waiting coming up with ideas, but when I entered the room, they'd all gone.

All I had now was a need, a delicious need. A heat between my legs that had to be dealt with before I could put some of my plans into action. I didn't have Marcus's patience; I was a multi-orgasmic woman and I'd learned to be proud of that.

"I've got plans for you two," I said. "But first, you're going to deal with a little problem I have."

I made Marcus sit on his haunches with his back to the end of the horse and stood in front of him. I lifted my skirt a little, although it was so short it was hardly necessary.

"Pull them down."

He slipped his fingers into my briefs and slowly slid them over my boots. I stepped out of them and put my hand on his head. Moving forward, he wriggled until I felt his breath between my legs. It made me gasp and I twitched as his lips touched my wet folds. I beckoned Lucy, and twisted her hair around my fingers, pulling her mouth to mine.

We kissed until we were both breathless; my own being affected by Marcus's lips now sucking firmly at my pussy. I pushed Lucy down behind me and guided her head towards my bum. Hands grabbed my cheeks and pulled them apart, and I let out a long groan as a tongue licked all the way from my pussy, along that sweet path to my ass.

I knew I was going to come; I leaned over Marcus to rest an arm on the horse for support. My other hand held the crop and I used it to push Marcus's head further into me. I jumped as his lips surrounded my clit and his tongue began to flick it. Lucy's tongue pressed at my ass and I came. A sharp, powerful orgasm, while their hands held me steady so they could continue; I wanted them to.

"More," I commanded. They carried on, not letting me come down. They each knew how to keep me there and both together was almost unbearable. But I was brave, I bore it. My orgasm rose again and flooded me as fingers and tongues invaded my pussy and my ass. I had to put my other arm on the horse to avoid collapsing in a heap.

"Enough," I panted. They stopped. I stayed where I was to recover. I wanted to continue our roleplay, so I needed to stay in some semblance of character. I finally stood, sated for the moment. Looking at them, they were enjoying this as much as I was. They were trying to stay in their characters, but both were doing a poor job of hiding satisfied smiles.

"Stand up," I said. "That was quite good, for a start. I'm going to see how much you can give me before you beg for something for yourselves."

I walked around to face them.

"Nice as those costumes are, I think I prefer you naked." They removed their clothes. Marcus was nicely erect, and Lucy's thighs were beautifully moist. "I want you both over the horse."

They moved and bent over the leather top. Two bums sticking out. I tapped each one in turn with the crop, but it wasn't the tool I needed. I went over to the racks and picked a flogger, swishing it through the air. I bent beside Marcus.

"We'll start with you, darling. Make that bum of yours a little pinker."

Standing behind him, I trailed the fronds over his body then raised it, letting it fall softly on his bum. Repeating the stroke more firmly, building to a regular rhythm. He was letting out little grunts as the strength increased. It wasn't his thing, but as part of a scene, we both enjoyed it.

When I'd brought a little colour to his cheeks, I stopped and bent by Lucy's ear.

"I'd like to use this on you, but you've never felt it. Can I try?"

She looked at me, a delicious expression on her face.

"Yes."

I gave her a kiss.

"Stop me if it's too much."

I stood behind her. She looked so inviting, her legs slightly apart, her wet pussy exposed between soft cheeks. Marcus had spanked her a few times since the holiday but hadn't used an implement on her. That gave me a thought.

"Stand up, darling, and watch me flog Lucy. Something she hasn't allowed you to do."

I heard a stifled giggle from Luce, followed by a gasp as I brought the flogger down lightly on her bum. As she relaxed, I repeated the stroke, keeping it regular and light. Her body was moving with the impact, little gasps and groans, but nothing which alerted me to a problem. I increased the force; she reacted by moaning. Her bum was taking on little pink marks, and she spread her legs further.

I was surprised she hadn't stopped me by now but didn't want to push it. I lowered the flogger and gently put my fingers between her open legs. She jumped and let out a pleading groan. I went around the horse and squatted in front of her. Her face was flushed.

"Turned you on, did it?"

"Yes," she said, an embarrassed smile on her face.

"Need to come?"

She nodded hard. I gave her a kiss and looked at Marcus.

"Fuck her." I looked back into Lucy's eyes. "Fuck her hard. Fuck her until she comes on your cock." Lucy whimpered as Marcus's fingers spread her lips, and gave a cry as his cock went deep into her.

"Oh, and darling …" I said, looking at him. "You're not allowed to come."

He gave me a look which probably spelt trouble for me later, but I knew he'd comply. He grabbed Lucy's hips and fucked her, each stroke slamming her against the horse.

"Finger her ass," I said, still staring into her eyes. They opened wide as his finger penetrated her rear and she began to groan; that long deep groan which betrayed her approaching climax. Her head dropped, but I grabbed her hair and held it, still wanting to hold her gaze.

Her eyes rolled up as her orgasm hit; her body trembling, her breathing sparse and ragged.

"Keep going. Keep fucking her," I said. Her gaze settled briefly on me. She was bleating with every breath, a row of staccato chirps as her orgasm continued. Her head became heavy, wanting to drop and I gently let it as I stopped him.

She eventually raised her head, flushed and breathless. I kissed her hard and she put her hand behind my head and pulled me to her. Then pulled away, gasping for air. I looked at Marcus, still buried in her pussy.

"Want to come, darling?" He nodded; the need etched on his face. "Not like that, come out."

Lucy gave a little gasp as he slipped from her.

"Lie on the floor," I told her. Unsteadily, she slid off the horse and laid on her back. "I want to see him come over your breasts."

I made him straddle her tummy and knelt by him. Taking his cock in my hand, I stroked it firmly and rapidly, looking into his eyes. It wasn't long before he grunted, and the first stream shot out, Lucy giving a little shriek as it landed across her face. The next shots fell shorter, over her breasts, as he gradually subsided.

"Darling," I said, with mock disappointment. "You've come over Lucy's face."

I bent to kiss her, veering away to lick his cum from her cheek and forehead before giving her a lingering kiss. Her tongue surprised me by seeking his taste in my mouth. I moved my hand to her breasts and rubbed his cum into her skin.

We all took a few deep breaths and smiled at each other.

"I haven't finished with you two yet, but let's take a break."

We leaned against the nearest surface as Marcus got up to get some wine. As we sipped it, nothing much was said, but the shared looks were enough. After the break, I carried on; I was having fun. Marcus became the anvil, lying on his back with Lucy straddling his face.

While he went to work with his mouth, I put on a strap on and fucked her gently, bringing her to another intense orgasm. She was under strict instructions not to touch Marcus, but when she climbed off, he was hard again.

I took her place, and Lucy fucked me while his mouth got to work. I teased him. Gentle strokes between his legs, fingernails running along his shaft and over his balls. And the occasional nibble on the end of his cock. All interrupted by my two orgasms. After I'd come down from the last one, I lifted off him and smiled at them.

"That's enough."

Lucy looked at Marcus's cock, with a querying look.

"Oh, darling," I said. "Do you still need something?"

"It would be nice."

I bent and kissed him.

"I've got something special for you."

I whispered to Lucy and got him to lie back on the bench with his bum right on the end. She got between his legs, as he realised what she was doing. A bit of lube later, and she was easing the strap-on into his ass, his moans already coming. Lucy lifted his legs either side of her and they got into a comfortable position; they could be there some time.

I bent and took his cock into my mouth. As Lucy gently fucked him, I gave him a slow, teasing blowjob. He was especially vocal, little sounds coming with each of Lucy's strokes. His cock sometimes jerking in my mouth as she hit the right spot deep inside him. After a while, his groaning was almost constant, broken only by his need to take a breath.

His body was gently moving on the bench, hips occasionally rising to meet the actions of Lucy or me. As his orgasm approached, his cock seemed to swell; it was as rigid and swollen as I could remember.

His groans suddenly became rhythmic and I closed my lips around his shaft, using my tongue to press his frenulum. Lucy thrust deep, holding herself against his thighs. He exploded. His hips rose, pushing his cock deeper into my mouth, and his first surge slammed into the back of my throat making me gag, my eyes watering.

He was crying out, gripping the bench as his body took over. I had to release him for a second or two to catch my breath, but clamped around him again, his cum oozing between my lips and sliding down his cock. He was still coming, his whole body tightening with each spasm, my mouth overflowing.

I laid my hand on Lucy's tummy. She got the message and gently eased out, Marcus jerking again as the dildo exited. As he finally subsided, I licked all the cum spilled over his cock. He was still mumbling, his chest rising and falling as his breathing steadied. His fingers were still gripping the bench.

Lucy was stroking his thighs and looked at me wide-eyed, mouthing a silent 'wow'. We sat there for a couple of minutes, caressing him, and keeping body contact. I moved up by his head and when he finally looked at me it was with glazed eyes. He broke into a beautiful smile and I kissed him.

He was still too dazed to respond. All he did was hold out a hand to Lucy. She leaned over him and could just reach for a kiss. He laid one arm over her and the other around my shoulders. After several minutes, he looked at me.

"You should be in charge more often."

Chapter 4 – Lucy

The run-up to Christmas was busier than usual. After I took the stand at the play party, I'd had several inquiries from people who wanted to commission pictures of themselves, their partners, or a particular fetish. One or two were eye-opening but I accepted them anyway. And they all wanted them for Christmas.

It did surprise me how readily they sent me naked photographs, but I assumed they trusted Sally and Marcus, and therefore me by association. I'd delivered most of the works by early December and the positive responses filled me with confidence.

"Any left to do?" Sally asked.

"None before Christmas now. The remainder are going to need a live sitting or two in the New Year."

She was with me for two nights, the last time before Christmas. Marcus was away on his mini book tour.

"How's he getting on?"

Sally rolled her eyes.

"Grumbling and willing it to be over."

"He doesn't like it, does he?"

"He hates it."

"Will it do any good?"

"Eva thinks so, and she should know. He's in the best seller's list and she means to keep him there as long as possible."

"She's an interesting character," I said. Sally raised an eyebrow. "No, not like that. Not my type. But she wants me to draw her."

"She did like the pictures she saw."

"I think it's a bit different from those. Apparently, she's got lots of tattoos and wants me to do something showing them."

"She told Marcus she was into them; piercing, too."

"She didn't mention that bit."

"Will you need to see them?"

"We haven't discussed exactly what she wants but for accurate depictions, I'm going to need to see them myself, rather than rely on shaky photos."

"Ever painted tattoos before?"

"The odd one or two, but imaginary ones. I don't think it's going to be easy if she's got a lot."

"Could be fun …"

"Told you, she's not my type."

***

"Won't I be in the way?" I asked.

"Of what?" Sal replied.

"Well, you know."

"Luce, you're part of us now, you're never in the way. Come and stay until the New Year."

It was a tempting offer. We'd had so much fun in France and the idea of staying with them all over Christmas was intoxicating.

"I wouldn't come on Christmas Eve."

"Why not?"

"Because I'll have to leave on Christmas morning to go to Annie's with Mum and it'll seem worse."

"Come to us as soon as you leave them, then. Don't wait until Boxing Day."

"I'll think about it."

I knew I'd accept the offer but didn't want to seem too needy. We were driving to the Christmas munch. I'd done things the wrong way around. People usually went to the munches first, then the play parties. But this would be my first time. Sal and I were going alone, Marcus was doing another signing and hadn't been happy.

"Have you heard from Jacques?" I asked. Jacques was her recently discovered half-brother.

"Yea, we're telling each other about our lives with Dad. It's all remarkably similar."

"Has he told his mother?"

"He's told her Dad died, but that's it for the moment. He's waiting for her to ask before he tells her the rest."

"That's a bit odd isn't it?"

"He knows her best."

"I suppose so."

The munch was well attended. Sally knew nearly everyone there and I knew a few, some intimately from their photos. It was a fun and relaxing evening and I got to talk to people I'd only seen half-naked before. You saw a different side of them here, their everyday personality.

"Hello, you two." We knew the voice well.

"Hi, Penny."

After hugs and kisses, she looked around.

"Where's Marcus?"

"Not here," Sal said. "He's off doing some signings. Disappointed?"

"A bit." She gave us one of her cheeky smiles. "I can't tease him. How's his book doing?"

"Very well. I think he's a bit shocked."

"I'm not. It's good. Even Helen enjoyed it, and it's not her thing."

I tried to imagine the two of them, curled up in the evening, quietly reading. It was a strange image but one which had a certain charm.

"What are you doing for Christmas?" I asked and immediately regretted it as her shoulders drooped.

"A few days with my family," she replied.

"Sorry, didn't mean to pry."

She shrugged.

"It's okay. From what you've told me, you know what families can be like."

"Let me guess; they don't approve of your lifestyle."

"I haven't told them about it. I don't think they'd even understand, let alone approve."

"You go home, pretend to be someone you're not and leave again."

"Yup, that's about it."

"What about Helen?" Sally asked.

"She'll be staying on her own."

"No family?"

"Not that I'm aware of."

"Won't she be lonely?"

"No. She doesn't do Christmas. Well, doesn't do any celebrations, really. Not even her own birthday."

I was tempted to ask why but knew better.

"Penny," Sal said. "Please come over for a day when you get back. We're not going anywhere, and Lucy is staying with us from Boxing Day into the New Year. We'd love to see you."

"Thank you. I'd like that."

"And try and persuade Helen to come, as well."

"That may be more difficult."

***

As I left Annie's I took a few deep breaths and forced my body to relax from the neck down. The day had gone surprisingly well. Mum had mellowed over the last year. Even Sarah and Nathan seemed to be coming around to their grandmother. She'd bought presents they wanted; indeed, her presents had been a hit all round.

But I'd still been out of sorts all day. For years, Christmas had been all mine. Sometimes I'd had a partner, but when I was single, I'd always had offers from friends and joined them for the day. Now, ironically, I had two lovers and hadn't been able to spend the day with them.

"Hi, Sal," I said, as she opened the door. "I'm all yours."

She gave me a sultry smile which made me shiver, and hugged me as I came into the hallway. Marcus gave me a big hug and a kiss when I found him in the kitchen.

"How was it?" Sal asked.

I quickly recounted my day.

"Better than last year," he said.

"Much. Not bad at all."

"We've changed things a bit this year," Sal said. "We're not having another Christmas Day tomorrow. As you're here today, we can open our presents."

"You haven't waited for me?" I asked, aghast.

"We opened some, but we've left a lot. Come on."

In the living room, the table had a buffet supper laid out. Sal poured me a drink, we filled plates and sat on the sofas. Marcus handed out some presents. I knew what they were like now. Lots of little things rather than big ones, and I wasn't caught out this year.

At the end, he handed Sally and me a last present each and sat down, smiling.

"He's got that look, Luce," Sal said.

We unwrapped the parcels and compared. Two identical remote-control vibrators; U-shaped with one bulbous arm and one flatter. One pink, one blue. We looked at each other, then at him.

"I'm not sure we should give you the controllers, darling," Sal said.

"That's not what I had in mind," he replied.

"Oh?"

"I thought you could swap remotes." Sal and I looked at each other. "I'm looking forward to watching a vibe war tomorrow," he said with a wicked grin.

We waited until the afternoon. Sal was itching to try our new toys, but I wasn't too worried. I'd had a small cordless egg vibe before and hadn't been impressed. It wasn't very comfortable, and the vibrations had been weak. I'd tried it once or twice before consigning it to the back of a drawer somewhere. I preferred something a bit more powerful.

I soon discovered technology had moved on. The vibe was remarkably comfortable even under clothes, and perfectly shaped. After a few minutes, I could hardly feel it. But when Sally switched it on, I certainly could. The next half an hour was mind-blowing. Sal and I started slowly, but it rapidly became a battle. We were soon writhing around on the sofas as these little toys did their work.

Sal had two orgasms before I came, but that climax was powerful, and I wasn't in control of it. It was a strange experience, reaching a shattering orgasm while fully clothed. As I came down, she went over and kissed Marcus.

"I think these are a winner."

"Mmm," he replied. "I've got a few ideas where we might use them."

"You're not expecting me to go out wearing this?"

"Possibly."

"I couldn't."

"And I'd have the controller."

I could see she was in two minds. Shy Sally was terrified of the whole idea. But the new exhibitionist Sally was excited by it. I was prepared to bet he'd have his way.

"Of course, darling," Sal said. "What you should have got Lucy was one for her ass."

He pulled another present out from under the cushion and handed it to her. She pulled the wrapping off and I knew the grin on her face spelt trouble for me. She opened the box and lifted out a substantial black plug.

"Come on, Luce," she said. "Jeans down, bend over."

"Sal …"

"Do it."

I found myself bending over in front of them, as Sal lubed me up and slowly eased the plug into my ass, which was already sensitive from our earlier activity. It felt good before it was even working. As I went to pull my jeans up, Sal stopped me.

"Take everything off."

She was already stripping, and I followed suit. She sat back on the sofa and opened her legs, inviting me to sit between them, leaning back on her. She gave both controls to Marcus and wrapped her arms around me, slowly caressing me. Then they began to play me.

The butt plug started to tingle; gently at first, but I was already aroused, and it didn't take long for the feeling to spread. He turned it up and the pussy vibe started. It was already overwhelming me. Vibration in my pussy, my ass and over my clit, and Sal holding and stroking me.

I let go, I couldn't control myself. My whole groin was trembling, my legs shaking. Sal held me tight as my orgasm came. An orgasm like I'd rarely experienced. I could feel heat everywhere, my skin tingling and burning. I let my head fall back onto her and gave in. My bum was jumping around, my hips jerking from side to side. I heard a scream as I went rigid, my feet digging into the carpet, my hands pressing on her thighs.

I was aware of Sal's arms around my tummy, holding me to her. She was resting her cheek against my neck. My heartbeat pounded in my chest and my whole body felt cool and damp. I gradually became aware of my surroundings. I turned to look at Marcus, a smile on his face, as Sal kissed my neck.

"Okay?" she whispered.

"Was I out?"

"Briefly."

I looked at my body, covered in a thin film of sweat. I was warm and exhausted, a feeling of complete contentment. Sal suddenly tensed and her head left my shoulder. A couple of groans hit my ear and her arms tightened around me. I looked over at Marcus; he was holding her control.

She'd enjoyed my orgasm and it wasn't taking much to bring her there again. But I had other ideas. I undid her grasp and slid onto the floor. I held out my hand to him and he handed me the control which I turned to the lowest level. He wanted the same thing. Standing up, he removed his clothes as Sal watched. She lifted herself, slid her knickers off and went to remove the vibe.

"Ah, ah," I said. "Leave that there. You need something in your ass as well."

Her face told us she agreed. She moved forward and bent over the sofa with her bum in the air. I grabbed the lube and poured some over her ass. He knelt behind her, and slid firmly in, making her gasp and drop her head. I turned the vibe up full, held it in place and watched her writhe as he fucked her ass.

The whole thing was brief. She was already near orgasm and watching us had made his need urgent. He grabbed her hips and took her hard. Her climax when it came was almost as powerful as mine. I left the vibe going and she kept coming, pushing back to meet his thrusts. Her final howl was accompanied by his cry as he came, sinking into her.

He lowered himself over her and grabbed her hands, their fingers interlocking. I sat quietly, watching them come down. He held a hand out and pulled me close; I hugged their linked bodies, and they both put an arm around me.

We didn't do much else that day. Sal and I didn't have the energy. When we went to bed, we did show our gratitude to Marcus for our presents. He seemed to enjoy it. The next few days were a mix of fun, relaxation, and excess. Mary and Ken joined us for a day and, to our surprise, Penny persuaded Helen to join her for an afternoon visit.

Helen made her disdain for Christmas clear, but she was good fun and happy to join in the banter. She never seemed to fully relax unless she was in control. But I guess that made her who and what she was.

"Lucy," she said after I'd talked about the commissions I'd done. "I might want you to do a couple of things for me."

"Of course, Helen. Anything you want."

She looked at me with that mix of humour and authority.

"It might mean you have to study Penny in intimate detail."

"I'm an artist," I said. "I sometimes have to suffer for my art."

A faint smile appeared on Helen's face.

"Indeed. I'll think about what I want." She turned to Penny. "We've had a few ideas, haven't we?"

"Yes, but I'd still like to include you."

"We'll see," Helen replied. "We'll see."

Chapter 5 – Sally

The end of another year. And what a year. I was still trying to take in the changes in my life. Three years ago, I was happy. At least, I thought I was. I was independent, with a job I loved. Friends and colleagues who gave me their trust and their support. I'd been missing that one spark; I didn't even know what it was.

It turned out to be Marcus and everything he brought to my life. Everything he allowed me to discover about myself; everything he gave me the confidence and freedom to try. And I'd tried a lot. I'd done things I'd only ever imagined in my dreams and fantasies. They were part of our life now and we still had a long to-do list.

New Year's Eve was special, too. Just the three of us. We dressed up in party gear and had our very own party. A large buffet we could pick at through the evening. We played games, we drank, we danced to some music from our past. Lucy and I drank some more, and the dancing became more erotic.

I slowly stripped in front of them, then stripped Lucy and we made love in front of Marcus, before stripping him and making love to him. By midnight, we were mostly naked and enjoyed a warm snuggle as the year turned. By the time we went to bed, we'd enjoyed our first sex of the new year. The prospect of more beckoned.

Lucy left us on New Year's Day. We were both going back to work the following day, and she hadn't been home since before Christmas. Marcus and I cuddled on the sofa and went to sleep. When we woke, we made something to eat and talked about the old year. But more importantly about what the new year held.

His writing was finally reaping the reward I knew it deserved. He was ambivalent about the success of Shadows of Gold. He was pleased with its reception and sales; more than he would easily admit. But he wasn't enjoying the publicity side at all. Whenever he came home from signings, he was always grumpy, and he hated interviews.

"They all ask the same questions," he said, as he had on several occasions. "Why can't I do one and they share it?"

"Did you ask Eva?"

"Yes. That's not how it works, apparently."

"You haven't got any more booked in, though."

"No," he replied, grinning.

"Alright, why not?"

"I told her I'd make stuff up; I think she believed me."

***

Eva came to see us. She'd also arranged to visit Lucy, so we offered her a room for the night. When she arrived on Friday evening, she gave Marcus a big hug, which caught him by surprise.

"Well done," she said, pulling away. He looked confused. "Didn't you look at the best sellers list?"

"Uh, no," Marcus replied. Which, as far as I knew, was true. I hadn't either. Eva rolled her eyes and rummaged in her bag. She handed him a sheet of paper, which he studied. She turned to me.

"Bestselling fiction hardback in December."

"Is that good?" Marcus asked.

"Good?" she replied. "That's the jackpot for any author. It doesn't get any better."

Over dinner, I could see she was buzzing about his success. Marcus appeared to be taking it in his stride.

"It's our first best-seller at Christmas in four years," she said. "My management are very happy."

"And you?" Marcus asked.

She looked at him; they'd developed a good – if slightly combative – relationship and understanding.

"I'm happy too, Marcus. Alright; if you pushed me, I didn't think it would sell as well as it has. I liked it and was happy to take it on, but it has exceeded my expectations."

"Do you know, Eva?" he replied. "I think that's the first time you've been completely honest about that."

"Perhaps," she said with a grin.

"And now you want me to do more signings and interviews to keep the momentum going."

"No."

We both looked at her, surprised by her reply.

"No?"

"No. We've talked about this, and we think part of the success has been your air of mystery."

"Seriously?"

"Yes. You did the launch, a few interviews and four signings. Most authors spend weeks touring the country, signing anything put in front of them, appearing on local radio stations to plug their book. Your reticence may have been to our benefit."

"Ours?"

"Don't start, Marcus," she said. "You know full well we both benefit from your success."

He conceded, and they stopped sparring.

"But surely," I said, "most people don't know Marcus hasn't done much publicity. How does that encourage them to buy his book?"

"It doesn't directly. But the trade and press will know. They'll be intrigued by this rather mysterious author, and it encourages them to talk about the book. The more places it appears, the more people buy it."

It didn't seem to make much sense to me, but I was sure Marcus would be happy knowing he didn't have to do more interviews.

"Eleanor's nearly finished her work on Shadows of Silver," Eva said. "She'll be in touch in a week or two."

"Oh," Marcus replied. "Okay."

"And she liked the vulture thing."

"You told her?"

"Of course."

"Thanks."

"Relax. She's much more fun than she appears at first."

"A bit like you?"

Eva laughed and turned to me.

"Is he like this with everyone, Sally?"

"Not everyone, Eva. It depends whether he thinks you're worth it."

"Ah, I see. It's a compliment."

"Let's just say he expects you to give as good as you get."

"I do try."

"What's the plan now?" I asked.

"We'll see how sales go and keep the advertising up. I'm planning to release the paperback in time for Easter. We may need you to come back into the sunlight for that, Marcus."

"Okay," he replied. "But not for too long, I burn easily."

"I'd also like to look at your earlier stuff."

He'd reluctantly agreed to remove all his self-published books from sale prior to the launch of Shadows of Gold. We'd talked about it a long time; we understood why, but it had wounded him more than he would admit.

"What for?"

"To see if there's anything we could work on."

"You mean now I've had one success, you're suddenly interested in finding more product to see if it's a fluke."

"Marcus, I'm making no judgement about your earlier stuff. I've only skimmed a couple of them. But we weren't going to put all that effort into Shadows of Gold, and make it a success, only to find your own books let the side down."

I briefly saw an expression on his face I hadn't seen before. Anger. It looked like anger, anyway. There was a long pause before he spoke; slowly and deliberately.

"Eva, I worked hard on those earlier books, and I'm proud of them. I'm not prepared to have someone – however well-intentioned – rip them apart and rebuild them to some standard formula. I agreed to pull them, but it's not in my contract. I can publish them again whenever I feel like it. I could ask Peter to offer them to other publishers. Don't push too far."

Eva was clearly surprised by his tone as, indeed, was I. But she was experienced at this game. We already knew how awkward some of her other authors could be. She was used to this.

"Okay, Marcus," she said lightly. "I'm only thinking out loud. How would you feel about letting me have someone look at a couple; you can choose them."

He wasn't looking at her, or me; he was staring off into the distance. I tried to work out what was going on in his head. This was a side of Marcus I wasn't familiar with.

"I'll think about it," he replied sharply.

"Thank you," Eva said. We fell into silence.

Eventually, I knew I needed to break the impasse, and tried making small talk. I wasn't good at it, neither was Marcus. It was one of our shared hates, but Eva and I chatted about anything that came into our heads. Marcus excused himself and left the room.

"I'm sorry, Eva," I said. "I've never seen Marcus in this mood. He's never angry."

"It's alright, Sally. Perhaps I could have worded things better. But I have seen some truly awful self-published stuff. If someone enjoyed Shadows of Gold, then bought one of his own books and it was all over the place, it wouldn't be good business for us."

I understood her view, but she could have been more careful how she explained it. I moved us to the living room, and twenty minutes later, Marcus returned. He was carrying a fresh bottle of wine. Going to Eva's glass, he poured it as he spoke.

"I apologise, Eva," he said. "I was rude, and I shouldn't have been. I'm afraid it's that conflict between my position and yours."

"Between good business and not needing the money?" she replied. I held my breath, as it was another challenging statement.

He looked at her and smiled.

"Exactly."

Everything was fine for the rest of the evening. Marcus was back to his usual self, and by the time we went to bed, he and Eva were the best of friends again. I climbed into bed and laid myself half over him.

"Are you okay?" I asked.

"Yes, I am now."

"You looked angry."

"I was. Well, more upset, to be honest."

"I've never seen you like that before."

"Sorry."

"Don't apologise. I was surprised and I think Eva was, as well."

"I don't like being a business asset. I know that's what I am to them, but it hurts. They have this automatic assumption anyone who self-publishes is not good enough. They never think it may be their system that's no longer fit for purpose."

"Are you going to let her have a couple of your earlier works?"

He gave me a crafty grin.

"Oh, yes. And I know exactly which ones."

Chapter 6 – Lucy

Sally dropped Eva off mid-morning. She left her case in the hall and followed me into the kitchen as I made some coffee. As we settled in the living room, I studied her. She was tall and slim; slimmer than either Sally or me. Long black hair which was straight and currently tied back in a tight ponytail. A face which was interesting rather than conventionally beautiful; high cheekbones, a strong nose and from where I was sitting, her eyes were slightly different colours. But it may have been the light.

"What would you like me to do for you, Eva?"

"To be honest, Lucy, I'm not sure. I have a particular request, which I'll get to. But I loved the pictures I saw at Marcus and Sally's and one or two pieces in that style would look great in my flat."

"Any subject matter in mind?"

I wasn't sure what she was after, nor how much she knew about my more explicit work.

"Well, Sally did tell me you aren't afraid of any subject. But I've only seen those two works."

"What I can do is show you some of my pieces." I'd prepared for this. "I've pulled out some recent stuff to give you an idea. They're on the table."

We went over to the dining area, and I slowly showed her a selection of pictures. Several different styles, some simple, some more complex. The early ones were tasteful curves and soft bodies.

"They get more explicit as we go deeper," I said. "Don't be afraid to stop me."

She didn't and let me carry on to the end.

"They're interesting, Lucy. Do you use live models, or is it from your imagination?"

"A bit of both, although most of these are from life, or at least from photographs."

"Anyone I know?" I'd half-expected the question, but it still made me pause. I saw a smile on her face. "Don't worry," she continued. "I'm not expecting you to answer that. May I go through them again?"

I stood by her side as she slowly turned them over, occasionally holding one vertically, as if imagining it on a wall. Several she put to one side in a pile. By the end, there were about half a dozen. She laid these out at the end of the table. She had an eye; they were among the best I'd shown her.

A varied selection: two light sketches of a female nude, one completed painting of a naked girl from the waist up, an abstract of crossed, stockinged legs, and two much more explicit works. A detailed painting of an erect cock (Marcus's, as it happens), and one of my own masturbation works. I'd deliberated long and hard about what to show her, but neither Marcus nor I were identifiable from the pictures.

"I love all of these," she said. "You've got a good eye for the human form."

"Thank you."

"And these are all for sale?"

"Yes, but if you want anything specific, I can create it to order."

I waited as she perused the selection. She finally picked the two sketches.

"These for my hallway …"

Then she picked the legs.

"… and this for my bedroom. I do like the explicit stuff but haven't got anywhere to display it."

We agreed a price, and she put them safely in her case.

"Right," Eva said. "To the important stuff."

"Tell me what you're looking for."

"I've got photos of my tattoos, but I had the idea of letting an artist portray them. But I'm not sure how."

"It does seem a bit pointless painting a static representation of them, a photo would do that more accurately."

"How about you do a few sketches? No detail, just ideas of body pose. I can select one or two I like which you could add the detail to."

"Sounds like a plan. I think I warned you I've never painted tattoos before. Well, I've added one or two small ones from my imagination. But if you have a lot, or they're complex, I'm going to need to experiment to get them looking right."

"Well, you'd better see them."

***

"She just stripped off?" Sally asked, smiling.

I'd driven straight to Marcus and Sally's after dropping Eva at the station. I spent most Saturday nights with them now; sometimes Friday as well.

"Yes. She wasn't shy."

"I think I picked the wrong artform," Marcus added with a twinkle. "Nobody takes their clothes off for a writer, but if you're an artist, bam, they strip without blinking an eye."

"And?" Sally asked.

"I was speechless," I replied.

"Why?"

"I've never seen anything like it. Her whole torso is covered, and it's incredible work."

"Colourful?" Marcus asked.

"No. All black, except for a couple of tiny red roses."

"What sort of designs?"

"All geometric patterns, and so intricate. From any distance, it almost looks like she's wearing underwear and jewellery. I embarrassed myself a bit I think because I stood and gawped. But she took it well."

"Can you do it?"

"God knows. I studied it and took loads of photos. We're not sure how we're going to depict it. I'm going to sketch some poses and she can select the ones she likes. Then I've got to try and draw all the tattoos. It's a real challenge."

It would be. I was in awe of the designs on Eva's body. The artistry involved was amazing. There was nothing above her shoulders, or along her arms. A couple of small designs on her inner thighs, and a narrow trailing spiral down the back of each leg. But her entire front and back were covered, apart from her breasts and her buttocks. It did look like a tight lace body.

"Is she still adding to it?"

"Apparently not. It was all done a few years ago by her then-partner who was a tattoo artist. She says she's happy with it as it is."

"I told you there was something hidden about Eva, darling," Sally said.

There still was. Eva had stripped to a tiny thong to prevent any embarrassment at our first meeting. But she had several empty piercings running down her abdomen, all fitting neatly into the overall design. God knows what else was under that small piece of material. It seemed proper not to pass this information on.

"Um, I think I may have let one or two things slip," I said.

"Oh, yes," Sally replied.

"Well, she asked where I sold the racier stuff. Before I knew it, I told her about the kinky market."

"Go on …"

"Well, she knew you two were into the fetish world."

"Mmm …"

"She put two and two together."

"Ah ha …"

"I might have told her you two were in the local scene … and you might have dragged me along."

Sally was smiling, a wicked smile.

"Darling," she said. "Lucy's been giving our secrets away."

"So I hear," he replied.

"Shouldn't we do something about that?"

"I think we should."

"Any ideas?"

"Several."

"Care to share?"

"Later, perhaps."

He stared at me, a faint smile on his face. I knew whatever he had in store, we were all going to enjoy it. He loved leaving us in anticipation, and

Sally loved that. I was beginning to see why. You knew something incredible was going to happen, but you didn't know what or when.

"Have you told her about Jacques?" he asked Sally.

"Ooh, no. He's told his mother."

"The whole thing?" I said.

"Yes. Everything I told him."

"And?"

"Apparently, she laughed at first. Since then, she's been taking it in; a few tears, some reminiscences, more questions which he can't answer."

"Can you?"

"No. Some of the things she's asked are the same things we'd like to know. But he is grateful."

"What for?"

"She's told him a few things he didn't know. Filled in some gaps."

"What about?"

"I don't know. He hasn't told me, and I'm okay with that. He thinks if anyone tells me, it should be Genevieve."

"Are you going to meet her?"

"It's not been decided yet. He's happy with it, but he wants any invitation to come from her."

"Do you want to?"

"Yes ... I think so. My head says it's a great opportunity to fill in the holes. But my heart is nervous. This time, I'd feel like the intruder."

"What do you think, Marcus?"

"I'd go for it. Sal's come this far, answered lots of questions, met her half-brother. If Genevieve wants to meet Sally, it'll be the final piece of the jigsaw."

"Well," Sal said, "perhaps not the final piece. I've accepted I'll never know the whole story; what about the third identity? But meeting Genevieve would close off this part of the puzzle."

We found ourselves wildly guessing Genevieve's story, then what the third identity - Paul Doyle – got up to. The theories got wilder and wilder, until Marcus suddenly changed the subject. I wondered why but realised Sally had withdrawn a little. We'd overstepped the mark; this was her father we were talking about, after all.

She soon recovered and Marcus went to the loo. When he came back, he stood behind my chair, and I looked up at him.

"I believe you were due to atone for betraying our secrets," he said.

"Oh, yes," I replied, knowing the fun was about to begin. "So I was."

"Still want to?"

"Do I have a choice?"

"Lucy, you know you always have a choice."

"I always accept the consequences of my actions."

"Good. Go to our room and wait for us."

I didn't need telling twice and was sitting on their bed a few moments later. As I expected, they kept me waiting. When they finally came through from the playroom, they were both naked. Sal was wearing a strap on and Marcus was carrying a flogger and a few other things I couldn't make out.

Sally came over to me, bent and kissed me gently, before guiding me to my feet. She ran her fingertips lightly down my neck and looked into my eyes, lust already emanating from hers. "We're going to tie you to this bed and do wicked things to you. Any objections?"

"I'm all yours," I replied, so eagerly it caused Marcus to laugh.

"Strip," Sal said. They watched as I quickly took my clothes off and stood still. She came in front of me.

"We haven't tied you up before." I was very aware of that, and the thought was already exciting me. "We'll be gentle ... reasonably gentle. Promise you'll stop us any time you need to."

"Promise."

"Good. On the bed."

Marcus had cleared the cushions and pillows and they positioned me on my back in the middle and put some soft cuffs on my wrists and ankles. Ropes were attached to these and quickly clipped to something under the four corners. They had fun tightening the ropes until my arms were outstretched, and my ankles spread wide enough for me to be very aware of my own vulnerability.

Sally knelt beside me, holding a piece of colourful silk.

"Happy for me to cover your eyes, or would you prefer to see what's going on?"

"I ... I don't know."

"Try it. If you don't like it, tell us."

She folded the silk and laid it gently over my eyes. I could still see light around the edges, but that was it. She moved off the bed, and I waited for whatever was going to happen. I heard some soft music, then ...

Lucy

Nothing.

I knew them well enough to know this was part of the game. They were here, sitting somewhere. Waiting. It was Marcus's signature; Sally had told me. Building the anticipation, but also letting me relax into the situation. Letting me push everything else from my mind and concentrate on the now.

And it worked. I felt my mind clearing, focussing on the present. This was me, Lucy Halstead, lying naked, spread-eagled, tied to a bed, exposed to the gaze – and attentions – of two lovers. A broad smile grew on my face. My body had relaxed, comfortable on their huge bed.

I gasped as a searing cold hit my belly button. My breathing wavered for a while as I struggled to cope with the sensation. My tummy shivered as the cold spread, making little muscles twitch and spasm. It wasn't painful, but it was all I could think of.

Then my foot twitched at a touch. I tried to identify it; a kiss. Lots of little kisses on my right sole, joined by the same thing on the other. It was a stunning feeling, a mixture of heaven and hell. I couldn't move my feet away, and it sometimes tickled, sometimes sent a wave of pleasure up my leg. And the cold was spreading. I'd worked out it must be ice, and it was melting. A little trickle was running down between my legs, past my pussy and on over my perineum.

The kisses were working their way up my legs, over my shins, my knees, and my thighs. Just kisses; no fingers, no hands. They went over my hips, up my sides and along my arms to my fingers. I've no idea how long this went on, but occasionally, more ice was added to the melting remains. I felt a warm breath by my ear.

"Cold?" Sal whispered.

"Yes."

"Don't worry. You're going to be a lot warmer by the time we've finished with you."

But not right now. I jumped as that same searing cold hit both of my nipples at the same time. They were already hard, but now ice was being rubbed around them in slow circles, leaving cold trails as it melted and ran down my sides.

The cold slowly moved down my tummy, heading for … Oh, God. How would I cope if …? My hips squirmed as they took the ice either side of my pussy, running along that sweet alley, and gently pushed it under me

48

until it met my ass. My bum cheeks slammed together, but as soon as they relaxed, I cried out as a piece of ice was slipped into my ass. The feeling was extraordinary. The cold spread out instantly, almost numbing my groin.

It wasn't pain, but it wasn't pleasure either; somewhere in between. Where had I heard that before? I didn't have time to answer, as my clit almost shrank away from a piercing cold. I was suddenly aware of how awake it was; swollen and sensitive as the ice was rolled around it, never quite touching it, running over the hood, the meltwater running over my pussy.

I wanted to spread my legs but couldn't; they knew. My legs opened wider as the ropes on my ankles were shortened and I sighed as my pussy opened up. I could feel how wet I was, and it wasn't all from the melting ice.

The bed beside me moved, and I sensed Sally curl up by my side and let her fingers gently play with my nipples.

"Cold enough?" she said softly.

"Wow," was all I could reply.

"Time to warm you up."

She softly stroked my breasts, as a warmth suddenly hit my groin. Marcus had covered me with his mouth. He didn't move; his lips sealed around my pussy, warming it. It was almost too much, the change from cold to heat. I groaned as his tongue touched my flesh and explored my engorged folds. I thought I was going to come, but he had other ideas.

Taking my lips in turn, he licked them, sucked them, played with them. Sally was now doing the same to my nipples, and I was squirming under the attention. I didn't ever want this to stop. Heat and cold merged and fought in my groin as Marcus ran his tongue over me, pressing into me, running to my perineum. I moaned as another ice cube slid into my ass and he sucked my clit in earnest.

My orgasm built so rapidly it almost surprised me. No long groan, no gradual tension through my body. It hit me in a colossal bang. Wave after wave of spasms flowed through my groin, my ass joining in wildly. Sal was kissing my neck and even though I was tied down, my movements caused the silk to slide from my face. She looked at me, an intensely erotic look, and started to kiss my ear.

Lucy

My orgasm had subsided but wasn't over. Marcus had left my clit and slid a couple of fingers into me, gently massaging that sweet spot. Another slid into my ass and I came again. Gently, intensely, my body relaxing onto the bed as if every ounce of energy was being sucked out of me.

I lay there, breathing deeply. No gasping for air, no twitching. Just an amazing peace. My eyes were closed, and when I opened them, Sally was on her side looking at me, and Marcus was lying between my legs, gently stroking my thigh. Both were smiling.

"Wow," I said. "I ... I don't ..."

"Then don't," she replied.

Chapter 7 – Marcus

It was several minutes before anything was said. Sal looked at me and we shared a warm smile. We'd decided to do the opposite of what Lucy would be expecting and gone for the soft option. It appeared to have worked.

"Enjoy that?" Sally finally asked.

Lucy looked at her, then slowly down at me.

"Couldn't you tell? That was wonderful. Not what I was expecting, though."

"Disappointed?"

"Not after that."

"Good. Shall we untie you?"

"I need the loo, yes."

We helped her up and she went off to the bathroom. Sal came up to me and put her arms around me.

"That worked," she said, running her hand down to my cock.

"Sure did."

"Are you as horny as me?"

"No-one's as horny as you." I jumped as she squeezed my balls hard. "Ow! But yes, I am."

She kissed me, and dropped to her knees, lifting my hard cock, and running her tongue along the base. When Lucy came back in, Sal had most of it in her mouth. Luce came up behind her and stroked her hair. I pulled

Lucy towards me, and she wrapped her arms around me as we kissed. Sal pulled off me.

"You were expecting us to use you tonight, right?" she asked Lucy.

"Yea."

"Still want us to?"

Lucy looked down at Sally's strap on, then at my erection.

"As much as you want."

***

I sent Eva manuscripts of two of my earlier books. I'd selected two which were radically different from each other, and from Shadows of Gold. I needed to see what she was really after. If she wanted me to churn out books in a similar vein, she wouldn't touch these two.

I heard nothing from her for two weeks. Her secretary was sending me regular sales reports, and I began to think Eva had looked at the books and put them in a file called something like 'bargepole needed'.

Then she rang me. She was coming down at the weekend as Lucy had done some preliminary sketches. Could she come and have a chat? I suggested she brought an overnight bag, and Lucy brought them over for dinner when they'd finished their discussions.

The weather was foul when they arrived, and we let them dry off before we sat down. Sal plied them with coffee and cakes. After a few pleasantries, I asked Eva if she'd read the books.

"Yes," she replied, giving me a long stare. "Are they representative of your earlier work?"

"How do you mean?"

"Well, they're a bit leftfield."

"That's the benefit of self-publishing, Eva. You don't need to stick to a formula."

She knew I was teasing.

"Did you choose those two randomly?"

"No. I chose them as a challenge."

Eva smiled, Sally laughed, and Lucy looked puzzled.

"I thought you might have," Eva replied.

"Don't worry, Luce," Sally said. "Marcus and Eva like to have fencing matches. Well, Marcus does."

"I do too," Eva replied, "when I have the time."

"So," I said. "You're not interested."

"I didn't say that. I've given them to Eleanor to look at."

"Is that wise?"

"I told you, she's not what she appears. I have a suspicion she might like them."

"But you couldn't publish them as new."

"No, we have a sister imprint which specialises in reprints and books we inherit from other publishers. If we take them on, we'd use that."

"Okay, but I'll be tougher on changes to these, and in any new contract."

"We're not there yet. It'll take Eleanor a while to work on them, as they won't be her top priority."

"I don't know, one bestseller, and I'm already down the priority list."

"No, Marcus. Her top priority is Shadows of Silver."

"Hasn't she finished yet?"

"No" she replied, shaking her head wearily, "but she'll be done in a week or two."

"Come on, what did you think of them?"

She frowned, and I expected a poor review. I knew she wouldn't soft soap me.

"They're good. I enjoyed Fuchsia Spring more than Lady Bard."

"You wouldn't have taken them, though."

"Probably not. My job isn't to enjoy the submissions I get, it's to decide if the paying public will enjoy them."

"Why take them now?" Sally asked.

"Business," Eva replied, shrugging. "Strange as it may seem, Marcus is now a best-selling author, but to most people he only has one book. We want to give them more; if these can fill the gap until Shadows of Silver, we're interested. Provided they're good enough."

I didn't argue; I knew her position and understood it. I was glad I didn't have to do her job.

Over dinner, we forgot all about my books, and Eva and I stopped sparring. It was a relaxed, convivial affair and by the time we moved to the living room, my companions had all managed to consume a fair bit of alcohol.

"Can I ask a question?" Eva said.

"Of course," Sally replied.

"I don't know if it's okay with Lucy present."

"Oh, she knows all our secrets."

"When I talked to you about your friend Penny at the book launch, you said you had a foot in her world."

"Yes," I replied.

"Through her?"

"Not exactly," I said, looking at Sal. She nodded. "I'm guessing from what you said you know a bit about that world too. Munches, play parties, that sort of thing."

"Yes, I'm familiar with them."

"We got involved in a local group after we started exploring things. Now it's an important part of our lives. We met Penny there, and her mistress."

She looked from me to Sally, then to Lucy.

"Is that how you met Lucy, as well?"

"No," Sal replied. "Luce and I have been best friends since uni, but we are responsible for pulling her into the whole thing."

"I assume from what I've seen you don't live it twenty-four-seven."

"No, neither of us is interested in that, although we now know people who do. For us, it's fun. Well, a bit more than fun. It's important, but it's a part-time thing."

Eva looked between us slowly.

"Who's in charge?"

"We switch," Sally replied. "But he's a much better top and that's the more usual setup."

"Do you ever find places to play out scenes?"

Sally looked at me, and I nodded.

"We don't need to. Come with me."

She led Eva downstairs to show her the playroom. Lucy and I stayed in the living room.

"She's not afraid to ask questions, is she?" Lucy said.

"No, but at least we're seeing her human side. And if she's experienced similar things, I think we can trust her."

"Oh, I wasn't worried about that. There's something she's hiding though."

"Think so?"

"Yea, from her manner, and one or two things she's said to me."

A little later, Eva and Sal returned.

"Well, that was a surprise," Eva said. "That's some room."

"We enjoy it," I replied.

"I bet you do."

"Come on, what's your interest?"

"It probably won't surprise you to hear I was a Goth as a teenager." She was right, I wasn't surprised. She always wore black, with an occasional white shirt. "I got involved with a group who also crossed over into the fetish scene, and it intrigued me. But I made a rookie mistake and hitched up with an abusive guy."

"Sorry, Eva," I said. "Don't tell us if it's painful."

"Oh, it's okay. I dealt with it long ago. I didn't know what or who I was, but he convinced me I was a sub, and treated me badly, though I didn't know it at the time. He was no dom, just a guy who used it as a cover. Too many of them."

"Unfortunately, yes."

"Luckily, I got away before he hurt me too badly, but I know he went on to hurt at least two other women. It put me off the whole scene, put me off men, until I met Dizzie, who was a tattoo artist. It was him who got me into body art, and I've had one foot, as you put it, in that world ever since."

"He did your tattoos?" Lucy asked.

"Yes, the whole lot."

"How long did they take?"

"Three years."

"Wow. Are you still with Dizzie?"

"No, but he did a lot to restore my faith in men. Our paths still cross occasionally."

"Are there tattoo groups like the fetish ones?" I asked.

"There are, but they're few and far between and I find them a bit cliquey. A lot of fetish groups welcome us, but some don't."

"There are people with tattoos in our group, aren't there?" Sally asked.

"A few, yea," I replied.

"I have some tatt friends I meet up with," Eva said. "But it's become a bit too trendy recently and there are a lot of wannabes. I avoid most of the groups now, but I do miss it."

"Why not join a fetish group?" Sally said. "They'd welcome you."

"I'm not sure I've got the nerve now. I haven't been to anything like that for a long time."

"Come along with us." Eva frowned and looked at Sally, then me. "They're a friendly bunch and welcome anyone who respects the scene and its players. We were terrified the first time we went; Lucy was too."

Eva was clearly interested; she didn't respond immediately.

"We have a munch every month," Sally said. "Normally on the first Tuesday. Then there's a play party every two months, always on a Sunday afternoon. The next one is three weeks tomorrow. We'd love you to come."

"Thank you, I do miss the freedom in these groups, but I'll need to think about it."

***

The Eurostar emerged from the tunnel and travelled on through the French countryside. The invitation from Genevieve had come, and Sally accepted with little hesitation. I nudged her to arrange the visit as soon as possible, so she didn't have too much time to dwell on it, and two weeks later we were on our way to Paris. We were only staying a couple of nights. The city wasn't the attraction this time, we were there with one purpose. We'd booked the same hotel we'd used when we travelled up from the fort. The address was close to the café where we first met Jacques.

We settled into our room and asked the concierge to recommend a quiet local restaurant. It was a good choice. Good food, warm, cosy, and casual. I tried to imagine how I would feel in Sally's position. We'd talked a lot about this meeting, and she seemed to be looking forward to it. But she was apprehensive, which was understandable, but I thought it might be for the wrong reasons. Although she hadn't said it, I got the feeling she was worried about what Genevieve thought of her. She wanted to make a good impression.

I wasn't sure that was the point, but in the end, this was about Sally, and she had to play it her way. All I could do was support her and offer suggestions or advice if she asked. I was surprised she seemed more relaxed about this meeting than the initial one with Jacques.

"Want to talk?" I asked after she'd been quiet for a while, contemplating her wine glass. She came back from her thoughts.

"Sorry, I was making a decision."

"About what?"

"How much to tell her."

"You mean the money and the shadow."

"Yes."

"And?"

"If we get on, I'll tell her most of it."

"Sure?"

"I'm fed up with secrets. I've overcome the shadow, but it's traces are still there. They don't hurt any more, but if I can bring everything out into the open, I can kick it out for good."

"What about Mary?"

"That might be one element of the story she won't hear from me. It wouldn't be fair on Mary."

"There's one more thing to consider," I said, wondering whether to say it or not.

"What?"

"Genevieve might have her own surprises to tell."

"I've wondered about that. Jacques did say there are things he hasn't told us. But whatever they may be, I want to hear them as well."

We fell silent again.

"I do love you," I said softly. She looked at me. "I'm proud of you. Living with the shadow for fifteen years, keeping it to yourself, then going through this voyage of discovery with its mysteries and revelations. Never sure what's around the next corner. I couldn't have done it."

"Yes, you could. Because without you, I wouldn't have done it."

"That's not the same. I can help other people, but I'm hopeless at helping myself."

"Then we're a perfect match."

I reached across the table and she held my hands.

"Sal," I said. "You're everything I ever dreamed of. I still pinch myself every day to make sure it's not a dream."

"It's not a dream, darling. I feel the same. I love you so much." She paused and those gorgeous green eyes pierced me. "Are you happy?"

"Happier than I've ever been."

"Even with ... Lucy?"

"You've got more than enough love for both of us. I'm totally happy with Lucy."

"You would tell me if you weren't, wouldn't you?"

"Yes. Besides, she gives me a rest."

She gave me a flirty smile.

"And another lover," she said.

"The situation has its advantages."

"Well, she's not here tonight. Will I do?"

"Let's head back; I'll let you know in the morning."

Chapter 8 – Sally

We lounged in bed the following morning. Our meeting with Genevieve wasn't until two o'clock.

"Well?" I asked as Marcus came back from the bathroom.

"Morning," he replied, not yet fully awake. "Well, what?"

"Did I do?"

He whipped the duvet from the bed, and I watched his eyes trail over my naked body, a smile growing on his face.

"You did."

"Want to do it again?"

The answer was an hour of soft, gentle sex, interrupted halfway through by the arrival of a breakfast trolley, as I was riding him to my second orgasm. I had to lift off to let the maid in and was closing the door, when he came up behind me, pushed me forward, lifted my robe and slid straight in. I had to hold the door handle to steady myself and started giggling, but that stopped as my climax came. He led me back to the bed, my legs still shaking, and we resumed where we'd left off.

We decided to find Genevieve's address, then have some lunch nearby until the time came. She lived in Montmartre, parts of which were achingly beautiful, in one of a terrace of stunning apartment blocks ranged up a long sloping street, which had steps on one side and a cobbled path on the other. There was a convenient café at the bottom, and we settled in until two o'clock.

"I'll tell you one thing," Marcus said, as we sat at a table on the pavement. "I don't think they were left penniless if she lives here."

"You never know. It was a long time ago; we don't know what she's done since."

But I knew what he meant. The area was one of the most eclectic and desirable in Paris. I could imagine living here myself. As we ate lunch, I realised how calm I was. I wasn't sure why. A year or two ago, I couldn't have done this. But here I was, about to meet my father's other wife. I laughed out loud, and Marcus gave me a puzzled look.

"Just thinking how weird this situation is," I said. "I hope it's not too frosty."

"Let's see how it goes. If it is, we do the minimum and make our excuses."

"I suppose you're going to leave it all to me?"

"Yes, Sal. She may not even want me there when you talk."

That gave me a moment of panic; I hadn't considered it, but if it happened, I thought I would cope. I looked at Marcus; I don't think he knew how much strength he gave me. But he'd been right last night. We gave each other strength.

We walked up the hill. Almost all the blocks were in wonderful condition, with one or two still black from the pollution of the previous hundred years. There were flower beds along the pavements; bare in February, but it must be beautiful later in the year. One of the blocks was shrouded in scaffolding, with the unmistakable sounds of stone-blasting coming from behind the covers, along with the inevitable streams of stained water running down the hill. Our destination was the block next door.

I pressed the button on the intercom, and within seconds, I heard Jacques's voice.

"Oui?"

"Bonjour Jacques. Sally."

"Ah, come up Sally. Third floor."

The door buzzed, Marcus swung it open and we went into the lobby. It was grand in a typical Parisian way and we walked over to the lift, an old, elaborate affair filling the centre of the grand staircase. He pulled the gates open, ushered me in, and selected the third floor. The cage slowly rose through the building before coming to a halt. I stepped out to see Jacques standing in front of an open door.

"Sally," he said, "welcome. Marcus, too."

He gave me a hug and a kiss, then shook Marcus's hand. He looked as immaculate as he had the first time we met. Not a hair out of place, his clothes fitting perfectly.

"Come, my mother is waiting for you."

For the first time, a little nervous shiver ran through me. I followed him through the doors of the apartment and immediately felt at home. It was grand but warm and lived-in, decorated in a sumptuous style. This was one old apartment which hadn't had the character sucked out of it. Huge mirrors, gilt edging, oil paintings, antique furniture. But it all worked together and wasn't at all over-powering.

We followed Jacques along a corridor and through the door at the far end, into a fabulous space. High ceiling, richly decorated, and with tall windows along one wall which looked out on a fabulous view of Paris. Standing serenely a few paces into the room with a faint smile on her face, was a woman. A striking woman. We'd worked out she must be at least sixty but seeing her now you wouldn't know it. Tall, with dark hair piled loosely on her head, a timeless face, and a figure many younger women would envy.

"Mama," Jacques said. "This is Sally Fletcher. Sally, this is my mother."

"Bonjour, Madame Mahoney," I said, as confidently as I could.

"Welcome, Sally," she replied in almost perfect English, with a slight French lilt. "Call me Genevieve. And this must be Marcus."

"Bonjour, Madame," Marcus replied.

"Please," she said, turning to a square of four sofas. "Come and sit."

"Thank you, Madame," Marcus said. "But would you and Jacques prefer to speak to Sally alone?"

"No, no," she replied. "You are welcome to stay if Sally is happy. It is my son who is leaving us."

I was surprised; I'd expected him to stay in case anything went wrong, but I was already getting the feeling Genevieve could look after herself. Jacques left us and she led us to the sofas, and I saw she'd prepared tea. A teapot, and a few plates of cakes and pastries.

I waited for her to seat herself and chose the sofa at ninety degrees to her. I was briefly annoyed when Marcus sat away from us, but I understood why. This was my gig, not his.

"So, Sally," Genevieve said. "You are Tony Crowther's daughter."

"I am."

"Or Brendan Mahoney's."

She was testing me; I'd half expected it.

"Both, I guess. It's a strange situation."

"It certainly is. What shall we call him?"

"Whatever you like. You knew him as Brendan, I'm fine with that."

"Good. Now, I want to thank you."

"Thank me?"

"Yes. For giving us an end to his story. When your father - Tony - died, you knew about it, could deal with it, even though it was a tragic story. For us, there was no such end. Brendan simply disappeared. We imagined all sorts of things."

"That he'd deserted you?"

She looked at me sharply, then gazed out of the window.

"No," she finally said. "In my heart, I never thought he deserted us, although Jacques did. They weren't close."

"My father didn't seem close to anyone."

She turned back to me.

"He was a man of his time; he wasn't easy to know. The Lord knows, this situation proves that. And now the work you've done on his childhood perhaps tells us why."

"Yes, I guess it does."

She'd been studying me, weighing me up. And now, she'd made her decision.

"Sally, you have kindly given us the results of your search, and I know Jacques has told you some of our story. If you would like, I suggest we complete the picture."

"I'd like that. To be honest, there's not much more to my story, but there were a few things I kept back."

"I understand, Jacques did the same. He's a good boy. But before we start, let's have some tea. That's one thing Brendan did introduce me too, and I'll be forever grateful. Marcus, please help yourself."

She poured the tea and handed me a cup. I didn't feel like eating anything.

"Shall I begin?" I asked. She nodded assent. I'd been truthful, there wasn't much I hadn't told Jacques. I quickly recounted the story, but this time I told her about the money, though without quantifying it. I told her about the shadow and how Marcus had helped me come to terms with my father and the money and supported me in my search for his reality. She studied him carefully, until I could see he was getting uncomfortable under her gaze.

When I finished, I sat back in my chair, and the pastries suddenly seemed attractive. Genevieve sat quietly while I picked up a plate and took a couple. They tasted heavenly. Finally, she chuckled.

"That's quite a story. I must confess, I'm not much surprised by it. I loved Brendan, but I always knew I didn't have all of him. I'm only finding out now how little of him I had."

"I'm sorry," I said feebly.

"Oh, you've nothing to apologise for. No one is responsible for the actions of their parents, as Jacques often tells me. Anyway, I won't bore you with my whole life story, but it is enough to say my childhood wasn't a happy one and by the time I became an adult, I was something of a – what would you call me? – a tearaway."

She smiled and I returned that smile.

"But I had one thing going for me, I'd turned into a beautiful woman, and I ended up using that asset. I went to the south of France and attached myself to any man who'd pay. I hope that doesn't bother you?"

She looked from me to Marcus; we both shook our heads.

"Good. I was successful, but it wasn't secure. A few weeks with one man, then a rush to find another before the money ran out. A friend of mine told me about a club – well, a brothel – in Cannes."

"Le Sphinx?" I asked. She turned to me sharply.

"You've heard of it?"

"Visited it. Well, the building where it used to be. We found a membership card among Dad's effects."

"Oh, did you? I went to work there, and that's where I met Brendan. He used to come in from time to time, and gradually only visited me when he did. He was very generous."

"That," I said, "seems to be a common theme. He wasn't mean. But where did the money come from?"

"I'm getting to that," she said, smiling.

"Sorry."

"He was a courier. In those ancient days, important documents and urgent things had to be physically carried around the world. He travelled all over the place delivering perfectly legitimate items. But it was all a cover; he was a smuggler. An exceptionally good one. As far as I know, he never got caught."

"What did he smuggle?" My heart sank a little. I'd suspected this might be the answer, but there were things I hoped he wasn't involved with.

"Small things mainly; gemstones, jewellery, precious metals, that sort of thing."

I must have breathed a sigh of relief; she picked it up.

"Oh, never drugs, he was always adamant about that. He only carried things he could conceal on himself or in a vehicle. He had a strong reputation among … well, among the criminal fraternity. If they wanted a special delivery, he was usually the first person they called. But he also smuggled stuff for himself; that was where he made the big profits."

It was then I noticed she was wearing some fine jewellery; a pearl necklace, large earrings, a couple of delicate rings studded with diamonds. They reminded me of my own treasure trove. Hardly surprising.

"Then we fell in love. I suppose now I have to question whether he ever loved me, but I loved him. I left Le Sphinx and we set up the house in Beaulieu …" She paused, looked at me, then Marcus. "I suppose you've been there, too?" I nodded. "I became his assistant, his secretary, and his business manager. Jacques came along two years later."

"About the time I was born."

"Probably, though I knew nothing of that. I assume your mother knew nothing about me."

"No, I'm fairly sure she didn't. From what I remember of her – she died when I was eleven – and from what my aunt tells me, she was a very naïve woman. I suspect, if you'll forgive me, almost your total opposite. I've always wondered why he married her."

"I wouldn't try and analyse your father too much. He was a mass of contradictions. I never worked him out. But he did a lot of trade between the continent and England. I suspect he wanted a convenient base."

"And a cover story."

"If you like, yes. He was always a meticulous planner. He never jumped into things. I guess having a family in England made good sense; business sense, anyway."

So, my mother, Charlie and I were a business asset. Something to cover his tracks. The man had some nerve.

"When he died," I said, "or disappeared as far as you were concerned, were you okay financially?"

"Oh, yes. That was one thing I didn't have to worry about. We'd spent years investing the money he made into legitimate things. Property, businesses, that sort of thing. It seems he was doing the same in England. We even bought Le Sphinx."

"No …"

"Yes, very profitable it was too. For a while."

"What happened?"

"The Berlin Wall fell."

I was flummoxed.

"How did that affect you?"

"When I first helped him, he was working mainly for long-established groups. Criminal gangs, if you like, all over Europe. But after the Wall fell, East European and Russian gangs began muscling their way in, and they didn't follow the rules. Cross them and you tended to disappear."

"Is that what you thought happened to Dad?"

"It was one of the possibilities, but it seemed unlikely. He'd given up the smuggling years before and we were respectable businesspeople."

"What happened to Le Sphinx?"

"We were made an offer we couldn't refuse. The place was too successful. The Russians were taking over the sex market in the south and they wanted Le Sphinx. They offered us a price and we knew what would happen if we said no. Brendan could look after himself, but he knew he couldn't win a war."

"But it closed down later."

"Yes!" she hissed with delight. "They didn't understand the place. They got rid of all the girls we'd recruited and brought in a load from Russia. Much cheaper for them. But the clientele of Le Sphinx weren't after quick sex. They wanted an evening of entertainment and companionship with women who could talk and discuss meaningful things. Or they were looking for girls with special skills, if you know what I mean. The members deserted the place, and it ended up with few customers. It was too expensive to run as an ordinary brothel, so they closed it. I think they sold it off."

"It's been turned into apartments."

"Pity, it was a beautiful building."

"Sorry, I interrupted. You were talking about the time after he died."

"Not much more to tell, Sally. Some of the businesses were in joint names, some he'd put in my name and I was able to carry on as before. After seven years, we applied to have him declared dead, and it all came to me … and Jacques, of course.

"A few years ago, we decided to simplify everything. I'm not getting any younger. We slowly sold off property and businesses in the south and bought a few in Paris. I was born here and wanted to come back. Jacques had one or two ideas he wanted to explore, and Paris was the best place for that, as well. We still have a few properties in the south, but we're disposing of them when the time is right."

A thought occurred to me.

"You own this block?"

"Yes," she said. "And the one next door, and the one two down from that. Amongst others."

"He provided for us all."

"He did. Strange, isn't it?"

"Yes. I still don't feel as if I know the man."

Genevieve looked pensive for a few moments.

"You know, Sally, I thought I did when I was with him. But now? All I can say is I knew a part of him."

Chapter 9 – Marcus

I relaxed as Genevieve told Sally her story; there wasn't anything I thought would upset Sal. It was a story we'd already guessed in outline. As the conversation moved to more general topics, they began to include me. Genevieve asked about us; how we met, what we did. She asked for a copy of my book, and I promised to send her one. Jacques joined us, kissing his mother before sitting down. They appeared to be close.

"Is everything alright, Mama?" he asked.

"Yes, Jacques. It is. We now know as much as we ever will about your father."

"Has it helped?" he asked Sally.

"It's much as I expected, to be honest, Jacques. But it does confirm a few things. I think it brings my search to a close."

"Can I ask …" he began hesitantly. I saw Genevieve frown slightly. "The other identity …"

"Paul Doyle?" Sally replied. "I'm not planning to pursue it. Again, we only have the documents, and most of the information relates to the far east. It would be difficult to follow any of it up."

"We might have other brothers or sisters," he said, looking at his mother as he spoke. He seemed to be pushing some unseen limit.

"It's possible," Sally said, placing her hand on his knee. "But I'm happy with the brother I've found."

He smiled, took her hand, and kissed it.

"He's happy to have found a sister, Sally," Genevieve said. "Happier than he will easily admit." Jacques gave a gentle nod. "I hope you will come and visit us, and we can get to know each other."

Sally looked at Jacques, then turned to Genevieve, before smiling her most open smile.

"I'd like that," she said.

After we left, we walked down the hill. Sally hadn't said a word since we emerged into the open air, and I stayed quiet. When we turned the corner at the bottom, she stopped, and I waited. When I looked at her, there were tears in her eyes. I pulled her to me, and she let go, sobbing onto my shoulder. A few passers-by gave us a wide berth, but I didn't care. The tension was coming out.

After a few minutes, I took some tissues from my pocket and put them in her hand. She pulled away from me, looked at them and shook her head. I'd half expected to need them earlier. She was smiling in between the tears, her eyes sparkling, and used the tissues to dab her face.

"Well?" I said.

"Now I know."

"And?"

"It's good. It could have been a lot worse."

"True."

"I need a drink."

There were bars and cafes along the street, and we went into the first we came across. I ordered some drinks and waited for her to talk. After she'd taken a few sips, she dabbed the last moisture from her eyes and put the tissues down.

"She was lovely," Sal said.

"She was. I think she likes you."

"I like her ... and Jacques. You won't mind if I keep in touch, will you?"

"It's none of my business, Sal." She went to object. "But, for the record, I like them too."

"Thank you." She leaned over and kissed me. "For everything."

We went back to the hotel, had a shower, changed, and headed out for dinner. Over the course of the evening, we dissected what we'd been told. It fitted what we knew and confirmed some of our guesses. Genevieve had been right; we knew as much as we ever would about Tony Crowther.

***

Eleanor had been busy. When I got back, she'd sent me her annotated copy of Shadows of Silver, as well as her initial thoughts about my two older books. Eva had been right; she had enjoyed them. Well, been intrigued is better. She suggested we get together and talk about them, rather than her putting her thoughts on paper. Sally encouraged me to accept the invitation.

When I went through her work on the Shadows book, my reaction was the same as before. Initial scepticism and tutting, but on close examination, most of her comments were constructive. I had some re-writing to do. I had time; Eva wasn't looking to launch until the autumn.

I travelled to London the following week to meet Eleanor. We sat in an office for three hours talking about the books, and I was impressed. She knew what she was talking about.

"I loved them, Marcus," she said. "But from a commercial point of view, they're difficult."

"I know. I'm not sure why Eva is even considering them."

"She's treading a thin line. She wants to keep you in the spotlight, but she can't afford to turn readers away in droves."

"Thanks."

"I've got some suggestions which would make them more saleable."

She spent the rest of the meeting going through a detailed analysis of both books. It was spot on, and by the end, I had some ideas to improve them without changing their essential character.

Towards the end of the meeting, Eva popped her head around the door.

"Oh, good," she said. "You haven't killed each other yet."

"No," I replied. "We were just joining forces to come along and kill you."

"Why ever would you want to do that?"

"Because you're our common enemy."

Eleanor laughed as Eva rolled her eyes.

"So, what do you think?" Eva asked.

"Eleanor's made lots of good suggestions, and I'll go away and work on them."

"Good boy."

I gave her a challenging look which Eleanor didn't see, and she flushed slightly. Eleanor had another appointment and we prepared to leave, but Eva called me back and closed the door.

"I'm coming to see Lucy this weekend. She's got the first finished picture for me to see."

"I'm sure it'll be good."

She looked nervous for the first time since I'd known her.

"Your offer …"

"Oh, yes."

"Still open?"

"Of course."

"I'm thinking about coming."

"Well, why not stay overnight with us? Then you can decide on Sunday."

Saturday evening was dinner for four, once again. Eva had liked Lucy's first picture, but they'd agreed to something a bit different and Lucy seemed to be enjoying the challenge. Eva fitted in easily now, knowing some of our secrets, and I knew Sally was desperate to tell Lucy about our visit to Paris. They hadn't been able to get together since we returned.

"Was Paris okay?" Lucy asked casually, obviously wanting to hear.

"Yes," Sal replied. "It was."

"Weekend break?" Eva asked.

"Not exactly," Sal replied, pausing as she decided how much to say. She went for it. "I was searching for my father."

Eva frowned.

"Would you like to hear a real-life mystery story?" Sally asked her.

She started at the beginning for Eva's benefit and brought her and Lucy up to date with our meeting with Genevieve. I watched Sal as she related the tale and saw she was actually relishing the details, enjoying the reaction she got to the more scandalous parts.

"I now know a lot more about my dear father," she said, as she concluded her telling.

"More than you wanted to know?" Lucy asked.

"No. I'm happy. I'm at peace with him now. I'd like to have had the opportunity to talk all this through with him, because there's a lot more we'll never know."

"The third identity?" Lucy said.

"Yes. Who knows, there may be a fourth or a fifth."

"You should write a book," Eva said. "People love real-life mysteries. False identities, gem smuggling, bigamy. It's got everything."

"I'm no writer, Eva," Sal replied.

"You don't know until you try. Or perhaps it's Marcus's next project. Turn it into a work of fiction."

I noticed Sally looking at me with a strange expression on her face. I suspected the idea hadn't occurred to her. It had to me.

"I've got enough to do," I said, "with your rogue editor's input."

"If you don't mind me asking," Eva said later in the evening. "What did you do with all the gemstones?"

"We sold a lot of the smaller stuff," Sally replied. "And I had the best made into jewellery. Would you like to see?"

"If you don't mind. I love jewellery."

The three girls disappeared downstairs and were gone some time. It was nearly an hour before they returned.

"I was about to organise a search party," I said.

"We got distracted," Sal replied. "Eva's been rifling through my underwear."

"She had the same reaction I did when I first saw it," Lucy said, giving me a wink. "How can one woman need so much underwear?"

"Something for every occasion," Sally protested.

"Yes," Eva said, eyeing me suspiciously. "I can't imagine what those occasions must be like."

"Don't play the innocent, Eva," I replied. "It doesn't suit you."

"Oh, alright. I'm rather jealous, and of the jewellery. At least I know you weren't lying when you said you weren't writing for money."

"Did you ever doubt me?"

"I've had writers tell me that before."

"To try and increase their credibility?"

"I guess so."

"I didn't have any to begin with."

"Eva loved the jewellery, particularly the emeralds," Sal said as we were lying in bed. "I let her try it all on."

"She was visibly excited," Luce added. "It was so unlike her usual self."

"I think she's forgotten how to have fun," Sal said.

"Or something happened to take the fun away," I replied. "I'm not sure she told us the whole story about her fake dom."

"True, I'd forgotten that."

"We'll need to look after her tomorrow, just in case."

"She's nearly ready," Sal said, coming into the living room. "You'll hardly recognise her."

Eva had said she needed a long time to get ready, and they'd gone downstairs nearly two hours ago. As usual, Sal was wearing a relatively normal dress; she'd take it off when we got there, and I'd have to wait and see what was underneath. Lucy came in, followed by Eva.

"Wow," came from my lips before I could stop it. Sal was right, I'd have passed her in the street and not known it was Eva, but I'd have noticed her. Her long black hair was loose, but glossy with red streaks through it. Her makeup was exquisite; thick black eyebrows, heavy black eyeliner with another red streak through it and deep red lipstick. She was wearing heavy, heeled ankle boots, and a long … well, what was it? A cross between a dress and a coat. It was tight around her torso, a row of small buttons running up the front to a high stiff collar, sitting on her shoulders. It split into four at the waist, with slashes down the side and at front and back. Underneath, a short flaring skirt, and bare legs. All finished off with black lace gloves.

"Well, darling? What do you think?"

"You look incredible, Eva. Sorry to gawp."

"That's okay. I haven't got done up like this in a while."

"Wait until you see the rest," Lucy added.

"The rest?"

"Not now, darling," Sally said, "later. And only if Eva feels like it. Are we ready?"

When we arrived, the girls went into their changing area. Eva didn't need to do anything, but Sally and Lucy came out in a couple of stunning outfits as usual. But I knew, for once, they were going to be outshone. I had a suspicion Eva was going to be the centre of attention today. We went through to the main social area and bumped straight into Yas, one of the organisers.

"Hi, Marcus," she said, hugging me, before doing the same to Sal and Luce.

"Yas," Sal said. "This is Eva, a friend of ours."

"Welcome, Eva. You're going to shame us all today. You look fab."

"Thank you, Yas."

"I'm guessing this isn't your first time at this sort of event."

"No, but it is my first for a while."

"Enjoy it. These three can show you the ropes, they're old hands now."

We went through to look at the events list and spent a few minutes noting items of interest, then went back to grab a drink and circulated. Yas was right, we did feel like old hands now; at least, Sally and I did. Lucy was still feeling her way. Eva seemed relaxed and as time passed, appeared to grow in confidence and stature. She was tall anyway, and the heeled boots added to her height.

After an hour, we'd chatted to lots of people and watched a couple of demos. People were interested in Eva; a new face, and a style which wasn't common in the group. I suddenly realised the four of us going around together might be putting people off approaching her.

I took Lucy to one side and explained. She immediately understood, and I steered Sally away, leaving Lucy and Eva to mingle.

Chapter 10 – Lucy

I still only knew a few people, but that number was growing all the time. I was happy in the group now and the two of us introduced ourselves and chatted. Several people seemed to make a beeline for Eva, people I might not have met without her. At one point, a guy with heavily tattooed arms walked past, and I saw Eva watch him. She looked thoughtful.

"Can we go back to the changing area?" she said.

"Of course. You okay?"

"Yes. I want to dump this dress."

When we arrived, I opened our locker and she carefully unbuttoned the bodice of her dress and slipped it off her shoulders. I smiled at how she now looked. Just her short skirt, boots and a bralette specifically cut to fit between her tattoos, which were now visible in all their glory. But there was more.

She had a vertical row of bars through piercings on her abdomen, with chains attached on each side hanging down. They originated under her bra – clearly attached to nipple rings – ran down her tummy and disappeared into the waist of her skirt. Sally and I had seen her in her underwear, and there were clearly piercings there but exactly what, we weren't privy to. When she'd posed for me, she hadn't been wearing anything in them, so I hadn't noticed.

"There," she said. "That's better."

When we returned, she drew glances from just about everyone. I'd spent the last few weeks carefully studying her tattoos closely and they were an artistic tour de force. A few people stared, but Eva was unfazed, and several people stopped her and politely asked to have a closer look, or who did them. She happily dealt with all their queries.

We went to get something to eat and found a couple of beanbags to sit on. A guy walked by who made us stare. Built like an athlete, in nothing but a tiny leather thong, which struggled to hide what must have been a larger than average piece of equipment and did nothing to hide a tight pair of buttocks.

"That's some bum," Eva said.

"If you like that sort of thing," I replied, then winced. I wasn't sure if Eva knew my sexuality. She gave me a questioning look.

"I usually prefer the female variety," I said.

"Ah, forgive me, I hadn't twigged."

"Oh, it's fine," I said, smiling. "It's always risky making assumptions here."

"True. Do you have someone?"

How do I answer? Would Sally and Marcus mind?

"Well, it's complicated," I replied.

"It's okay, I was being way too forward."

"No, you should probably know." She looked at me expectantly, and I wasn't sure how to explain it. "Sally and I have been friends for donkey's years, but recently, we've been … a bit more."

"Oh …" She wasn't sure what to say, thinking through all the possible chances to say the wrong thing. "Does Marcus … know?"

She looked startled when I laughed.

"He encouraged it." She went to say something, but nothing came out, her mouth gaping half-open. "And now … well … the three of us are … sort of …"

Her mouth closed and she slowly smiled.

"I see. There's more to Marcus than meets the eye."

"There certainly is. Until I met him, I'd been gay for fifteen years."

"He must be something special."

"They both are. Let's see if we can find them."

We found them watching a demo and shuffled in beside them. Marcus's eyes widened when he saw Eva, but she sat by Sally and he couldn't see without making it too obvious. I winked at Sally, and she smiled back. When the demo finished, he leaned forward.

"I'm sorry, Eva, but I'm going to be rude and look at your tattoos."

"Be my guest," she said, standing and slowly turning in a full circle. "Like them?"

"I'll be honest," he replied, "I'm not usually a fan. But the artistry and skill in those are incredible. They flow over you, almost as if they've been there since birth. They're stunning."

"Thank you, that was the intention. To make them look a natural part of me. I'm not into figurative stuff or too much colour. I've just got two tiny spots of red."

He looked back at her, scanning the designs.

"Oh," she said, smiling, "you wouldn't see those unless we got very friendly."

"There's a challenge," Sally said.

"I've got enough trouble keeping up with you," he replied.

"I don't know about that, Marcus," Eva said. "I hear you've got your own little harem here."

I gave Sally and Marcus an apologetic smile; I knew immediately they didn't mind my indiscretion.

"I don't think that's true," he replied. "I think Lucy and I are Sally's harem."

"How do you work that out?" Sal said.

"First you seduced me, then Lucy. We're the innocents in all this."

"You nearly had me there, Marcus," Eva said. "Until you claimed to be innocent. I know enough about you now — about all of you — to be quite sure that's one thing you're not."

"I think she's blown our cover, darling," Sal said and kissed him.

"Hi, guys," a familiar voice said. Penny was standing in front of us in that dress. The pink latex dress she was wearing when we first saw her at one of these events. She gave each of us a hug and a kiss but was looking sideways at Eva and frowning, as if digging a memory from the depths of her mind.

"It is you, isn't it, Eva?" she said.

"It is, Penny. Hello."

Penny gave Eva a hug and a kiss as well, which surprised her.

"You look stunning," Penny said, still openly studying Eva's body. "That's … wow. I know someone who would love to see these designs. He'll be here later if you're still around. I'll introduce you."

"No Helen today?" Sally asked.

"No," Penny replied. "Something came up she's having to deal with."

"And you're not there helping?"

"She's probably glad to be rid of me for a few hours."

"Who'd want to get rid of you, Penny?" Marcus asked.

"Depends what I'd done, wouldn't it, Marcus?" she replied with a gorgeous cheeky smile. "I must go to the loo. See you later."

She walked off slowly, knowing we were watching, and we all followed every move of her hips.

"Sometimes I wish I had a bum like that," Eva said.

"Gorgeous, isn't it," Sal dreamily replied.

"Someone else you'd like to add to your harem?"

Sal turned to Eva and looked her in the eye.

"We already have, once or twice."

Eva took a second or two and collapsed into laughter.

"You three are going to get me into trouble," she said.

We'd arranged to leave at a reasonable time, as Eva had to change and get back to London. As we drove away, she was the most relaxed I'd seen her. She'd disappeared with Penny for a while.

"Did Penny take good care of you?" Marcus asked.

"She did. She's a lot of fun." We kept quiet. "She introduced me to a guy who's in the middle of a full-body design. He's only using geometric patterns, and he looks terrific."

"Did he like yours?"

"Yes, he did. His aren't as intricate as some of mine, and he wanted some pictures." These events had strict bans on cameras and phones. "Lucy, can you send me copies of the pictures you've taken?"

"Sure."

"I've got his email, and I'll send him a few carefully selected ones."

As we arrived at Marcus and Sally's, a thought struck me. Usually, when we got home, we were all ready for some fun of our own. This afternoon seemed to be different. I guessed it was because Eva was with us, but it was strange. Marcus asked if Eva wanted to stay another night, but she had to work early the following morning, so we all changed, and he drove her to the station.

"Sal," I said, as we lounged around, waiting for him to return. "How come we didn't get as turned on this afternoon?"

"Speak for yourself."

"Did you?"

"Yes, but it does change over time. When we first went, we were desperate by the time we got home. I think it's the novelty of being in a place with half-naked people, watching the demos and things. But you get more accustomed to it."

"That's a shame."

"I don't think so. It means you get more out of the event. You watch, you listen, you learn. Doesn't mean you can't have as much fun when you get home."

"That's a relief."

"Staying the night?"

"How can I turn down that offer?"

"Good. Fancy giving Marcus a treat?"

She left him a note on the table, and we had a quick shower. Leading us, still naked, into the playroom, she lowered the lights and put some quiet music on.

"Right," she said. "Lock me to the bar."

She lowered the bar from the ceiling, and I put some cuffs on her wrists. She gripped the bar, and I locked them to it, raising it until her feet were flat on the floor, her arms stretched high above her.

"What about me?" I asked.

"Unfortunately, I can't now lock you to the bar. Not a good idea, anyway."

"Why?"

"What happens if we're both locked in place, and he gets delayed?"

"Good point. How about this?"

I stood facing her, raised my arms to the bar, and pressed my body to hers. Breasts to breasts, groin to groin, thighs to thighs.

"Perfect," she said.

It was. The feeling of being skin to skin was warming me. Perhaps the afternoon had affected me more than I realised. We were soon gently kissing, and I had the advantage. Leaving one hand on the bar, I lowered the other, and ran it delicately down her back, causing her whole body to flex and ripple.

She let her head fall back, as I let my fingers explore the body helpless in front of me. Her exposed neck was asking to be kissed, and I let my lips trace over her skin from ear to breast. By the time my fingers trailed from her bum, around her hip and inched between her legs, she was moaning gently.

A door closed in the corridor outside. I removed my fingers and replaced my wandering hand on the bar as the playroom door opened. Marcus walked in, wearing a pair of black boxers. He took one look at us and smiled. Sally had put a glass and a bottle of wine on a table, and he walked slowly over to it, poured a glass, and sat down. Sally found my mouth and started to kiss me; I responded eagerly. The warmth of her body against mine was working its magic.

After watching us for a few minutes, he came over, gently kissing us in turn. His hand began to stroke us, gently, softly, running over our skin. He checked our hands and found mine were loose. Going over to the racks, he picked up another pair of cuffs and clipped them around my wrists, before locking them to the bar.

I'd not been tied like this before. There was an excitement about it, a vulnerability. Not a word had been spoken. The trust they had in each other had been extended to me. And I trusted them; if I said stop, I knew they would.

He walked around us; two naked women, helpless, pressed together, anticipating his next move. I could see the euphoria in Sally's eyes and understood it now. I didn't think I'd ever feel it as strongly as she did. She gave in to it, luxuriated in it. Sometimes, she seemed to be in a trance. I decided to let myself go, to see if I could follow her.

As he circled, his hand trailed over us, lightly rolling over our skin, from neck to bum. Being Marcus, especially our bums. Sally suddenly jerked as I heard his hand come down on hers. A few slaps, eliciting a series of little whimpers. Then it was my turn, and I tensed as his hand came down on my cheeks several times. He moved around us, spanking us in turn, allowing us to relax between each flurry of strokes.

The flogger was next. He started with me, gently, allowing the fronds to wrap around me. Moving to Sal, there was no such consideration. The crack of the leather on her skin echoed around the room, as did her grunts with each stroke. Before I knew what was happening, the bar rose, and I gave a little shriek as my feet left the ground, my hands gripping the bar tighter.

We were suspended and swinging free. The feeling of vulnerability increased; and increased again as he spun us gently. I wasn't prepared as the flogger struck. He stood still and flicked it as we spun, randomly striking my skin or Sally's.

As the spinning stopped, I looked at Sal. Her eyes were sparkling, and she gave me a passionate kiss, almost a bite. Her mouth sprang open, as another sound echoed around the room. A crop. I soon found out this was much more precise. Again, I knew he was being gentler with me, but the little burning patches were spread further over my body.

When the impacts stopped, the sudden peace was overwhelming, and I had a moment of panic. But I saw this was what it was all about. I'd forgotten everything else in my life. I was here, now, enjoying the sensations, the feelings, the intimacy. It was a feeling I'd never experienced before getting involved with these two mad people.

I came back to the present as my ankle was moved, and Marcus attached a cuff to it, followed by the other. A bar now held my legs apart. He did the same to Sally, though her bar was wider than mine. The ceiling bar descended, and my feet came to rest on the ground. It continued to drop, and a touch of the crop made me shuffle my feet back. By the time we settled, we were bent forward so far, we were only held up by our grip on the bar between us. Sal and I were facing each other on either side of it.

I felt vulnerable. My hands locked, my legs spread open and my bum sticking out. I smiled as I considered how much Marcus must enjoy us in these positions. My thoughts were brought to a sudden halt, as a cold, wet object slid firmly into my ass. A lubed plug; a large one. I watched as he walked around and repeated the operation on Sally. We could see each other clearly in this position, our faces a couple of arm's lengths away. The look on her face was so sensual and erotic, shivers ran through my groin.

Then I saw Marcus holding a cane. My heart missed a beat; was I going to feel that? I'd thought about it often. I'd watched him using canes on Sal and although I knew what it did for her, it still made me wince. But I had to admit watching it turned me on like crazy; I still hadn't fully come to terms with that.

He stood in position behind Sally and was watching me, his eyes focussing on my face. Sally's eyes were closed, a dreamy smile on her lips. I noticed he was holding a thin whippy cane, not one of the heavier ones, and he gently tapped it on her rear. No force, just teasing her. Her whole body tensed as he gave her the first meaningful stroke, but her body relaxed again, and I saw her adjust her feet to stick her bum out further.

He started to place rhythmic strokes on her bum and thighs. I couldn't see the impacts, but the sound of cane on skin echoed around the room and I could see her body moving in response. He ran his hand over her bum, eliciting a long, low moan from her. Then he moved around behind me.

I knew I could say no. A small part of me was tempted to. I didn't fantasise about pain, never really considered it. But I found myself enjoying the sessions where he spanked me. Sally and I sometimes did it, too. It wasn't the pain for me, not in the way Sally or Penny got off on it. It was the whole experience; the fun we were having, the pleasure that came with it. I wasn't going to say no, not yet anyway.

I flinched at the first touch of the cane, then felt foolish when I realised he'd simply laid it across my bum. Sally was watching me, her eyes fixed on mine, those green eyes so wide, I hardly recognised them. I knew she'd fantasised about watching me being caned; she'd told me several times. It appeared that particular fantasy was about to come true.

The cane lifted away from my cheeks. I closed my eyes, waiting for the first touch. It came, much lighter than I expected. Just a fleeting nip, nothing really. Then again, and again. Slightly firmer now, moving up and down, occasionally flicking my thighs and one or two in that delicious spot where they met my bum. The individual strokes weren't painful, but the heat was growing, and I could feel warmth gradually spreading. I opened my eyes and saw Sally with a gorgeous grin on her face. She blew me a long slow kiss; I couldn't help smiling.

Marcus moved back to Sally and this time, he didn't hold back. The strokes were stronger and more regular. Sally was soon swaying under their impact, and the whimpering was much stronger. But the look on her face was one of ecstasy. She jumped as his fingers landed between her open legs, squirming under their actions, and I realised she was close to orgasm. Marcus stopped, and her body dropped in exasperation. Watching her receiving the cane had made me horny as hell.

But as he moved behind me, I froze. Would he use the cane on me as hard as he had on Sally? I wasn't sure I'd be able to take it. As this went through my mind, I relaxed. Then let out a loud whine as vibrations hit the plug in my ass, closely followed by his cock sliding into me. Within a few strokes, my orgasm rose and flooded through me. I was desperately hanging on to the bar, my legs shaking as he continued to fuck me, the vibrator sending spasms from my ass through my whole groin.

Just as it was getting too much, the vibration stopped, and he stilled, stroking my back gently. He waited until the trembling subsided before slipping out of me and running his hand over my bum, letting it slide between my legs, causing me to gasp as his fingers ran over my aching clit.

As I recovered, I looked at Sally, a pleading look on her face. She wanted him; she needed him. In this mood, she'd do anything for him. I recognised that mood from our own sessions. She was desperate to come; once, twice, who knew? He dropped behind her, and I couldn't see what he was doing, but the sounds and expressions she made told me it was working.

Her back arched as her orgasm hit, her head dropping. A series of little chirps filled the room, followed by a giggle, then a cry as he rose and drove his cock into her. At full depth, he paused, bringing the wand into contact with her plug. That was it, she was gone. I struggled to stay upright as her writhing was transmitted to the bar which was the only thing holding us up.

He began to fuck her, the wand still in place. Her body was shaking in spasms as he kept her orgasm going, curious noises coming from her throat, interspersed with funny little giggles. They were so strange, I found myself laughing. She heard and raised her head enough to look at me, but her eyes were glazed, rolling upwards as another climactic wave washed over her. Her head dropped again.

Marcus moved the wand between her legs, and the noises went to a whole new level. He stopped his movement, pulled her back onto him, and held her there while he let the wand do its work. I'd seen her like this on several occasions now, once or twice under my ministrations. I didn't know whether she experienced one long orgasm or a series of them, but it was astounding to witness. He ignored me now, treading a fine line between pushing her further and knowing when to stop.

Her hands left the bar, and she drooped, the cuffs now the only thing holding her to it. He had one hand around her waist, holding her firmly in place while the wand took her to another peak, producing violent trembling and a long, piercing cry which was almost inhuman. He removed the wand, which dropped to the floor and laid his hand on her back. Then there was stillness.

Sally came down, the trembling slowing, and after a minute or two, she tentatively reached for the bar. His free hand went under her tummy and he lifted her enough for her to grasp it. It was moments like this which made me realise how well they understood and trusted each other.

He looked over at me and gave me a slow wink. A wave of emotion went through me that made me a little uncomfortable, but it passed. Sal's head slowly came up. Her face was heavily flushed, and she had that look. Her 'fucked' look. The look that said she'd been somewhere special. She looked in my direction and I could see she was trying to focus. When she did, she smiled vacantly; I tried not to laugh.

Marcus had slipped out of her and now nudged the back of her knee and she sank to the floor. He quickly undid her ankle cuffs and removed the spreader, allowing her to sit on her heels, and released her wrists. Her arms fell by her side. She was exhausted.

Chapter 11 – Marcus

Sally's response in this session had surprised me, and I'd switched to safety mode as her orgasms flowed, thinking she might pass out. Now that she hadn't, and was safely squatting on the floor, I could carry on. When I'd returned to the flat, I'd found a note from Sally. 'We're in the playroom. All yours. Silent mode?' It was something we'd tried once or twice, a whole scene where nothing is said. This time there'd be three of us.

Sal was safe, but Lucy was still fully restrained, and all mine. She'd reacted positively to the cane, and now I was getting to the point where I wanted to take my pleasure. But I could still wait a little longer. I picked up the wand, and moved behind Lucy, turning it on and letting it rest on her butt plug. I loved how sensitive her ass was. When she was in the mood, you could make her purr just by stroking it. I wondered how she would respond to it being fucked, but the invitation hadn't come, though I knew Sal did with a strap-on.

The vibration was soon affecting her, and she was moaning freely, trying to press her ass harder against the wand. I slid into her pussy, eliciting a low growl. This time, I wanted to fuck her, so holding the wand, I began to rock. I moved the wand to her clit, and she groaned, her head dropping. I looked over to Sal, who was watching with an intense expression on her face.

Lucy's head reared up, and that long groan began deep in her chest. As I switched the wand back to her ass, it roared from her throat as her climax came. She began shaking and I watched her bum cheeks wobble deliciously. She began grunting, and as the grunts slowed, I stopped, gently stroking her back. Her head slowly dropped, as her orgasm ebbed away. I slid out and guided her to her knees.

As she recovered, I removed her ankle cuffs and released her from the bar. She squatted in the same position as Sally, who now shuffled across to us, and put her arms around Lucy, kissing her. Sal looked up at me, then at my cock, at her face level. She opened her eyes wide and smiled, as her hand reached out for it, and she encased the head with her lips.

I groaned as she slid it further into her mouth. My climax wasn't far away, and this was as good a way as any I could think of. She slid a hand between my legs and stroked my balls as she sucked. No gentle teasing this time, but soft firm strokes.

Lucy was now back with us, and she had one hand on my bum, sliding a finger gently down the valley, over my ass and down to my perineum. Sal came off my cock and swung it towards Lucy who took it in her mouth, looking up at me. This was almost too much. They let it jut between them, licking and kissing the sides, occasionally sliding their lips over the head. I was the one making the noise now.

Sal knew I was close and nudged it towards Lucy, who took the head into her mouth, clamping her lips around it. Her tongue started to flick and that was it. My balls tightened and my cum rushed along the shaft.

"Luce …" I managed to grunt in warning, before it shot into her mouth. I heard a cough at the back of her throat and her eyes blinked, but she carried on as my balls continued to empty themselves. After the first few spasms, Sally leaned forward and kissed her cheek, and Lucy came off me, their lips coming together.

I could see my cum spilling from her mouth, covering her chin as she shared it with Sally. She pulled away, looked up at me and they both licked me clean. It was one of the most erotic things I'd ever experienced. They shared a long, lingering kiss, their tongues seemingly searching for the last vestiges of my tang.

I bent down, gave each a kiss, and slowly left the room to end the scene. Standing in the corridor outside, my legs were still shaking, and I had to lean against the wall to stop them. I waited a couple of minutes, before going back in. Lucy and Sally were still on the floor, with their arms around each other.

"Here he is," Sal said, patting the floor beside them. "I've told Lucy what was on the note."

"She didn't know?"

"No."

"How come you didn't speak?" I asked Lucy.

"The funny thing is, I didn't even notice we weren't talking. I didn't think about it."

"Are you okay?" I asked Sally.

"Yes, I was close to passing out."

"I thought you were."

I kissed her.

"Are you okay?" I asked Lucy.

"Certainly am. That was some session."

"The cane?" Sal asked.

"Not bad," Lucy replied, with a grin.

"Can he use it again?"

Lucy looked at me.

"Yes, and a bit harder."

"There, darling," Sal said. "Imagine the two of us bent over the horse at your mercy."

"I already have, frequently."

***

Two weeks before Easter, and I was in London again, doing interviews before the launch of the paperback version of Shadows of Gold. Eva and I had an understanding now. She carefully selected the promotional work she asked me to do and I did it, always on my best behaviour. I rapidly got fed up answering the same questions time after time, but it was only for a few days. I took the opportunity to do a bit of shopping and visit a couple of exhibitions, which lightened my mood.

I spent a tiring afternoon at Eva's office. She had a couple of boxes of the paperbacks for me to sign. It was nowhere near as many as the hardbacks, as the demand for signed paperbacks wasn't there, but they were more difficult to sign and took almost as long. Eva let her secretary deal with my grumpiness before putting in an appearance. We were joined by Eleanor. I'd done some re-writing on my older works and sent them copies.

"I think they're much tighter, now," Eleanor said. "I like them."

"I'm still not sure," Eva said and saw my reaction. "Marcus, I've got my business head on here. I liked them, but I'm still not sure how people who've read Shadows of Gold will react to them. My focus is on Shadows of Silver, and I want everyone who bought Gold to be gagging for Silver. If they read one of these and it puts them off, Silver won't sell."

I knew what she was saying, but it was frustrating.

"Eva," I said. "You know my position; I don't really care. If you want these two, take them, if not, don't. But at some point, I will be making my old works available again."

She raised her eyebrows.

"Blackmail, Marcus?"

"No. You know me better than that. But I'm not hiding them away forever. You can either work with me or leave me to it."

It sounded a bit like an ultimatum, but I was getting fed up with the delay. Prior to Shadows of Gold, I sold my books online and via my website. My sales were good for an indie, and although the money wasn't important any longer, I was a writer. I wanted people to read my work.

"Okay," she said. "We'll work with you. But we'll initially only publish them as e-books. If there's enough demand, we'll look at physical copies."

"No, thanks," I said.

"Why not?"

"I can do that myself. What I can't do is get physical copies into bookshops, to get them in front of new readers. If I accept your offer, I end up in the same position I was before, except you take a huge cut."

"I didn't think you needed the money."

"I don't, but there's a principle here."

I could see Eleanor was getting a little uncomfortable, but Eva and I were used to this. Robust discussion, you might call it. Eva tapped her pen on the table, frowning at me.

"I'll do some calculations," she finally said. "To see what it would cost us to do a short print run, to test the market. Would you be happy with that?"

"Yes. Provided I don't have to sign them."

The ice broke, and Eleanor took the opportunity to leave us.

"Eva," I said. "One more thing. My website."

"Oh, yes."

She'd already offered to bring it in-house and have her team manage it. I suspected the idea was to keep it well away from me.

"I'm replacing it," I said.

"Let us do it for you."

"Is that in my contract?"

"No," she replied, shaking her head.

"You know, for someone who likes control, your contracts are surprisingly leaky."

"I'll tell our legal department. Are you doing it yourself?"

I had built my current site. It didn't have any bells or whistles, but it was simple, elegant, and fit for purpose, but it needed freshening up. And it was getting a lot more traffic.

"No, I'm going to ask Penny to do it."

"Penny? Penny as in ..."

"As in the bum you envied." She rolled her eyes, but there was a grin on her face. "She's a web designer. I've seen some of her stuff, and it's good. A bit quirky sometimes, but good. I'd prefer to work with someone I trust."

Eva looked slightly hurt.

"You don't trust me?"

"You, yes. But you wouldn't be building or running the site, would you? Some faceless teenager in your media department would, following a set of rigid, boring style guidelines. My site would look the same as all the other authors you run websites for."

"Alright, but can I please ask you to run it by us before you launch it?"

"Helen's coming over this evening," Sally said when I got home.

"Oh?"

"Yea. I got an odd call from her, asking if she could speak to us."

"What about?"

"I don't know. But she asked if Lucy could be here, as well."

Helen didn't just pop in; it wasn't her style. The times she'd visited us had been arranged well in advance. She didn't do anything on the spur of the moment. Lucy arrived from work, equally mystified. At six-thirty on the dot, as arranged, the doorbell rang. I opened the door to find Helen and Penny and ushered them in.

Helen was immaculate as always, but looked tired, and proved frostier than usual. The barest of greetings followed. Penny was subdued.

"Sit down, Helen, please," Sally said.

Helen waited until we were all seated, then looked at the floor.

"I'm sorry to invade your home like this," she said, waving away an attempted protest from Sally. "But I need to give you some information." For the first time, she looked uncomfortable and glanced at Penny. I wondered what could have happened. "Ben has left us. Well, I've kicked him out."

We were all on tenterhooks now. Something had obviously led to this abrupt action. I glanced at Sally and Lucy, but they were watching Helen, waiting for some explanation. Penny was looking at her mistress with concern.

"He picked something up and passed it on to Penny and me."

Sally, Lucy, and I looked at each other, our minds thinking the same thing.

"From what I can ascertain," Helen continued, "this happened within the last three months, well after Penny holidayed with you. But I wanted to let you know in case the little bastard was lying. I'm sorry, but I suggest you all get tested."

She was being very formal, and clearly still angry. I dreaded to think of her reaction when she first found out. There was silence in the room, Sally and Lucy looking concerned.

"Thank you, Helen," I said. "We appreciate you telling us. May I ask what we're dealing with?"

"Gonorrhoea," she replied, enunciating every syllable. "And lice," she spat out. I suspect Sally and Lucy relaxed at the same time I did. Gonorrhoea wasn't great, but it could have been a lot worse.

"We'll get checked out. Thankfully, those are easily curable."

"That's not the point, Marcus," Helen said. "I've always prided myself on being a shrewd judge of character. I got it wrong with Ben."

"None of us is perfect," Sally said softly. "We all make mistakes …" Helen went to say something, but Sally carried on, "… even you, Helen."

Helen tensed, and I saw Penny wince, but she relaxed again, and a faint smile appeared on her face.

"Yes, Sally, I guess I'm not perfect, after all."

"It's the imperfections which make us who we are," Penny said, then blanched as we all looked at her. Helen laid her hand gently on Penny's leg and they shared an endearing smile.

"Helen," Sally said, "will you stay for dinner?"

"Thank you, no. I'm afraid I'm not good company at the moment."

"Okay, but you're not leaving until we've set a date for you both to spend an evening with us."

"Three doctor's appointments, then," Sally said after Helen and Penny left.

"Yes," Lucy replied, looking thoughtful.

Over dinner, we were quiet, thinking about the implications. The three of us were committed to our relationship; we trusted each other. When Penny had joined us, we'd perhaps let our guard down a little too much. We knew Helen and Penny were a committed couple as well and trusted each other. We'd forgotten about Ben and his other relationship. It was a chink in our armour.

Chapter 12 – Sally

Helen and Penny came to dinner on Easter Saturday. We'd been tested and were massively relieved when everything came back negative. I made sure I spoke to Helen a couple of times, as she was upset by the whole episode. When I told her we had the all-clear, I think she was as relieved as we were.

She seemed back to her usual self when she arrived with Penny. Over dinner, the subject was avoided, but Helen was still a bit withdrawn.

"Still brooding, Helen?" I asked.

She gave me a fierce look, then softened.

"A little," she replied.

"She still blames herself," Penny added, surprising us.

"I guess that's the danger of a shared relationship," Lucy said.

"Not really," Penny replied. "Ben didn't get it from Jason."

I looked at Lucy and Marcus, who looked blank.

"Jason's an old friend of mine," Helen said, seeing our confusion. "Ben's master." She put her glass down and looked at Penny who nodded gently and turned to us. "It was Penny who noticed the problem first and went to the doctor. When the results came back, I got tested as well. At first, we questioned each other, which hurt, then we realised it must be Ben. I went to see Jason."

"That was the day of the play party," Penny added.

"He was as surprised as us," Helen continued. "We waited for Ben to get home and confronted him. Eventually, he told us he'd met someone at a party and seen him a few times. We presume that was the source, but we can't be sure he hadn't messed about before. That's why I told you."

"So, he's not part of your set up anymore?" Lucy asked.

"I'll throttle him if I ever see him again," Helen replied; we believed her. "And Jason's told him to leave as well."

"Think he's learnt his lesson?" Marcus asked.

"Frankly, I don't care. I'm annoyed he fooled me. With everything I've experienced, I thought I was a good judge of character ..." she looked at Marcus, "... especially men."

"Are you going to replace him?" he asked.

"No," Helen replied sharply. "Not at the moment, anyway, whatever this little thing might want." Penny blushed and looked down at the table. We knew what her appetites were. "We'll leave it for the moment, and perhaps discuss it. I'm willing to accommodate Penny's needs," Penny smiled sweetly, "but not at the risk of my own health, or hers."

I saw her point, but knowing Penny, I wondered if it would cause a problem for them. To me, their arrangement with Ben had always seemed a little odd, but if we'd learnt one thing on our journey into this world, it was that nothing was odd.

We left the table and moved to the living room, taking the wine with us.

"How's the book doing?" Penny asked Marcus.

"Quite well," he replied.

"Very well," I said, "he's being modest. The hardback's still selling well, and the paperback was launched on Thursday." I waited for him to say something, but he didn't. "And he needs to talk to you, Penny."

She looked puzzled, and Marcus gave me a frown.

"Me?" Penny asked.

"Yes, Penny," he said. "I'm replacing my website and wondered if you had time to do it for me."

Her face took on a look of pure delight; her soft spot for Marcus was all too evident.

"Of course," she replied. "I'd love to."

"Lucy needs to talk to you, as well," I said. Her turn to frown at me. Penny looked from Lucy to me, puzzled again.

"She needs a website, too," I said. "Her kinky artwork is proving extremely popular. It's time she had a wider audience."

"Ooh," Penny said, "we could have fun with that. I'll ring you both in the week to arrange meetings."

"Are you busy, Helen?" I asked.

"Very, the party event brought in a lot of business."

"Have you always been a corsetiere?"

"No, I came to it later in life."

"What did you do before?" Marcus asked.

"Oh," she replied airily, "this and that."

We were intrigued by Helen. We still couldn't decide how much of the person we saw was the real thing. Sometimes, it seemed to be an act. We'd imagined all sorts of possible pasts for her and dearly wanted to know the truth.

"Anything interesting?" he asked, clearly offering a challenge.

"Plenty," she replied. "But I'm not sure you're ready for it, Marcus."

"Try us."

Penny had been watching this exchange with an amused expression. We had wondered how much Penny knew about her mistress's past life. Helen looked at each of us in turn and held out her glass for a refill. She took a couple of large mouthfuls and started talking.

Nearly two hours later, she stopped and emptied her glass. We had sat for all that time, mesmerised by her story and her telling of it. Nobody said anything, taking in the things she's told us.

"So you see, Marcus," Helen concluded, "trust is something I don't give easily."

"I can see why," he replied. "Thank you for trusting us."

She straightened her skirt.

"I don't know about that," she said, turning to Penny, "but this one trusts you, and that's good enough for me."

They shared a private moment, which touched me more than I expected. Although they were vastly different, there was a strong bond between them.

Now the tale was over, we all needed to stretch or visit the loo. I found myself alone with Penny.

"Did you know all that?" I asked.

"Most of it," she replied, smiling gently. "All the important stuff. But it's the first time I've known her tell the whole story, and there were a few details new to me."

"I hope she won't regret it."

"No, she doesn't do regrets. You can be sure there are still things she didn't reveal."

"You should write your memoirs," Marcus said to Helen after we all returned. "I reckon people would love that story."

"No, thank you," Helen replied. "I value my privacy too much. I'm not ashamed of anything I've done, but I've had my time in the spotlight. Now, I prefer quiet anonymity."

We knew what she meant; we felt the same way.

"It's time we talked about holidays," I said the next morning over breakfast. It was Easter Sunday, and we were already eating chocolate from the eggs we'd given each other.

"We're not going to beat last year," Lucy said.

"Probably not," I replied. "What does anyone fancy doing?"

As I suspected, Lucy stayed quiet. She still wasn't comfortable about the financial side of things, however hard I tried to convince her.

"Darling?" I said to Marcus.

"The first thing is to work out how much time off you two can get."

"True," I replied. "I get twenty-five days."

"Same here," Lucy added.

"Right," he said. "How much do you want to keep in reserve?"

This led to a long, circular discussion, as we tried to fit a quart into a pint pot. Lucy and I had been lucky the year before when we'd been able to take unpaid leave.

"Could we do it again?" Lucy asked.

"I'm not sure," I replied. "David was happy last year, as I had nothing to do during the library move. But I doubt I can do it every year."

"Okay," Marcus said. "Let's assume you're both putting twenty days into the equation. Anything else will be a bonus."

"Fair enough."

"You two will want to go away for a couple of weeks."

"Not two weeks, surely," Lucy said. "That's half our time."

"How about a week?" I said. "And one or two weekend breaks."

"Sounds good."

"That leaves three weeks."

"You'll want to visit Jacques and Genevieve," Marcus said. He was right. We had an open invitation to visit them and I couldn't leave it too long. Besides, I wanted to.

"So, a few days in Paris."

"Leaving two weeks," he said.

Compared with the previous year, it seemed horribly short. We came up with a few suggestions, but our hearts weren't in it.

"Lucy," Marcus finally said. "Could you afford to take unpaid leave?"

She considered it for a moment. I was tempted to offer help but thought better of it.

"Yes," she replied. "I managed last year, and I'm making some money from my art."

"Right," he said. "You two need to find out if you can take unpaid leave, and if so, how much. Then we can make some decisions."

"Good idea. Luce?"

"Yea," she replied. "Why not?"

"And how about we have a trip to Paris before the end of the Easter break?"

***

This time, we hadn't needed to book a hotel. When I spoke to Jacques, he insisted we use an apartment in their block.

"We keep one free for visitors," he told me. "It's not very grand and it's at attic level, but it's got quite a view."

I couldn't refuse but warned him we wanted to stay a few days and take in the sights as well. He had no problem with that, nor my request to bring a friend. So, we found ourselves on the Eurostar again, but with the addition of Lucy. She wasn't sure about coming, worrying she might be in the way, but I convinced her it would be fine.

When we arrived, Jacques greeted us on the top floor, and I introduced Lucy. He showed us the apartment. It was typical of a Paris attic, all sloping ceilings, and odd-shaped rooms. But they'd done it up beautifully. Two bedrooms, a bathroom, a small kitchen, and an almost circular lounge. But the best bit was a small outside space on the roof, overlooking half of Paris. It was wonderful.

"I'll leave you to settle in," Jacques said. "When you're ready, go down to Mama's. She's eager to see you. Just go in, she's left the door open."

We unpacked and freshened up, before descending a couple of floors to Genevieve's apartment. I'd wondered if I should bring a present but couldn't think of anything appropriate. Just before we left, I found the perfect thing.

I knocked on the door and pushed it open.

"Genevieve," I called out, "it's Sally."

"Come in, come in," the reply came.

We walked along the hallway, and Genevieve appeared at the doorway of her reception room, a broad smile on her face. She gave me a hug and a kiss and did the same to Marcus.

"This is Lucy," I said, "an old friend of mine."

"Bonjour, Madame," Lucy replied very formally.

"Welcome, Lucy," Genevieve said. "I'm Genevieve, please. Another pretty face. Come in."

She led us to the sofas, and we sat closer this time. I thought I'd better clear any embarrassment upfront.

"Just to let you know, Genevieve. Lucy knows most of my secrets and story. But I've only told her the bare bones about you and Jacques. I didn't want to betray confidences."

Genevieve chuckled.

"You mean about working in a brothel," she said. "And being married to an international smuggler who had more than one wife?"

There was a moment's silence before we all joined in her laughter.

"I think that brings you up to date," I said to Lucy.

"Lucy," Genevieve said. "If you're a friend of Sally's, that's enough for me."

"Thank you," Lucy replied, a little nervously.

"Genevieve," I said. "I have something for you."

"You didn't need to bring me a present."

"It's not exactly a present."

I took a leather roll out of my bag and handed it to her. She saw the initials 'BM' embossed in the leather, and slowly looked at me.

"I wasn't sure if you'd want it," I said, suddenly aware this could backfire spectacularly.

She undid the straps and unrolled the leather. Inside were the passport, credit cards, business cards, driving license and a few other things in the name of Brendan Mahoney. She slowly picked up each item, examining it, turning it over. At the end, she came to the membership card for Le Sphinx and held it up.

She looked at me, and I saw her eyes were moist.

"This," she said, waving the card, "was where all the trouble began."

I thought I'd made a mistake, but a broad grin filled her face.

"Oh, Sally. This is wonderful. Thank you. Is this what you found in the bank box?"

"Yes. This one, and two more."

"Without this, you wouldn't have found me?"

"No."

"And that would have been a shame. Come and give me a hug."

I went over and she held me to her for some time, before releasing me. At that moment, Jacques came in.

"Bonjour, mama," he said and came and kissed her. I used the opportunity to retreat and sit down. She silently passed him the leather roll. He sat on the arm of the sofa and opened it. At the first object, he looked at his mother, then continued to examine all the items. When he finished, he gave his mother a look I couldn't read.

"A gift from Sally," Genevieve said.

"Thank you, sister," Jacques said, and came over to give me a kiss.

"I thought you should have them. I should tell you most of them are fakes."

Genevieve laughed.

"That doesn't surprise me at all."

Chapter 13 – Lucy

Sally had told me more about Genevieve and their earlier meeting than she admitted, but without dotting the 'i's and crossing the 't's. As they chatted, I studied Genevieve. I didn't know her age, I don't think Sally did, but they'd told me she was at least sixty. If you concentrated, you could see the age in her face, but she had a timeless look which was classically French. Elegantly dressed in an understated way, with hair that looked carelessly styled but annoyingly perfect.

I also studied Jacques. Marcus and Sally had been right, he was beautiful. Tall and slim, with perfect posture, and precise, delicate movements. When he walked around the room, he seemed to glide. But it was his face which drew you in. It was delicate and sculpted, every feature perfectly shaped. I looked from him to his mother, and you could see some of her features in him.

His hair was short and tousled, as if he'd just got out of bed, but I was sure it had taken him some time to achieve that look. At one point, he caught me looking at him. He just smiled, and nodded his head slightly, before returning to their conversation. At the next pause, he turned to me.

"Lucy," he said. "Excuse us, we are leaving you out."

"No," I replied. "You all have so much to talk about which I'm not privy to. Please, don't mind me."

"I will get some tea, then I must leave you."

He returned a little later with tea and a plate of gorgeous Parisian patisseries, placed them on the table in front of us and kissed his mother.

"Adieu," he said, rapidly scanning all of us. "I will see you all tomorrow."

"He's off to work," Genevieve said as he left. It was five in the afternoon.

"What does he do?" I asked.

"He runs a couple of clubs, Lucy," she replied. "But I will leave him to tell you about them. Perhaps you can visit while you're here."

"Of course," Sally said. "We'd love to."

Over tea, Genevieve asked us if we'd been to Paris before, what we'd seen, what we wanted to do while we were here. She discovered my love of art and recommended a couple of smaller museums which weren't as crowded as the more famous ones. I made a mental note. On our way in, I'd noticed the art on the walls. It was an eclectic collection, but all original. From nineteenth-century works, through the twentieth, to a few contemporary items.

"Genevieve," I said. "May I be rude and look at some of your pictures?"

"Of course, Lucy. Be my guest."

I wandered around the room, examining each one as they continued their conversation.

"And we'll want to do some shopping as well," Sally said. "Won't we, Luce?"

"If we must," I replied. I knew what that meant; we'd both shop, she would pay. I accepted it now with a shake of my head but still wasn't comfortable with it.

"I have an idea," Genevieve said. "If you're happy to traipse around with an old woman, I'll take you to a few of my favourite places."

"We'd love that," Sally replied.

So it was, that next day, Genevieve, Sally and I set out on a shopping expedition, leaving Marcus to his own devices. He didn't mind shopping, but tactfully suggested three was the optimum number; four would be a crowd. We headed out, and Genevieve took us by the arm as we walked along. It felt a bit strange, but it seemed to be common for friends to walk along arm in arm, and it meant we didn't get split up in the crowds.

We went to shops we wouldn't have found as tourists, little boutiques in tucked away arcades, as well as the larger department stores, hosting the famous names. Genevieve was known in many of them, and obviously a welcome customer. I gave in and joined Sally in trying things on.

By noon, we had accumulated a collection of bags and needed a rest.

"Are you okay to carry on?" Sally asked Genevieve, who showed no sign of tiring.

"Oh, yes," she replied. "I can shop all day."

"What about all the bags?" I asked.

"I have an idea. Genevieve, is there somewhere for lunch around here?"

"Oh, yes. There's a lovely café around the corner."

As we walked, Sally called Marcus.

"Where are you?" she asked. "Fancy lunch? … We're heading for Café Amerigo on Rue de Mezieres … Okay, see you there."

"Where is he?"

"The Luxembourg."

"Oh," Genevieve said," that's not far away."

When we arrived at the café, it no longer surprised us Genevieve was known to the staff – and some of the customers. She ordered something I didn't catch, and we took the weight off our feet. A few minutes later, Marcus joined us, giving us each a kiss. To my surprise, he had a few bags of his own.

A waiter brought a huge jug to the table. The liquid it contained was pale orange, with some fruit and ice bobbing about. I could see bubbles.

"I find this so refreshing," Genevieve said. "It's orange and mango with a little lemon juice and a touch of mint."

"Just what I need," Sally replied.

"Oh," Genevieve added, "and a little champagne."

As we found ourselves sharing her liking for this particular drink, another waiter brought a couple of platters to the table, one with hot food, one with cold. It looked like a feast. Some breads arrived, and we tucked in.

"What have you been up to?" Sally asked Marcus.

"Wandering around," he replied. "It's a joy in this city."

"Isn't it? Been doing some shopping?"

"A bit."

"Darling …" she said in her best seductive voice. I knew what was coming.

"Yes?"

"You're not going back to the apartment, are you?"

He knew what was coming but put on his innocent face.

"Why?"

"We've got more shopping to do, but we've got a lot of bags."

"Have you?"

"Yes. I was wondering ..."

Genevieve was watching the conversation with amusement.

"Pass them over," he said.

As we left the café in one direction, I looked back at Marcus heading off in the other, laden with umpteen bags.

"Where now, Genevieve?" Sally asked.

When we returned to the apartment, Marcus was sitting on the roof terrace with a bottle of wine and three glasses. We kicked our shoes off and sat down as he poured.

"Had a good day?" he asked.

"Yes. I'm knackered," Sally replied.

"Me too," I added.

"Well, get some rest, because we're heading out in a couple of hours."

"Where are we going?"

"To Jacques's club. Well, one of them. Club Beaulieu."

"What sort of club is it?"

"Cabaret, I think. I met him as I came back and he invited us any evening, so I suggested tonight."

"Is there a dress code?"

"No jeans, but beyond that, apparently anything goes."

We needed a taxi to get to the club as it was some distance away in a grand old building which looked a little run down, but there was evidence of work going on to improve it. Arriving at reception, Marcus told them Jacques was expecting us, and shortly after a waitress led us to a table set slightly apart on a raised area of the floor.

"Monsieur Jacques will join you when he can," she said.

She gave us menus which were small booklets. We flicked through and found a history of the building and how it became a club. Then a food menu, followed by page after page of drinks. I'd never seen a menu like it.

Lucy

We spent some time deciding before ordering, then sat back and looked around. Although the club felt warm and cosy, it was large. Booths around the edges, and tables in the centre running to the stage, which was larger than I'd expected. To one side of it was a band, currently playing ambient music as people ate. We realised we were in Jacques's own booth.

Our drinks arrived, followed by the food. The service was remarkably efficient. The staff were quick and silent, unusual in a Paris club. The lights dimmed a little, the band struck up a rousing tune and a spotlight shone on the edge of the stage.

"Mesdames, messieurs, ladies and gentlemen … your host … Jacques Mahoney."

To the beat of the music, Jacques appeared, bowed, and glided to the centre of the stage. He was wearing black trousers with a multi-coloured, satin jacket and bow tie. He welcomed everyone to 'an amazing night of cabaret' and told a few jokes in a relaxed style, wandering the length of the stage, catching people's eye. He seemed in his element.

He introduced the opening act – 'the Beaulieu girls'. No French cabaret would be complete without them. It was a varied bill, but every act was top class. There were no amateurs, no slip-ups. A comedian, a deliberately terrible magician, a vocalist, with the girls appearing briefly between each act.

Jacques arrived at our booth.

"Hello," he said. "Is everything alright?"

"Yes, thank you, Jacques," Sally replied. "This place is fabulous."

"We're not quite there yet, but I'm happy with how it's going. We need to finish the outside and find one or two more performers."

"The ones you've got are good," Marcus said.

"I only employ the best. Unfortunately, there are too many poor cabarets in Paris. It puts people off."

"Do you host the show every night?" I asked.

"No, I only do a couple of nights a week. But as you were here …"

"Oh, Jacques," Sally said. "Thank you."

"It's my pleasure. I must leave you; I need to keep everything moving. If you need anything, ask one of the team."

I was enjoying myself. The patrons were having fun, the performers were good. A couple of acrobats made the audience laugh, then gasp as they tumbled between the tables, even somersaulting over a few, making the occupants shriek.

A guy came on and sang three songs; all impressions of famous singers and if you shut your eyes, you'd believe they were there. The girls did a couple of numbers, wearing less each time, but always tasteful. I was too far away to get a good look, but enjoyed them, nonetheless.

The stage went dark, the music stopped, and the house lights went out. The band played a plaintive melody, and a female voice filled the club. I didn't know the song, but it was instantly moving.

A spotlight pierced the darkness, and a woman entered the stage from the wings. Tall, elegant, and beautifully dressed in a full-length clinging dress, her face framed by cascading dark hair. The audience were instantly spellbound; nobody moved, not even the staff, who I noticed were standing still wherever they were.

Her voice was remarkable; rich, clear, and sultry. The first song finished, and she launched into another, more upbeat number. She moved around the stage, making eye contact with members of the audience. Another couple of songs followed, both I recognised as Bertolt Brecht; songs of decadence and cynicism. Funny, witty, drawing laughter from the patrons. She was playing with the crowd, who were hanging on her every word, every expression.

The girls joined her for a beautifully choreographed medley of some classic Hollywood song and dance tunes. When they left, the stage darkened, as she came to the single spotlight in the centre and began to sing a medley of French chansons. I couldn't follow all the words, but the tunes were all well-known. The timbre of her voice fitted them perfectly, and it was very moving.

I suddenly heard a gasp beside me; Marcus heard it as well, and we both turned to look at Sally, who was sitting upright with her hand over her open mouth.

"What's wrong?" he asked.

"That's Jacques," she replied.

Chapter 14 – Marcus

I looked back at the stage and knew instantly Sal was right. It was Jacques. I looked at Lucy and her face betrayed her surprise as she took it in.

"He's … gorgeous," she said and laughed.

"He sure is," Sal replied.

I had to agree. The medley was coming to its climax now with the inevitable 'Non, je ne regrette rien'. Jacques's performance would have given Edith Piaf a run for her money. As he took his bows, the audience showed their appreciation and we stood, applauding him. At one point, he looked over, gently inclining his head to us.

It was the end of the show, all the performers came back to take their bows and the band returned to playing background music. We talked animatedly about what we'd seen, about the beauty we'd previously seen in Jacques. When Sally saw him coming towards us – now dressed as he had been as host – she got up, and ran to him, throwing her arms around him. It took him by surprise, but he quickly recovered and, smiling, brought her back to us.

"You were brilliant, Jacques," she said. We joined in the praise.

"Thank you," he replied. "I wasn't sure how you would react."

A waitress appeared and handed Jacques a glass of champagne, which he downed in one, before handing him another. This one he put on the table and sat down.

"How long have you been performing?" Sally asked.

"Most of my life, one way or another," he replied. "I always loved dressing up, even as a child. It was one thing …" he paused and looked at Sally, "… one thing our father didn't … encourage." She nodded. "But now, I can be myself."

"And your mother?" Sal asked.

"Oh, she encouraged me. Always has. She was the first person to show me how to apply make-up."

"She was a good teacher," Lucy said.

"I have had others, but Mama was the first."

I thought about Jacques and his mother. They'd had a lot to deal with, but it had clearly created a deep bond between them.

"Did you enjoy the show?" Jacques asked.

"Yes," Sally replied. "It was wonderful."

"And the girls?" Jacques asked, turning to me.

"They were … appealing," I replied.

"Lucy liked them too," Sal said.

Jacques turned to Lucy, who was grinning.

"Ah," he said, "I see."

"Jacques," Sally said, seeing Lucy's embarrassment. "You said you own another club."

"Two actually, but I don't have much to do with one of them." He saw her puzzlement. "I acquired it by accident as it shares a site with the one I was interested in. It's a contemporary club, which doesn't do anything for me, so a couple of friends run it."

"And the other?"

She looked at him expectantly; he gave in. "Well, as you've taken my transformation tonight in your stride. It's a drag club."

"Is anyone welcome?"

He looked at each of us in turn.

"Yes, not everyone comes in drag. But I guarantee you won't know who has and who hasn't."

We didn't get home until about two in the morning, but we weren't tired. We went out onto the roof terrace, opened a bottle of wine, and discussed the evening. As the conversation slowed, we looked out over Paris at night.

"Fabulous, isn't it?" Lucy said.

"Like a scene from a film," Sal replied.

There were still faint sounds of people enjoying the nightlife, the odd siren, and trains in the distance. We fell silent. I wasn't sure what the girls were thinking, but for me, it was another moment of disbelief at how my life had changed.

"It's getting cold," Sal said. "This dress is a bit thin."

I turned to her, this beautiful woman I loved. She looked ravishing. Next to her, Lucy looked as delicious.

"Take it off," I said to her quietly. She frowned at me and raised an eyebrow.

"Take it off," I repeated. "Lucy and I will warm you up."

And we made love, the three of us enjoying the warmth of each other's bodies on a Paris rooftop.

"Ready, Luce?" I asked.

"Yup, all set."

"See you later," I said to Sally as we left.

Lucy and I were setting out on our own for a few hours, leaving Sal to spend some time alone with Genevieve. I'd offered her the chance over breakfast, and after a little thought, she accepted the idea. I didn't know whether they had anything else to tell each other, perhaps prevented by our presence, but even if they didn't, they could still share things we couldn't hope to understand.

We went to the Musee d'Orsay and spent a pleasant morning wandering around, with me trying not to pester her with too many questions. But I could see her delight in the impressionist works which lined the walls. I'd always been ambivalent about the genre, but her gentle commentary allowed me to see them in a different light.

We had lunch in a pavement café and crossed the Seine to wander through the Tuileries Gardens.

"How do you think Sally feels about Genevieve?" Lucy asked.

"I'm not sure," I replied. "I've been wondering the same thing. They seem to have taken to one another."

"They do."

"I hesitate to think she sees Genevieve as a sort of surrogate mother …"

"That's Mary still."

"And always will be. But I think she sees her – and Jacques – as family."

"Funny, isn't it? This is her father's other wife, yet Sal doesn't seem bothered by that at all."

"No, she's got the measure of her father now."

"You'll never know how good it is to see that." We paused by a modern sculpture and attempted to work it out. "God," she said suddenly, "Mary. Can you imagine Mary and Genevieve together?"

"They'd get on well. They're both feisty women of a certain age."

"Yes, and they've got a lover in common."

We looked at each other and burst out laughing, the sculpture forgotten. She put her arm through mine, and we strolled on.

By the time we returned to the apartment block, we'd had a text from Sally telling us to join them, so we went into Genevieve's door.

"Had fun?" Sal asked after our greetings.

We told them where we'd been and joined them for tea. It seemed to be an important fixture in Genevieve's routine. Sally's mood indicated they'd enjoyed their time together. A little later, we returned to our apartment. We didn't ask anything further of Sally; if she had things to tell us, she would in her own time.

We had dinner in a restaurant Genevieve had recommended and we could see why. Although she'd only returned to Paris three years earlier, she was a mine of information about the city. The next day, we played tourists again, taking it in turns to nominate our next destination. We returned in the early evening, as we were visiting Jacques's other club. We rested, as he'd told us it wasn't worth turning up until at least ten.

We dressed as best we could, completely unsure what to wear. He'd told us not to worry, but we didn't want to let him down. When we arrived, we were surprised by the interior. It was very minimal and industrial in style. No plush furnishings. But I guess that wasn't what people came for; it was to see and be seen. It was a place full of beautiful people.

Jacques had been right; it was impossible to tell the gender of many of the guests. Some flaunted their cross-style, and a few were spectacular. But many were subtle and understated. We found Jacques talking to a group of people and I was surprised to see he was dressed in male clothes.

He spotted us, excused himself and came to greet us.

"Jacques," Sally said. "I was expecting to see you in feathers and frills."

"I don't always dress up," he replied, smiling. "It depends how I feel. Tonight, I've come as myself."

"Are there any rules?" Lucy asked. "I don't want to offend anyone."

"Just be yourself," he replied. "Unlike the Beaulieu, most people here will be from Paris. If you say the wrong thing, they'll act like all Parisians; think you're an ignorant English person and pretend they don't understand you."

Well, that was the Parisian way in most things. Jacques led us to the bar where we ordered some drinks and he stayed with us for a while, introducing a few people. Then he left us to it.

By the time we got home at four the next morning, we'd had a fabulous time. We'd realised early on it was like the fetish group. Everyone was there to enjoy themselves and looking to have a good time. Keep the discussion general, compliment people, and ask questions. Just don't make them too personal.

We managed to survive the evening on our rather poor French, although both Sally and Lucy were more fluent than me. And we didn't disgrace ourselves.

We left all our clothes on the floor, flopped into bed, and fell asleep.

The next day was our last, we were heading home the following morning. We asked Genevieve if we could take her and Jacques out to dinner.

"If you want him to come," she replied, "we'd better make it early. As you've seen, his evenings are generally occupied."

"Okay," Sally replied. "Where would you like to go?"

Genevieve thought for a moment.

"Le Servan would be nice, if you can get in."

We could, and we did, booking early to allow Jacques to join us. We spent a pleasant couple of hours over a fine dinner before he departed to begin his evening's work. We said goodbye, and he was sincere when he asked us to come back soon, and often. After the rest of us returned home, we saw Genevieve into her apartment, and settled on the roof terrace for the last time, over a bottle of wine.

"I have a feeling," I said, "we'll be spending quite a few nights on this terrace in the future."

Sally turned to me.

"Yes, if that's alright."

"I don't know," I replied. "Not sure I can cope with slumming it in some grotty Parisian garret."

"I'll come on my own, then," she said, sticking her tongue out.

"You know you can, if you want."

"I was joking."

"As was I. We can come as often as you like."

"Thank you. Luce, happy to come back?"

"Well, yes. But I'm not sure I'm entitled to."

"You're a part of this setup." Lucy went to protest, but Sally stopped her. "And Genevieve knows that."

"Oh," Lucy said. "Did you …"

"Yes, I told her about the three of us and how we got here. My past has had too many secrets. Genevieve and I have been honest; she needed to know about me, about how my life is now. I hope you don't mind."

"No, I don't. Not at all."

***

"That's about it," Sally said, as she finished recounting our visit. Mary and Ken were our guests for dinner, and Mary had already told him the back story. More or less; we didn't know if she'd told him of her affair with Tony and thought it best not to ask.

"How does it feel to find your brother?" Mary asked.

"It's great, Mary, to be honest. It's a positive ending."

"You're not continuing your search?"

"No. Paul Doyle is a dead end. Let's leave it that way."

"You have family in Paris now."

"Yes, not a bad result."

"No," she said. "Free accommodation."

"You should come over," Sal casually said. Mary frowned.

"I'm not sure. I have no connection with them."

"Perhaps, but you both knew Dad, and I think you'd get on well. Don't you, darling?"

"Yes," I replied. "But the two of you together could be a danger to Parisian society."

Later in the evening, Sal took Mary downstairs to show her something. They were gone for half an hour and I guessed they were talking rather than showing. After Mary and Ken left, Sally came and sat on my lap and gave me a long, gentle kiss.

"I'm in such a good place," she said.

"Yes?"

"I've dealt with the shadow and accepted my father for what he was. I've found a second family who've welcomed me with open arms. I've got you; I've got Lucy. I can't imagine things being any better."

"Want to tell me about your chat with Mary?" I asked.

"I wanted to make sure she was happy with the situation. After all, she's been my only family for years. I didn't want her to feel left out."

"And?"

"You know Mary, she's smarter than that. She's fine. She'll always be my rock, and she knows it. I can never repay her for what she's done for me. I wanted to tell her again, and we got a bit emotional."

"Ah."

"She's really happy for me ... for us, all of us."

"Will she meet Genevieve?"

Sal went quiet for a while, thinking.

"I don't know. She's curious, she's bound to be. Think of all the times Dad was away for weeks on end, all the mystery. Genevieve is a big part of the answer to that."

"Would Genevieve want to meet Mary?"

"Yes, she told me so."

"Did you tell her about Mary and your father?"

"No. I didn't feel I had the right to divulge that."

"We leave it to Mary?"

"Yes."

She snuggled into me, and I kissed her neck. She was at peace, completely at peace. Probably for the first time since I'd met her. No shadow, no secrets, no fears. She shifted in my lap and raised her head, and I saw a seductive smile on her face.

"Fancy an early night?" she asked.

Chapter 15 – Sally

"Come on," Marcus said, rolling his eyes. "Out with it."

Lucy and I had asked about unpaid leave, but we'd refused to tell him the answer. His reaction had made me laugh. Now we were discussing holidays again during our regular Saturday night date with Lucy.

"Well," I said, "we've gone and done something you might not like."

"I'll tell you when I know," he replied, shaking his head.

"We've booked something."

"Oh, yes."

I looked at Lucy, who was chewing her lip nervously.

"Yes," I continued. "We've booked the fort again."

His face betrayed the merest hint of a smile.

"Have you?"

"Yes. For eight weeks."

"I see," he said. "So, I'm there for eight weeks; will you two be able to join me for a week or two?"

"Fool!"

"That's wonderful," he said. "You sure you didn't want to go anywhere else?"

"We talked it over and over, but we couldn't think of anywhere that could be better. Whatever ideas we came up with, they always fell short of last year. I hope you're happy with it."

"Absolutely."

"Good. We did think we might go off somewhere else for a few days while we're there, but we'll see how we feel."

"Are you with us the whole time?" he asked Lucy.

"Certainly am."

"Good."

"We might invite one or two people again," I said.

"Have anyone in mind?" he asked, a challenging smile on his face.

"Mary and Ken."

"Mmm."

"And, well, Helen and Penny."

"Knowing full well Helen won't come."

"She might this year."

"Want to bet on it?"

"No."

"Anyone else?"

"What about Eva?"

"Really?"

"Yea, she's fun when she switches off from work."

"We'll see."

"That's about it."

"When are we going?"

"Second week of July."

"I hope Eva hasn't got anything planned for me. You know what she's like, working me into the ground."

"Then you'll either have to do it remotely or say no."

"Now that, I like."

"Oh, and because we're taking unpaid leave, we've still got our paid holiday which we can use the rest of the year."

"That's great."

"Which means Lucy and I are going to St Petersburg next weekend."

"You are?"

"Yea, her birthday's the week after, but we couldn't get the tickets we needed, so we're going early. Is that alright?"

"Of course it is."

"Sure you'll be alright on your own?"

"I'll manage."

Our few days in St Petersburg went without a hitch. We spent the whole time wallowing in culture. The Hermitage, the Russian Museum, and various palaces during the day; the theatre and the ballet in the evening. We lost count of the number of times the beauty and history almost overwhelmed the senses and brought tears to our eyes. The time whizzed by and we were home all too soon.

Once again, Lucy went out to dinner with her mother and sister's family on her birthday. She arrived at our front door on Friday evening to stay for the weekend.

"How was the birthday dinner?" Marcus asked.

"Rather nice," Lucy replied. "They took me to Pizza Express and we went early so Nathan and Sarah could come."

"Oh, wow," I said. That was a surprise.

"Yea. It felt like a real family occasion."

"How's it going with your mum?" he asked.

"She's surprised us all. The change over the last year has been dramatic. She's made some friends at the church and even joined a couple of clubs. Annie says she's a different person; I wouldn't go that far, but she's not an emotional drain anymore."

"Freedom," Marcus said.

"I think so. She hasn't mentioned Dad to Annie or me for ages and we don't mention him either."

"Strange."

"Yea. I'm afraid she may be hiding something, but I'm not in a position to question it."

"Has Annie?"

"No. We've talked about it because we both think the same. But she's doing so well, we don't want to knock her back."

"Seems fair. If she wants to talk, she will."

After dinner, we gave Lucy a few presents we'd held back from the actual day. She was suitably embarrassed.

"The weekend is yours, Luce," I said. "We've not planned anything; what would you like to do?"

"Oh, I don't know," she replied. "Let's just have fun."

"I'll guarantee that, and we can go out somewhere tomorrow. But is there anything you fancy doing in the evenings? Any fantasy you've got you haven't told me about?"

She knew I was half-joking, but there were fantasies I hadn't told her. Even one or two I hadn't yet revealed to Marcus. She was bound to have some of her own. She didn't reply for a minute or two, thinking, but I could tell from her demeanour there was something, and she wasn't sure whether to tell us.

"Come on," I said. "Out with it."

She smiled coyly.

"You know when you wear your collar?"

"Yes."

"When you submit to Marcus?"

"Yea."

"Would it work with someone watching?"

I looked at Marcus.

"Would it, darling?" I asked.

He considered for a moment.

"I honestly don't know," he finally said. "It's a very intimate thing. You shut out the world; well, I do too, I suppose. I'm not sure if it would work with someone else present."

"If you don't want to," Lucy quickly said, "it's fine. I completely understand. I don't want to intrude."

"And," Marcus continued, "would Lucy be a spectator, or would we include her in the scene?"

"I don't know," I replied, ideas and images racing through my head. Most of them delicious.

"And if you watch," Marcus said to Lucy, "what do you get out of it?"

"I … I don't know," Lucy replied. "But … it's something I've thought about a lot."

"Have you?" I said, smiling at her.

"Yes, sorry."

"Never apologise for your fantasies. Particularly when they include me."

I looked at Marcus, clearly deep in thought.

"Well?" I asked him.

"If you're agreeable, I don't see why we couldn't try it. It might not work – it'll certainly be different - but I can't see any dangers in it."

"Tonight?" I asked. In truth, I was already keen on the idea. It hadn't crossed my mind before. Marcus was right, our submission sessions were the most intense, intimate moments between us. We didn't do it often. But the thought of someone watching – or participating – had awakened my whole body at a surprising speed.

"No," he replied, and I sank a little. "Tomorrow night. We need to think about it a bit before we jump in."

I knew he was right, sadly. But I was worked up now, and before long I was working them up too. Marcus and I concentrated on Lucy, making her the centre of attention. Doing things we knew she couldn't resist until she was exhausted and sated. We almost had to help her to bed.

As we lay there, Lucy already asleep, I thought about the scene we were planning the following night. Submission was a private thing, between Marcus and me. It always had been. We even had a special collar no one else knew about, not even Lucy.

It had a massive sapphire in it, one of the spectacular stones my dear father had acquired; somewhere. I'd had the collar made just for us, fully believing no one else would ever see it. Just as I never imagined anyone watching my submission.

But here I was, keen to be watched. Wanting my submission to be witnessed by my lover. The idea was exhilarating, filling my mind with images. But I was unsure how it would work. I knew now submission meant different things to different people; all of them valid.

For me, it was largely a mental thing. Slowly losing myself in Marcus's imagination, giving him everything of me. When I was in my special place, only he existed. I was aware of nothing else; almost an extension of him. It was a wonderful feeling. No cares, no responsibilities, nothing. That special place was the safest in the world. He was the only person there, and whatever he did to me or told me to do, took us to a different plane.

How would it be when someone else was there? I didn't think I would be able to block them out completely; I'd be aware of their presence all the time. Would that mean I wouldn't reach my special place? Or, knowing it was Lucy, would it heighten the experience? How would it affect Marcus? Would he concentrate on me, or involve Lucy?

All these questions and no answers. We'd have to wait and see, but the thought of it meant I had to wake Marcus and ride him to a gentle orgasm, while Lucy slept alongside.

We hadn't been quite honest with Lucy about our plans. On Saturday afternoon, we took her to a local historic house and spent a couple of hours wandering through the maze of rooms and the gardens. It was a beautiful May day, sunny and warm.

"How about a cream tea?" Marcus asked.

"Sounds good," Lucy said. "My treat."

"It's your birthday," I replied. "We'll be doing the treating."

We headed to the restaurant area, and just before we got there, I said I needed the loo, and Lucy joined me.

"I'll find a table," Marcus said and walked on.

When Lucy and I entered the courtyard in front of the restaurant, where several tables were laid out, Lucy went towards the door, but Marcus was waving from the end of the building, as I expected.

"Luce," I said, "he's found a table."

She followed me around the corner into a grass area surrounded by flowerbeds. And stopped. Waiting for her at a long table were Mary, Ken, Helen, and Penny, the usual birthday culprits. Lucy smiled and screwed her face up at me.

"Well," I said. "We didn't have a birthday dinner for you, and this seemed like the next best thing."

We spent the next couple of hours enjoying our cream tea and the company. Lucy got embarrassed when everyone gave her little presents, and we sang Happy Birthday. Quietly, given the setting. After tea, we all went for a walk around the gardens. It was interesting to watch the differing strolling partners.

At one point, I spotted Ken talking to Penny, and a little later her place had been taken by Helen. I'd love to have overheard those conversations. Ken was lovely, and much less naïve now, but I wasn't sure he had any idea of the basis of Helen and Penny's relationship. I found Mary at my side and hugged her.

"Watch out, Mary," I said, nodding towards Ken and Helen. "He may be picking up bad habits."

"Oh, I'm not worried," she replied. "I've already taught him a few."

"I believe you."

"He's fun. Quite good, actually."

The smile on her face told me what she meant, and we giggled together. Rather too loudly, as Marcus and Penny turned to see what had amused us.

"He's a keeper, then," I said.

"Yes, darling. We've even talked about living together."

"Wow. And …?"

"It's a big step at our age. We've agreed to keep our own houses for the moment, but we rarely spend a night separately." I grinned at her, and she laughed. "It's not just you youngsters who know how to have fun, you know."

"Talking of that, we're going to the fort again this summer."

"Are you?"

"Yup."

"I guess it'll be a shorter holiday this time."

"No. Eight weeks."

She stopped and turned to me.

"Mary," I said. "I'm in the happiest place I've ever been. And I'm well off. I want to enjoy the money now, while I can." She was beaming. She understood what I was saying, and how far I'd come to be able to say it. "We'll be expecting you and Ken to come over at some point."

"Ken loved it last year; I don't think I'll have any trouble persuading him. But we won't get in your way for too long."

"You're never in the way," I replied.

She gave me a shrewd look.

"You know what I mean," she said, before putting her arm through mine and leading me forward.

Chapter 16 – Lucy

It had been a lovely afternoon, and the surprise tea party topped it off. As we drove home, I thought about the evening. Perhaps I shouldn't have raised the idea. I knew from what Sally had told me that their submission sessions were important to them. A time when they were at their closest. Should I have left well alone?

When we got home, I took Sally to one side.

"Sal, I'm not sure about tonight. It might be better not to do it."

"Why's that?"

"I don't want to spoil anything. I know what it means to you and I don't want to cause trouble."

"Luce, I want to do it. I want you to see it. We don't even know if it'll work. Just relax and enjoy it."

"What are you two scheming?" Marcus asked from the next room.

"Lucy's worried she might have asked too much for tonight," I replied, leading her back into the living room.

"Still want to do it?" he asked Sally.

"Yes."

"Still want to see it?" he asked me.

"Yes … but …"

"That's settled then," he said. "We'll have dinner and relax. There's no hurry."

I knew him well enough to know he'd have thought about it all day. If he was happy, I needn't worry.

118

"Why don't we dress for dinner?" Sally said.

Marcus showered quickly and had disappeared by the time we returned to the bedroom. We spent some time choosing what to wear. I hadn't brought anything formal with me, so we had to find underwear and a dress from Sally's vast collection which fitted me. Then we did our makeup and hair; we were going the whole hog.

"What about jewellery?" Sally asked. She had a lot of that, as well, including her special collection. She opened the box with the emerald set. It was sensational and suited her perfectly.

"Want to wear it?" she asked.

"Me? It's your signature set."

"But it's your birthday," she replied, handing me the first earring. "And you are wearing green."

I watched in the mirror as she hung the necklace around my neck and did it up, then set the bracelets on my wrists. It was thrilling and I felt like a princess, something I didn't normally aspire to, but once in a while …?

"There," she said. "What do you think?"

"It looks wonderful," I replied. "The necklace is much lighter than I expected."

"You can always borrow it, you know. Borrow anything."

"I couldn't Sal. I'd always be aware of how much it's worth."

"It's only money," she replied, giving me a wink in the mirror. She chose some jewellery for herself, we checked ourselves – and each other – in the mirror and went upstairs.

Marcus was finishing off the table as we appeared; he was in a dinner jacket and bow tie. He turned to us, and whistled, a broad smile lighting his face.

"Well," he said. "That's a sight to make a happy man feel very old."

"Idiot," Sal replied. "What do you think of Lucy's jewellery?"

He looked at me and his eyes went from item to item before he looked at my eyes.

"It suits her," he said. "But if she'll forgive me, not quite as well as it suits you."

"The eyes," I said.

"Yes," he replied, smiling. "But you still look ravishing, Luce."

They went to work in the kitchen, not allowing me to do anything but hold my glass of champagne. I saw a whole salmon ready for the oven, and some langoustines ready to cook. They were indulging me with some favourites.

"Do you wear this set often?" I asked Sally.

"We don't go to many places that warrant it," she replied. "But I do wear it sometimes."

"Oh, where?"

I caught a grin from Marcus.

"Right here," she replied. "With nothing but a dab of perfume."

Dinner was glorious; all my favourites, light conversation and wine and champagne. Sally stopped me when I went to refill her glass.

"No, thanks. I don't want to drink too much. It spoils the effect."

I must have looked puzzled.

"We learnt that, didn't we, darling?" He nodded. "We started one submission session after I'd drunk rather a lot; it didn't work. I wasn't drunk, but my head was a bit fuzzy, and I found my mind wandering. I couldn't concentrate on Marcus. We had to give up."

"Well," he said, chuckling, "we had to change the plan a little."

She leaned over to whisper conspiratorially in my ear.

"He took me downstairs instead, gave me a good whipping and fucked me raw."

"You know what she's like when she's pissed, Lucy," Marcus said.

"Yes," I replied. "A bitch on heat."

Sally pursed her lips and frowned.

"I am not," she said, trying to maintain her innocence. We both stared at her until she crumpled into laughter. "Alright, alright. But I don't remember either of you ever complaining."

After dinner, we settled on the sofas and chatted. Sally was curled up by Marcus, leaning on him. He asked us about St Petersburg, and we told him of the places we visited, the ballet we saw.

I realised partway through I was doing most of the talking; Sal was only adding small snippets. She seemed reserved, and it suddenly hit me she must be thinking about what was going to happen. Was it a mistake? I shouldn't have asked.

Later in the evening, Marcus turned to her.

"Ready?"

"Yes," she replied, and slowly lifted herself from the sofa. "What would you like me to wear?"

He looked at her and thought for a moment.

"Nothing," he replied. "Nothing at all."

She bent to kiss him and slowly walked from the room.

"Marcus," I said. "Is it best not to do this? She seemed very withdrawn."

"It's fine, Luce, she's mentally preparing. She'll go and run a bath. We won't see her for at least half an hour while she relaxes in it and gets into the right place."

He disappeared downstairs and returned with a black velvet bag and a thin cane. He put them both on the sofa beside him.

"A couple of things," he said. "Don't be surprised if she seems different. If she gets into it, she might appear stoned or spaced out. Don't worry, that's normal. If I involve you, stay calm and relaxed. Finally, if it works, when she comes out, it's a slow process. It can take an hour or more. During that time, you may see all sorts of emotions, and she normally cries."

"Cries?"

"Yea. We don't know why, though it's quite common. Probably emotion coming out. But she tends to be exhausted and when I'm happy she's back with us, we usually go to bed."

"Shall I use the spare room?"

"No. You're one of us now, but don't be surprised if she doesn't interact until the morning."

Taking all this in, I wondered what I'd let myself in for. Sally had told me a little about how she felt when she submitted. But it sounded heavy as Marcus explained it. It both worried and excited me. Whatever happened, I was going to see something I'd never witnessed before. He lowered the lights and put on some soft, instrumental music.

It was forty-five minutes before Sally appeared, wearing just a robe, and carrying what I assumed was her collar in her hand. She'd left her make-up on but tied her hair in a loose ponytail. She almost glided over to Marcus, bent and kissed him, then offered him the collar.

"Happy to proceed?" he asked softly.

A gorgeous smile betrayed the answer before she gave it.

"Yes," she replied, equally softly.

She undid the robe, and let it slip off her shoulders before laying it on the sofa. Her naked body had a silky sheen to it, she looked stunning. I wasn't sure what she'd used, but I was going to ask her. She dropped to her haunches in front of him, letting her hands rest on her thighs. The way she was looking at him was intensely personal, and I felt the urge to look away, as if I was intruding. Which was exactly what I was doing.

He lifted the collar, laid it around her neck, fastened it and turned it until the clasp was at the back. I held back a gasp. On the front of the collar was a huge blue stone, glinting in the pale light. It must be a sapphire. I remembered there being one in her father's collection and I hadn't seen it in any of her usual jewellery. They must have used it for this intensely private piece. I felt even more of an intruder.

"Is that comfortable, Sally?" he asked.

"Yes, thank you, sir," she replied.

The word resonated around the room. I'd heard her use it to him in jest many times, I'd even teased him with it myself. But it was always part of the fun, an act. The way she said it now seemed real; she meant it.

"Good," he said, "hands behind your back, close your eyes."

She moved her hands behind her and let her head drop, her eyes shut. Then nothing.

For what seemed like an age, she knelt motionless in front of him, while he sat still. Initially, I froze, afraid to move a muscle, but I gradually relaxed and found myself entranced by the tableau in front of me. It looked like the cover of a few books I'd read recently. Although I didn't think I'd ever be as interested in this world as they were, I was intrigued by it and had been doing my research.

"Sally," he finally said softly. She raised her head, opened her eyes, and looked at him.

"Yes, sir."

He patted the front of the sofa and she turned, curling up on the floor, and leaning against his leg, with her head on his knee. He laid his hand on her shoulder and slowly stroked it. I could see her face clearly, and her expression was unreadable. She didn't look at me; she wasn't focussing on anything, as far as I could tell.

His hand moved further, across to her other shoulder and gradually up to her neck. A couple of long sighs betrayed her pleasure at his touch. I knew her neck was a trigger for her when she was in the right mood. He undid her ponytail, letting her hair flow through his fingers. Again, time seemed to stand still; their interaction happening in slow motion.

He turned to the bag he'd brought in and took out some rope and a couple of other items I couldn't see. Bunching her hair, he threaded it through some sort of mesh. When he finished, it was woven into her hair, ending in a double loop near the end, to which he attached a length of rope.

"Sally, stand up."

She rose slowly, standing in front of him, her hands still behind her back. He stood as well, kissed her forehead, and led her into the middle of the space in front of us. For the first time, she looked at me, and the warmth of that look made me shiver. He gently turned her away from me and moved her hands by her side.

"Bend forward."

She obeyed, leaning forward enough to offer a tantalising glimpse of her pussy between her thighs and her soft bum. He'd positioned her to give me the best view in the house. He went to the bag and came back with some lube and what I now knew was a butt hook. He gently stroked her bum before putting a little lube on her ass and slipping the hook in. She made no sound.

Taking the rope hanging from her hair, he slipped it through the hole on the hook and back up again, putting it through the double loop. He gently tightened it until her head was tilted slightly back.

"Turn around."

She was facing me again, staring into my eyes, but I saw Marcus was right. Her eyes were glazed, as if she wasn't seeing me. He put the bag on the small table by us. Reaching inside, he took out a couple of chains, with clamps on their ends.

He stood to one side of her and gave her a gentle kiss, then cupped her left breast, its nipple already hard and swollen. He took it between his lips; her mouth fell open and her eyes closed. But again, no sound. Pulling away, he took a clamp and gently attached it to the nipple, eliciting a brief whimper as it gripped.

He repeated this on her other nipple, and let the chains hang in front of her. A single chain ran to her belly button, with three chains trailing further. A chill ran through my groin as I realised where they were going.

He turned her slightly, so I could see as he stood in front of her. Dropping slowly, he kissed his way down her abdomen.

"Spread your legs."

She moved her feet, and I could now see her sex clearly, already glistening in the low light. He was on his knees and took one of the clamps in his hand. She let out a delicate moan as he ran a finger across her pussy to separate her lips and gently squeezed one to allow him to place a clamp on it. A sharp gasp from her made me wince, but she didn't move. He repeated the action on the other side; the same response.

The final clamp was different. It looked like a small pair of tweezers. He leaned forward and the first loud sound came from her, as he put his lips around her clit and sucked it. Pulling away, he laid the clamp either side of her swollen bud and tightened it, watching her face. When she winced, he tightened it a little more and stopped. A few short breaths followed before she stilled.

He stood and gave her a long, gentle kiss.

"Okay?" he asked.

"Yes, sir. Thank you."

He turned her to fully face me and stood behind her. The rope meant she was looking over my head, not at me. She shivered as his hand landed under her right breast and caressed it before he tightened the clamp a turn or two, then the other.

Her eyes were now more often closed than open, as his hand rolled over her tummy, his fingers sliding over her pussy, gently opening her lips. Sally let out a loud groan this time, followed by three or four panting breaths. His fingers spread her open and I could see the clamps, her entrance, and her wetness, already coating the inside of her thighs.

Two of his fingers continued to run up and down the valley, making her shiver, her face etched with need. I now had needs of my own. I wasn't sure what I'd expected, but he'd surprised me with this slow and gentle approach. It was incredibly erotic. I couldn't take my eyes off them.

He continued to slowly rub his fingers into her, and I knew she was building to orgasm. He was close behind her, letting her lean against him.

"Look at Lucy," he said. Her eyes lowered to look at me, her head still held back. "Straight at her." Her mouth fell open as her attempt to lower her head caused the butt hook to pull. "Hold her eyes."

I couldn't move, her gaze piercing right through me. He was bringing her to orgasm, and the view, the situation, the atmosphere made me wish it was me.

But he didn't. He stopped just before she reached the peak. But there was no hint of frustration as there would have been normally. She continued to focus through me; it was almost uncomfortable.

"On your hands and knees," he said. She dropped. "Follow me." He walked slowly around the room, and she crawled behind him. Watching them was exhilarating, it was beautiful. She was beautiful.

I focussed on her, naked on all fours, clamps in sensitive places, the chains linking them hanging under her. Her head held up by the rope attached to the butt hook. He brought her back and stopped when she was right in front of me, facing away. The view of her bum and clamped pussy was delicious.

He knelt by her, and slipped his finger between her legs, bringing her close to orgasm again. Her body began to tremble as she neared, and he stopped. This time, her body slumped, and she let out a long breath.

"Stand up."

She got to her feet and he turned her around. "Hands behind your head." She clasped them in place. Then he knelt in front of her, put his hands on her hips, and leaned forward. She instantly began panting as he used his tongue between her lips, flicking it over her clit, now hugely swollen by the gripping clamp. She was moaning, her eyes closed. She was near.

And he stopped. Her whole body seemed to shrink, a long sigh escaping her lips. He turned to me.

"Would you like a taste?" he asked.

Would I? I slid off the sofa as he stood and moved behind her again. I knelt in front of her, put my hands on her bum, and nuzzled into her, letting my lips kiss her clit, and my tongue slide around her entrance. Her response was instant, her body rising and tensing. I panicked; was I allowed to take her to orgasm? She wouldn't need much.

I pulled away and looked up at Marcus; he smiled back.

"Would you like to come, Sally?"

"Yes, sir," she replied, shuddering. "Please."

He nodded to me, and I leaned in, finding paths for my tongue between the clamps. His hands appeared at her groin and gently pulled the chains, spreading her lips apart. They were swollen and red; her clit was massive, bigger than I'd ever seen it. When I touched it with my tongue, she cried out.

"Gently," I heard him whisper.

I enclosed her clit with my lips and let my tongue flick it softly. To my surprise, this one touch triggered her orgasm, and she let out a long cry, as her legs shook. Another cry echoed around the room as Marcus released the clit clamp with one hand and let it hang loose. 'Carry on' he mouthed to me, and I let my tongue explore her entrance, eliciting a whole new bout of spasms, groans and shaking. I stopped as her orgasm subsided and sat back against the sofa.

She was leaning against him for support, her eyes closed, a dreamy expression on her face. He guided her hands to her side, and she slowly regained her balance and opened her eyes. He reached around and gently took both labia clamps off, Sally gasping each time. Then he removed the nipple clamps, again a brief flash of pain on her face as the blood flowed back. The rope was loosened, and her head dropped to its normal position.

"What do you say?" he asked.

She looked down, and her expression melted me. It simply confirmed the love I had for this wonderful woman.

"Thank you, Lucy," she said. I was so flustered by her look and the sound of her voice, I had to look away. He undid her hair and removed the butt hook.

"Are you okay, Sally?" he asked.

"Yes, thank you, sir."

"Need the loo?"

"Yes, please, sir."

She left us, and Marcus gave me a hand and helped me up.

"That was … well, I'm not sure of the words," I said. "Thank you."

"We're not finished yet," he replied.

"No?"

"No. She's fine to continue. Want to get involved?"

I thought I already was but eagerly agreed.

"Good, happy to follow my instructions?"

"Anything you want."

Chapter 17 – Marcus

When Sally returned to the room, she came and stood in front of me. Her neck was still flushed from her orgasm, and the look on her face was one of pure contentment.

"Strip me," I said.

She slipped my jacket from my shoulders and laid it on the sofa, undid my bow tie and pulled it from my collar. Unbuttoning my shirt, she ran her hands over my chest as she removed it. Dropping to her knees, she undid my trousers and I stepped out of them as she let them fall, taking my socks off at the same time. She looked straight ahead as she slid my trunks down, my cock close to her face. She sat back, looking up at me. I knew what she wanted, but not yet.

"Stand up."

She rose and looked into my eyes, making me pause and wallow in her stare. She knew it.

"Now strip Lucy," I said. I saw a brief flash of surprise, but she turned and went over to Lucy who stood. Sal went behind Lucy, undid the zip, and lifted the dress up and off with a little wriggling help from Lucy. The bra came off next.

"Now from the front," I said. Sal knelt in front of Lucy and slid her briefs down her legs and off her feet, undid the suspenders and unclipped the belt. Lucy was getting into it now, and she put her leg onto the sofa to allow Sal to roll the stocking down. In doing so, it brought her groin close to Sally's face. She did the same with the other leg. When that stocking was off, Lucy left her leg where it was, with Sally kneeling a few inches from her sex.

"That looks inviting, doesn't it, Sally?" I said.

"Yes, sir. It does."

I went over and knelt beside her. Holding her chin, I turned it to give her a lingering kiss, then moved forward and engulfed Lucy's pussy with my lips, licking and sucking on it. Lucy's reaction told me she'd enjoyed what she'd witnessed so far, and she was very wet. I pulled away and kissed Sally again, my mouth still covered in Lucy's moisture. Sal moaned as she tasted her lover on my lips.

I repeated the action, with Sally's eyes glued to my every move, eagerly kissing me as I offered her my mouth a second time. I ran two fingers over Lucy's labia, and she moaned as I let them sink into her. Removing them, I offered them to Sal and she greedily sucked on them, her eyes closed.

"Make yourself comfortable," I said to Lucy, and she sat on the sofa, lying back and opening her legs, one on the floor, one up on the cushion. Sally was staring between Lucy's thighs, eager to enjoy the feast, but I was going to disappoint her. I bent down and started to lick Lucy's wet flesh, making sure Sally could see every move.

Lucy was reacting to my touch, and I knew her well enough now to know her orgasm was near if I wanted to take her there. I did, but slowly. After enjoying her taste for a few minutes, I knelt up, pulled her to the edge of the sofa and slowly entered her, eliciting a satisfied groan as my whole length filled her.

I slid in and out slowly and turned to look at Sally. Her eyes were fixed on Lucy's groin, watching my cock penetrate her lover. She would have been happy with either at that moment; Lucy's pussy or my cock. I reached over and slid my fingers between her legs, and she gasped as I encountered a mass of engorged, soaking flesh. Her thighs were wet, moisture dripping onto the ankles they were resting on. I paused as she looked into my eyes. I tried to read her, but it was difficult when she was in this state. But I saw love, need, and lust, a heady mixture.

I returned to the present and fucked Lucy more firmly, placing my fingers over her clit and gently teasing it. It was enough. That familiar groan began, and she tensed as her body rose from the sofa. She let out a long groan as her orgasm came, her body pushing against me to maximise my depth within her. She grunted a few times, then slowed and I let my hand rest on her tummy.

I leaned down and kissed her, a huge smile on her face. We kissed a few times before I pulled away and winked before turning to Sally.

"Did you enjoy that?" I asked her.

"Yes, sir," she replied. "I always do."

"Would you like to lick us clean?"

Her eyes widened.

"Yes, please, sir."

I slipped out of Lucy, and Sally shuffled forward, grabbing my cock, and taking almost the whole length in her mouth. She looked up at me as she licked and sucked every trace of Lucy from me. Then, still holding my cock, she turned to Lucy and began to greedily eat her. Lucy was still sensitive from her orgasm, but it didn't stop Sal, as she encased Lucy's pussy with her mouth. She changed back and held my balls as she engulfed me again.

I recognised the little moans in her throat. Rolling her hair around my hand, I moved her head on and off my cock. I took her right hand and put it on my bum, allowing her to use our safe gesture, then held her head still and slid in and out of her mouth. Her lips sealed tightly around the shaft. Her eyes closed, one or two coughs died in her throat, and her climax took her. Strange sounds, deep within her chest, were muffled by my cock, and her whole body shook. Her legs trembled and her shoulders spasmed several times.

I pulled from her and she gasped for air, her head dropping as I released her hair. I looked at Lucy, who was wide-eyed with wonder. She shook her head. I watched Sal's body slowly relax and her head rose again.

"Did you enjoy that?" I asked.

"Yes, sir," she replied in between short breaths, "… I did." There was a satisfied smile on her face.

"I don't remember you asking permission."

Her smile turned to a pouting frown with more than a hint of defiance, and I had to hide my smile.

"Sorry, sir."

"I think you need a lesson."

"Yes, sir."

"Lucy," I said. "Fancy making her bum burn?"

Almost before Lucy answered, Sally was up, waiting for Lucy to get into position, before throwing herself over her lap. I knew they had spanked each other, but never witnessed it. Now I did. Lucy didn't hesitate, giving Sal a good, firm spanking, as Sal squirmed on her lap. Both were still highly aroused and that showed in their reactions. Sal was uttering deep grunts and the occasional squeal as Lucy spanked her, and Lucy was utterly focussed on Sal's reddening bum as she brought her hand down again and again on those rippling cheeks.

Kneeling watching this, I had time to sense how aroused I was. My balls were aching, and my cock kept jerking as I watched the action in front of me. I decided we were near the end of this session. I knew Sally was near orgasm again, but she'd have one or two in reserve. I raised my hand, and Lucy spotted it, stopping, and resting her hand on Sally's bum. Sally was breathing heavily.

"Is she wet?" I asked Lucy.

"What do you think?" she replied, holding up wet fingers after sliding them between Sally's thighs. Sally turned to look at me, a pleading look on her face. I returned her stare.

"Let her come, Luce."

We held each other's eyes as Lucy fingered Sally to another orgasm, her glowing bum quivering as it flowed through her, gradually settling as it passed.

"Need another yourself?" I asked Lucy.

"I might," she replied, smiling.

"Good, I need to as well, and this little thing is going to provide both. Sally …"

"Yes, sir." She was still breathing heavily.

"Between Lucy's legs."

She slid to the floor and Lucy moved forward, opening her thighs. Sally went straight for the target and I pulled her to her knees, plunging straight into her. She briefly lifted off Lucy as I did so but sank back down. I leaned over her.

"If you're a good girl and satisfy Lucy, we might allow you to come again."

Whatever her reply was, it was muffled by Lucy's pussy, but in truth, I doubted I could prevent it. I needed to fuck her, and I was sure in her state, she'd come at least once before I did. I hardly moved in her as she worked on Lucy.

Luckily, Lucy was near, and I heard the low groan, always softer if she was approaching a second orgasm. I slipped a thumb into Sal's ass; all she did was arch her back and push herself harder back onto me. Lucy suddenly stiffened, her body tensing as she reached her climax, allowing me to take what I needed.

Sally let out a shriek as I fucked her as hard as I could. She came almost immediately, dropping down, and I pushed her forward, her body now resting on Lucy's tummy. Lucy put her arms around Sal as I continued to fuck her, her orgasm rising and falling, those strange noises echoing deep in her throat and chest.

My climax came, and as Sally felt the first eruption deep within her, her orgasm peaked. As I spent myself, she flopped onto Lucy, suddenly still and I knew she'd blacked out. Lucy looked at me, panic on her face. I shook my head to reassure her, knowing it was momentary, and with that, Sal moved again, and let out a long sigh.

I leaned over her and kissed her neck, gently undoing the collar. Holding it in front of her face long enough to get a positive grunt, I put it on the sofa next to us. I slipped out of her, and gently pulled her back onto the floor, curling myself around her. She put her arms around my neck and laid her head on my chest.

"Okay?" I whispered.

"Mmm," was the only response, but that was all I needed to hear.

Nothing was said for twenty minutes, and the only movement was Lucy curling up on the sofa and Sally occasionally shifting against me to get comfortable. I held her, stroked her hair, kissed her neck and shoulders.

Eventually, she lifted her head, sat up and stretched. A long, vocal stretch accompanied by a deep breath, a loud yawn, and a beautiful smile. She put her arms around my neck, leaned in and gave me a sensuous kiss that seemed to last forever. Pulling away, she held out her arm, and Lucy leaned over, only for Sally to pull her onto the floor beside us. They shared an equally prolonged kiss, then she drew Lucy in and the three of us sat curled up in a warm heap, Sally in the middle.

When I woke in the morning, it was to sounds that took a few seconds to identify. But when I did, I rolled over to see Lucy lying on her back, her eyes closed. Sally was nowhere to be seen, but I knew where she was. I rolled the duvet off the bed, revealing her between Lucy's legs.

"Good morning, darling," she said. Lucy opened her eyes and smiled at me.

"Good morning," I replied. "You okay?"

"Definitely. Fancy sharing breakfast?"

I moved down the bed, and we gave Lucy a late birthday present.

When Lucy left that afternoon, Sally and I settled for the evening.

"What did Lucy think?" I asked, knowing they'd discussed it.

"She was intrigued," Sal replied. "She loved it but worried her being there spoiled it for us."

"Did it for you?"

"No. It was different, not as intense. I didn't go as deep. How about you?"

"It may be because it was the first time. Think how much better our sessions are now than when we started."

"True."

"But it will be different with a third person. I wasn't sure how much to include Lucy, either."

"You got it right."

"Hopefully. I'm glad I didn't go with my first idea."

"Which was?"

"To tie you up, and make you watch Lucy and me without giving you anything at all."

She narrowed her eyes at me, smiling.

"I'd have had to accept it."

"I know, but I'm not sure you'd have been as happy this morning."

"I'd have been very frustrated."

"Mmm, I know."

She swatted my arm.

"Would you do it again?" I asked.

"Definitely, but only in addition to our own sessions."

***

132

I spent a couple of days in London. I had to visit Eva and Eleanor, and speak to Peter, my agent. He had tentatively agreed a contract dealing with my earlier books. I'd insisted on several conditions, and Eva - or her management - had not been happy with some of them. They'd had to do a lot of negotiation.

"This is the best we can hope for," Peter said. "I'm surprised they agreed to as much as they did."

When we ran through it, it met most of my conditions, and I agreed to sign it.

"Right," he said. "I'll get this back to Eva."

"I'm visiting her this afternoon; I'll take it, if you like."

"Good afternoon, Eva," I said as her secretary showed me in.

"Hello, Marcus. How are you?"

"Not good." She gave me a querying look. "I've spent the morning going over this new contract and I see you're fleecing your authors again."

She rolled her eyes.

"I've had to work bloody hard to get that agreed here," she replied. "Don't tell me you won't agree to it."

"Signed and sealed," I said, handing her the envelope. Her shoulders slumped and she shook her head.

"I still can't tell when you're being serious," she replied.

"I rarely am."

"Except when you think I'm trying to stifle your creativity."

"Correct. You're smarter than you look."

"Thanks," she said, laughing. "I may have some news you'll like."

We were here to discuss the publication of the first two earlier works, the current plan for Shadows of Silver, and a loose discussion about the future. It was all amicable. The previously published books were going to be released without fanfare. A small number were going to be given to retailers Eva thought would have a potential customer base, but that was it. No advertising or promotion until we saw what happened.

Shadows of Silver was well-advanced. I'd completed what I hoped would be the final version, but Eleanor was joining us later with her views on it. We discussed the launch and promotion plans, most of which we'd already agreed. We were launching it on the same date as Shadows of Gold the previous year.

"Spewn Words," Eva said as we drew to a close.

"Oh, yes." I'd almost forgotten she'd had it.

"The chap I gave it to didn't want to run with it in the end."

"Surprise, surprise."

"But I had a thought."

"Careful."

"I know, I do, sometimes. How about we treat it in the same way as your earlier books? Work with Eleanor, and soft release it. No fanfare, no advertising, same print run, and see how it goes."

It seemed a good idea. Even I knew it was a book with a limited audience. It was an acquired taste.

"Sounds fair enough," I replied. "As long as Eleanor doesn't insist on too many changes."

"We'll see. She's been looking at that as well."

When Eleanor arrived, we got through business rapidly. The few issues she had with Shadows of Silver were easily dealt with. The two earlier works needed a final tidy up. Then we came to Spewn Words.

"I didn't know what to think of this when I first read it," she said. "I couldn't make head nor tail of it. I tried to find the threads in it, tried to work out the structure. Then I was in the bath one night and it hit me. I read it again, not looking for anything, just reading the words and letting them flow."

"How nice you think of me in the bath," I said, and Eva laughed. "But you're right, it's not a story or a progression. Just enjoy the words and ideas."

"Exactly," Eleanor said. "So, I read it again."

"And?" Eva asked.

"I wouldn't change a thing."

Eva and I looked at one another.

"Nothing?" I said.

"No. There are no character arcs, no plotlines, just leave the words to speak for themselves. If I'm honest, I don't fully understand it, and I'm not sure how I'd begin to edit it."

"Fair enough," Eva said. "Happy with that, Marcus?"

"Yes," I replied, secretly happy I'd stumped Eleanor, who left us shortly after.

"I suppose you've already got a follow up to Silver?" Eva asked.

"Actually, no. Though I've got something fairly concrete in my head."

"Better start getting it on paper," she said, goading me.

"I will, but not before the autumn."

"Another summer break?"

"Yes, we're going away for a couple of months."

"A couple of months?"

"Yes, it's becoming something of a tradition."

"Where are you going?"

"Same place as last year, a fort in the South of France."

"The three of you?" she asked, a curious smile on her face.

"Yes, with a few friends popping over from time to time."

"Lucky them."

"Why don't you join us for a few days?"

"Oh," she said, looking embarrassed. "I wasn't fishing."

"No, I know you weren't, but you'd be more than welcome. A long weekend if nothing else."

"Thank you," she replied, a little flustered. "I'll … think about it."

Chapter 18 – Lucy

My relationship with my mother had gradually improved since we'd been back in contact. Our meetings were still a little formal, but I was more relaxed about what I said, and she seemed less uptight. Her life had changed so much since my father died.

She'd moved into a new house, changed to a different, less rigid, church. She'd developed a real relationship with Sarah and Nathan, her grandchildren, who now liked spending time with her. Annie thought it was this which pleased Mum the most.

I was only seeing Jenny, my counsellor, every three or four weeks now, as I'd resolved most of the issues around my father. But I continued to see her because building my relationship with Mum sometimes triggered painful memories.

I didn't blame her. She wasn't attuned to other people's feelings; it was part of what I now saw as the indoctrination she'd been exposed to for most of her life. My father only believed in right and wrong, black and white. Mum was now coming to terms with the grey of most people's lives.

It wasn't uncommon for her to say something which appeared tactless or cruel. It wasn't deliberate, it was the way she was.

"How often do you see her?" Jenny asked.

"Every couple of weeks, it's no longer a big thing. Sometimes we meet for an hour or two over lunch."

"That sounds better. How do you feel about her?"

"I'm still working that out. I struggle to see her as my mother, it's more like meeting an elderly relative."

"Are you glad it's happened?"

"Yes. Partly because of Mum, but also because I'm closer to Annie and her family. That's nice."

"Do they know about your relationships?"

"No. I'm not sure what or how to tell them about that. They accept me for who I am now, but the setup with Sally and Marcus might be difficult for them."

"There are many who might struggle to understand," she replied, smiling.

"I know. I'm not sure I understand it myself, let alone feel able to explain it."

The next time I visited Mum, she'd cooked us a meal and I was surprised it was pasta. At home, we'd always had very plain food.

"I've been experimenting," she said. "I've had a few disasters, though."

"Really?"

"Yes. I'm using things I've never tried before and I'm learning from my mistakes."

"Such as?"

"I tried to cook a curry. It was so hot, I had to throw it away."

"Did you ever try new things on Dad?"

I noticed she paused before replying.

"No, he wasn't interested. For him, food was simply fuel. No frills."

"Pleasure was a sin."

Another pause, as she looked at me. Perhaps to see if I was mocking her.

"Yes, it was. Everything had to have a purpose. If it didn't, it was … unnecessary."

We ate in silence for a few moments.

"How did you cope with that?" I finally asked her.

"I was used to it, Lucy. It was how I'd been brought up by my parents. When I married your father, it seemed perfectly normal. I'd never known another way of life."

"When did you begin to doubt that?"

We'd finished eating by now, and she was resting her elbows on the table as we talked.

"Because of Annie and Tim. As they … pulled away from us, I tried to work out why. I saw how they lived their lives, and it was different. They were freer, particularly Annie. She was able to do what she wanted, without Tim's permission and didn't get punished for it." My ears pricked up at that. "They were always happy, having fun. Your father raged about it, but as I understood their lives more, I looked around and saw that was how most people lived. It wasn't Annie and Tim who were the odd ones out, it was us."

"What would have happened if Dad hadn't died?"

"I don't think I'd have changed. I didn't have the strength to fight him."

"Would you have left him?"

"It didn't even cross my mind. I was his wife and owed him obedience."

"Do you still think that?"

She was getting uncomfortable, but there was something hidden here which I feared but wanted to know. Her earlier comment had reinforced that fear.

"Since he died, I've come to see the world in a different light. We saw those outside our church as sinners. Everything they did was evil, and God would punish them. But now, I see it was all lies. People want to enjoy life, enjoy their family and their friends. For sixty years, it was drummed into me we weren't on this earth to enjoy ourselves, and I believed it."

"You didn't have a choice, Mum."

"No, but now I do."

"Has that affected your view of Dad?"

She stayed silent, and I could see she was battling with something.

"He's gone now," she finally said, "best to leave it."

"Mum, you've not got a single picture of Dad in this house, nor anything, as far as I can tell, which reminds you of him. Why not? What are you not telling me … or Annie?"

"I don't want to speak ill of your father."

I laughed, a bitter laugh.

"Mum, I hated him. He cast me out for who I was, for what I was. He was a blinkered, embittered, cruel man. Over the years, I came to pity him. That was how I dealt with it. Nothing you can tell me is going to affect my view of him."

She turned away from my gaze and I feared I'd gone too far. We were silent for a while, then she spoke.

"He was blinkered. He was embittered. He was cruel. I see that now. I see how married couples live their lives and compare it to our marriage. All the things I was told were normal ... well, they weren't."

I took a risk, sure of my suspicions.

"He beat you," I said quietly.

She turned to me, surprised, then softened.

"Yes," she replied.

"When he was angry?"

"No, not in anger."

"Often?"

"Once a week, on Saturday."

"Once a week?"

"Yes."

"Why?"

"He kept a book in his pocket. Every time I did something wrong, he marked it down."

"Then punished you for it? In cold blood?"

My blood was boiling now. This was what I'd feared, but hearing her say it, and in such a calm way, was chilling.

"Yes."

"How?"

"He used a bunch of birch rods." I couldn't believe I was hearing this. She could see I was fuming. "I thought it was what all husbands did. I'm sure it was normal in our church."

"I don't think anything was normal in your church."

"I see that now."

"Did he ... enjoy it?" She didn't understand what I was saying. "Did he ... get pleasure from it?"

She looked puzzled for a moment, then a glimmer of comprehension appeared.

"Oh, no. I don't think so. We didn't ... well, you know. Not after you two were born."

"Because it was sinful."

"Yes. That was only for procreation."

"Wasn't that a problem for you?"

She smiled for the first time, a rueful smile.

"No. I didn't know women could … enjoy it. I've only learned that recently."

"Did you think it was okay for him to hit you?"

"Yes, because he beat himself, too."

"What?"

"He kept his own faults in the book as well, and used the rods on himself."

It fell into place at that. Flagellation, self-flagellation, expunging sin. It was so fucked up.

"Then went to church on Sunday," I said, "and prayed away his sins."

We returned to our silence. Me, dealing with a resurgence of hatred for the man who had been my father. Mum, probably wondering whether she should have brought these things into the open. I didn't know what to say. I wanted to offer something profound, something helpful to remove the memories. But we weren't close enough and I knew from my own experience there was no magic phrase, no panacea.

"Are you dealing with it okay?" I finally asked.

"I think so," she replied. "I know now how wrong it was; that it wasn't part of God's plan for me."

"You still believe?"

"Yes, I still believe, but in a kinder God. A God who loves everyone, whoever they are, whatever they are."

Her look as she said this told me it was aimed at me. I wasn't sure how to take it; was she accepting who I was, or attempting to redeem me?

"Are you happy with your life now?" I asked.

"I'm at peace," she replied. "I feel safe. I'm … free, to do what I want, to go where I want."

"Have you told Annie?" She shook her head. "Are you going to?" She frowned, and the tears came, without warning, surprising me. I went over to her and put my arms around her awkwardly. I let her cry. "Would you like me to tell her?"

She nodded silently, wiping her eyes.

I went straight to Annie's house after my visit and sat with her while Tim kept Sarah and Nathan occupied, telling her everything mother had told me. She was aghast, but we'd suspected something of this nature, and it wasn't a complete surprise.

"How did we not know?" she asked.

"Why would we?" I said. "He knew it was wrong. Even if he believed he was doing God's will, he knew most people would see it was wrong. So, he hid it."

"There is one thing, though," she said. "How come he didn't beat us?"

It was a good question and thinking about it made me shudder.

"I didn't think of that. I don't know."

"Because if that's how they were brought up, why didn't they bring us up in the same way?"

"Perhaps we'll find out, but I suggest we let it lie for a while. I don't know if she'll regret telling us, so we'd better not push."

"What do we do?"

"Nothing. Perhaps check on her and let her know we'll help if she needs it. But I doubt she'll ask."

As I lay in bed that night, I thought about everything Mum had told me. I wasn't angry any longer but felt sorry for her. She'd lived like that for most of her life, controlled by either her father or her husband. No wonder she now felt free.

"Not a pleasant discussion," Marcus said, when I told them over dinner on Saturday night.

"No, but one I was expecting," I replied. "She'd said a few things which made me suspect something like this."

"Are you okay?" Sally asked.

"Yea. Dad means nothing to me, and although Mum and I are getting on fine, we're not emotionally close. I think that's helped."

"How can anyone do that in the name of religion?" Marcus asked no one in particular. We pondered the question for a few minutes, each with our thoughts.

"Sorry," I finally said. "Didn't mean to bring the evening down."

"It's fine," Sal said. "It's what friends are for."

We spent the evening quietly, talking about our forthcoming holiday. Mary and Ken were already pencilled in to come and stay for a week.

"And you invited Eva," Sally said to Marcus, grinning.

"I thought it would be okay," he replied, "you suggested it. I doubt she'll come, anyway."

"So what's the problem?" I asked, sensing I'd missed something.

"Nothing," Sal said. "I've been ribbing him about it. He clearly wants to see her in a bikini."

He rolled his eyes, and Sally blew him a kiss.

"I presume we'll ask Helen and Penny again?" she said.

"Don't see why not," he replied.

"Will Helen come this time?"

"I doubt it. I think she might want to, but it would seriously change the dynamic and she knows it. She's happy to let Penny spend her free weeks with us, provided she wants to, of course."

"Let's ask them tomorrow."

"Okay, but don't pressure either of them, they may have other plans."

Chapter 19 – Sally

"Everyone ready?" Marcus asked. We were heading to another play party, and there were four of us again. Eva had come down in the morning and joined us for lunch, then we'd spent an hour getting ready. Lucy and I marvelled as she did her make-up.

Again, she went full Goth, and it transformed her. She was wearing a similar outfit to last time, a bralette cut around her tattoos and a tight mini skirt. This time they were both bright blue. I noticed she hadn't yet done her hair.

"Not long, Eva," I said. "Time to do your hair."

"Nearly done," she replied, sweeping her long hair up. Reaching into her make-up case, she pulled out a net and stretched it over her head, holding her hair in place.

She pulled a blue wig out of her bag, carefully put it on and fiddled with the edges, before combing it out as she wanted it. It was a thick, long bob which framed her face perfectly, and she looked stunning. I made a mental note to try a wig or two myself; Marcus might like the transformation.

"You never cease to surprise me, Eva," Marcus said when she came into the living room.

"You're not the only ones with secrets," she replied.

When we arrived at the venue, Lucy, Eva, and I went to the women's changing area. Eva wasn't shy this time, and Marcus had three half-naked women to admire as we re-joined him. Throughout the afternoon, we did the rounds and introduced Lucy to a few people she still hadn't met, and Eva to everyone we came across. Her look and tattoos proved popular again, and she dealt calmly with lots of questions.

One of the demos we watched was about e-stim devices and how to use them. We hadn't tried them; it wasn't high on our priority list. But we were intrigued.

"We should try, darling," I said to Marcus.

"Fancy it?"

"Yea. Might be fun."

"It is," Eva said.

"Good?" I asked her.

"I had a guy who was into it. The idea scared me to death, but he persuaded me to try it." She laughed as she saw the querying look on Marcus's face. "Come on," she continued, "I'm no saint."

"Somehow," he replied, "I didn't think you were."

Their sparring had become playful, both enjoying the challenge of besting the other. There was no edge to it, and it was fun to watch.

As we returned to the social area, I saw red hair above the heads around it in the corner of the room.

"There's Helen," I said, and we headed her way. She was talking to a couple of people I didn't know.

"Hi, Helen," I said.

"Well, hello," she replied. I saw her look at Eva and give her the usual slow assessment. The couple she'd been talking to slipped away.

"This is Eva," I said. "Eva, Helen. Helen is Penny's mistress."

"Hello, Eva," Helen said. "I assume none of those are temporary."

"No," Eva replied. "For life."

Helen nodded. I hadn't warned Eva about Helen but thought she could handle her.

"Helen," Marcus said after a few pleasantries. "We're spending some time at the fort again this year. We'd like to invite you and Penny to come over again."

Helen raised an eyebrow, and a wry smile appeared.

"Us, or just Penny?" she asked, clearly winding him up.

"We'd love to see both of you."

"Well, I'll have to talk to Penny. I suspect she'll pack her bags tonight when she finds out."

It was said with humour and genuine warmth.

"And you?" he asked.

"We'll see, Marcus. We'll see."

As Helen left us, Eva turned to me.

"She was not what I expected as Penny's mistress."

"They appear an odd couple but see them together and there's real chemistry."

"She seems a bit cold."

"Outwardly, yes, but it's something of an act. Underneath, she's a rather wonderful person. She doesn't let people in easily, and if you cross her, she'll eat you for breakfast."

"She is impressive."

"Isn't she? She's a corsetiere, and Lucy and I have one or two of her creations."

"Did she make what she's wearing?"

"Undoubtedly."

"Wow."

A little later, a slightly breathless Penny appeared.

"Hi, guys," she said, giving us all a hug and a kiss. "I've been looking for you."

She was wearing a tight mesh mini dress, with just a thong underneath. We all took a moment or two to enjoy it; she paused to let us.

"I hear you're going to the fort again," she said.

"We might be," Marcus replied.

"And you've invited us for a few days again."

"We might have."

"Thank you." She was trying to hide her excitement but failing. "I … I'd love to come."

"Good, for how long?"

She looked down briefly, her tell she was nervous.

"The same as last time?" she said. Marcus stared at her; I knew he was teasing her, and she did too. "If it's not too long?"

"As long as you like, Penny," he finally said, and she broke into a broad grin.

"Thank you. Thank you so much. I'll agree the dates with you and Helen."

As she walked away, I caught up with her.

"Penny," I said. "Do you actually want Helen to come as well?"

She looked down again, then back at me.

"Yes ..." she replied quietly, "and no."

"Meaning you'd like her to, but you want your own time as well."

"Yes. I know it sounds bad."

"No, it doesn't, and it gives me an idea."

"When she was with you last year," Eva said when I re-joined the group, "was she fun?"

I turned to see an amused glint in her eyes.

"She was, rather."

"How come Helen agrees?"

"It's their contract. It's only for fifty weeks a year."

"And she's able to do what she wants in the other two?"

"Yup."

"Including ..."

"Including what?" I was enjoying teasing her for once.

"Joining your harem?"

"Penny's in her element, and she's got a big soft spot for Marcus."

"She has?"

"Yes."

"That doesn't worry you?"

"God, no. We trust each other, and it's all part of the fun."

"I was right," she said, shaking her head. "You lot will get me into trouble."

***

On our way to the fort, we stopped off in Paris for three days and stayed in Genevieve's guest flat. She and Jacques were kindness itself. Never expecting anything from us, and more than willing to share their knowledge of the city.

We took Genevieve out to dinner one night and visited Jacques's drag club again. This time, we'd taken some more appropriate clothes, and spent time getting into the spirit of the place. Jacques, who was dragged up this time, still outshone us all.

We invited them both to come and stay with us. Genevieve said she might, but Jacques politely declined. I'd seen how his life was his clubs and the friends who visited them. He gave almost all his time to them, and to his mother. I wasn't sure if he had a partner, but I assumed there was no one around currently. I believed he would have introduced us.

As we collected the key to the fort, we were excited. Our previous stay had been memorable for all of us, and the thought of another summer here was intoxicating. When we arrived, we unloaded the car which had been piled to overflowing, as we had Lucy with us this time, and made a quick tour of the place.

There had been one or two changes. There was now a small gym in one of the spare spaces downstairs, a huge waterfall shower by the pool and a few new pieces of furniture and artwork. We opened all the doors and sat on the terrace, with our first bottle of wine.

"Any plans?" Lucy asked.

"None at all," Marcus replied. "Though I guess tomorrow we ought to go and do some shopping and stock up for a week or so."

As before, we each had a short list of things we wanted to do and places we wanted to visit. We agreed before we came we'd follow the pattern of the previous year; one day of activity, the next relaxing at the fort.

Mary and Ken arrived at the end of the first week and stayed for six days. Ken had changed since he'd met Mary, he was much more worldly, but his sense of awe at new experiences was still touching. I was moved by their relationship. She'd sacrificed so much for Charlie and me, and I was delighted she'd found someone to share her life with.

The following week, Genevieve joined us for a few days. She was gracious as ever and tremendous fun. On the second day, we stayed at the fort, and I found myself alone with her after breakfast on one part of the terrace; Marcus and Lucy were giving me time with her.

"I hope you're not too disappointed Jacques isn't coming," she said.

"No, he's a busy man."

"Yes, he is. But he keeps busy for a reason." I looked at her, unsure of how to reply. "Shortly before you first met him, he lost his partner."

"Oh, I'm sorry."

"They'd been together for three years; it was one of the reasons he was happy to move to Paris. Raoul was a lovely boy." She laughed. "Boy; listen to me. He was the same age as Jacques. He was killed … in a car crash."

My chest tightened uncomfortably.

"Oh, God," I said. "I'm so sorry."

"Don't be silly, it's not your fault. He's coming through it; his clubs are his life at the moment."

"But now he's having to deal with Raoul's death and his father's."

"Yes, and he's still battling his father."

I must have shown my puzzlement.

"Sally, he never got on with his father … your father. You must know what it was like. A boy's father never at home, only appearing for short periods before disappearing again."

"Yes, I know that feeling. I didn't know him at all."

"Exactly. I brought him up, and Brendan – your father – didn't always approve of my efforts." I thought back to Dad's disagreements with Mary. "I think, and please don't be offended, your father should perhaps not have had children, but these things happen."

"I think you're probably right."

"By the time Jacques knew he was gay, your father tried to change him. All it did was drive them further apart. When he disappeared, Jacques tried to blank his father from his mind."

"I did the same. But my contacting him and filling in the gaps …"

"Made him think hard about what happened. He's still dealing with it."

"I feel awful, and he's being so nice to me."

"Oh, he has nothing against you, he likes you. He loves the fact he has a sister. But he's having to reassess his father. We've had many afternoons talking about him in the last year, more than we've ever had before. It's been good for both of us. The news you brought us allowed me to close the book. But for Jacques, he's still got a way to go."

"Is there anything I can do?"

"He looks at you and sees someone who's come to terms with your shared father, and he's not sure how. I wouldn't be surprised if he asks you at some point."

"I'll willingly help."

"Good, but let him come to you, let him ask."

"I will."

I recounted the conversation to Marcus and Lucy after we returned from seeing Genevieve safely onto the TGV to Paris.

"He's on the same path you were," Lucy said.

"Yes, and I didn't see it. I feel guilty about that."

"Don't," Marcus said and gave me a concerned look. "If you dwell on it, it won't do you any good. Jacques has his reasons for feeling the way he does, and he'll find his own way to deal with them."

"I shouldn't help him?"

"Of course … if he asks for your help. But his solutions won't be the same as yours."

"He's right, Sal," Lucy said. "You can't take responsibility for your father's actions."

I knew they were right; we'd known pursuing my father's muddled life could lead to pain. But if I hadn't contacted Jacques, perhaps he wouldn't have had to rake through painful memories. I was stronger now, though. I determined to help him if I could but wouldn't dwell on it. The next day, it was just something on my to-do list.

A few days later, Lucy and I headed to the airport as one of my plans came to fruition. We were going to pick up Penny and Helen. After the play party, I'd spoken to Helen. As she was always direct with us, I was with her.

"I suspect you'd like to come," I said. "But you don't want to intrude on Penny's downtime." Her brief expression of surprise confirmed my suspicion. "Am I right?" She softened into a smile.

"You are, Sally. I haven't been on holiday for years, apart from visiting a couple of old friends."

"Would you like to come over?"

"It does sound tempting. But this is Penny's time for herself, and that's important … to both of us. She loved last year, and I don't want to spoil her fun."

The last phrase was accompanied by a knowing smile.

"Well, Helen; I have a suggestion …"

So now, they were both coming, but Helen was only staying a few days, leaving Penny with us. They'd both liked the idea and it satisfied everyone's reservations. We'd talked a lot about how Helen might be on holiday. She was always perfectly turned out, never a hair out of place, and usually formally dressed.

Today proved no exception. We spotted the plait of red hair easily and went to greet them. Helen was dressed in a tailored skirt and jacket – we'd never seen her in trousers. The only concession to being in the south of France in mid-summer was a pair of sunglasses perched on her head.

They both had large suitcases as well as hand luggage and we shared the load between us as we headed for the car. Penny was holding her excitement in check; we all knew it, and I think even Helen was amused. Marcus, Lucy, and I had agreed we wouldn't tease or flirt with Penny while Helen was here, and we'd always remain covered. We weren't sure how relaxing the next few days would be. It would depend on Helen.

She turned out to be an ideal guest, more relaxed than we'd ever seen her. She didn't seem to control Penny in any way, although Penny made sure Helen had everything she needed.

She surprised us, too. First by appearing the next morning in a pair of trousers, a full, loose linen pair, reminiscent of the forties. But they suited her. We spent the day driving along the coast, having lunch in a small town perched above the Mediterranean. In the evening, we had dinner in a restaurant we liked in Hyères.

She surprised us more the next day, one of our relax at home days, by appearing after breakfast in a flowing robe, with her hair loose. She went to the pool, took the robe off revealing a one-piece costume, climbed down the steps, and launched herself under the water.

We looked at each other, almost in disbelief, then at Penny, who seemed almost as surprised as we were. Helen spent half an hour in the pool, where Penny joined her.

When they came back to us on the lower terrace, Helen's hair was still matted over her shoulders and back. Penny disappeared inside, and Helen sat on one of the loungers.

"I could get used to having a pool," she said. "Though not many have this setting."

"It's rather nice, isn't it?" I replied.

"Yes, I can see why you love it."

Penny returned with a couple of hairbrushes, sat behind Helen, and began to sort out her tangled mane, which was drying in the sun. Both seemed engrossed in what they were doing.

"Have you always had your hair as long?" Lucy asked.

"For most of my life, yes. I've cut it shorter a couple of times, but always come back to this."

"It's gorgeous."

"I hated it when I was young, but I've grown to love it."

Penny plaited Helen's hair loosely, tying it off with a band. I was looking at Helen in her swimsuit. If I looked anything like that at her age, I'd be more than happy. I didn't know her exact age, but we'd guessed she was in her early fifties. We knew something of her life story now, but she'd clearly taken care of herself.

The afternoon saw one of those tremendous Mediterranean storms. It appeared quickly, the clouds darkening and the air becoming heavy in a matter of minutes. The thunder rolled around the point on which the fort was built. Lightning flashed around us and the rain came. Torrential rain, rolling in off the sea.

The fort was partly built into the cliffs, and there was no exposed roof on the lower levels. It seemed strange to watch the power of the rain, without much sound. We left all the terrace doors open, as it was still hot, and sat inside, watching the light show, and listening to the thunder echo around the cliffs. It was dramatic entertainment.

Helen insisted on taking us out to dinner on her final night with us, and we found a restaurant by the marina in Toulon. It was a relaxed evening and Helen was on form, with none of her usual reserve. It seemed a holiday had done her good.

Chapter 20 – Lucy

Sally and Penny took Helen to the airport, and Marcus and I had a leisurely lunch.

"Are we stripping off now?" I asked.

"I'd like to wait until we've spoken to Penny. Just to make sure."

When Penny and Sal returned, they joined us on the terrace and tucked into the food we laid out for them.

"Safely on her flight?" I asked Sally.

"Yes, but she did leave Penny a surprise."

"Oh?"

Penny looked a little embarrassed.

"Didn't she?" Sal asked her.

"Yes. I thought I was here for eight or nine more days ..."

"The remainder of the two weeks after Helen went home," Sal said.

"... but the ticket Helen left me is for two weeks tomorrow. I wondered why she insisted on booking the flights." She looked around the table, failing to hide her anxiety. "Is that okay? I can always arrange an earlier flight."

"I told her I'd have to ask you two," Sal said, giving us a wink.

"I'm not sure," I said. "What do you think, Marcus?"

"They're winding you up, Penny," he said. "You're welcome to stay as long as you want."

She visibly relaxed.

"Thank you."

"But," he said, "let's agree the rules."

I saw Sally roll her eyes.

"Why would it be any different to last year?" she asked.

"Because Penny may want to change them."

"No, I'm fine with them," Penny said, rather too quickly.

"Sure?" he asked her. "You know you can change them anytime."

"Yes. I'm happy to do exactly what we did last year."

She was teasing him now and enjoying it.

"Exactly?"

"Other things, as well." She dropped her gaze. "I've brought a couple of things with me."

"Really?" Sally said.

"Yes."

"Want to show us?" Marcus asked.

Penny hesitated a moment before disappearing inside.

"Are we all happy?" Marcus asked while she was gone. Sal and I took our clothes off before he could even shake his head.

Penny came back onto the terrace, with her hands behind her back and a determined look on her face. She stood by the table between Sally and Lucy, seeing their nakedness. A hungry grin appeared.

"I knew you'd have a few toys," she said. "So, I've only brought things that are favourites of mine."

Her hand appeared and laid a short whip on the table; plaited leather with a mass of short loose strands at the end. Then she revealed a cane. It was short and very thin. Marcus picked the whip up and ran it through his fingers, looking at her. She was focussed on him. Then he picked the cane up, and ran his fingers along its length, bending it and letting it go. He passed it to Sally, who examined it.

"You need to tell us what you want to do," he said to Penny. "Don't be shy, I doubt we'll say no." She grinned. "But equally, speak up when you don't want to do something. Agreed?"

"Yes," she said softly.

"I know you're not used to it but speak up for yourself."

"I'm learning," she said. "And I want to use these things … and anything else you might have brought with you."

"You haven't seen what we've brought."

"Try me, I can always say no."

"You are learning," Sally said. "Helen's going to have to break you in again when you get home." Penny's face told us she wouldn't mind in the slightest.

"What do you think?" Marcus asked Sally, who was still playing with the cane.

"It's like our whippy one, but thinner and lighter. I don't think it would do much damage, but I bet it stings like hell."

"Let's find out," he replied, turning to Penny. "Bend over."

There was a moment's surprise on her face, followed by a look of pure delight as she threw herself over the edge of the table between Sally and me. We pulled our chairs back to let Marcus walk around and give him room to manoeuvre.

Penny was still clothed, and her loose dress came to mid-thigh, even when she was bent over. Marcus threw the hem over her back, leaving us with a gorgeous view of her bum, beautifully encased in a pair of white boy-shorts.

These he whipped down in one movement, leaving them at knee level. His hand moved back to her bum, and he stroked her cheeks, eliciting an immediate wiggle from Penny. He took the cane from Sally and tapped it lightly on her skin.

"He's going to enjoy this," I said to Sally.

"So am I," she replied.

His tapping got firmer, and rapid, moving up and down her bum, drifting over the top of her thighs. Penny's right foot came off the ground, lifting slightly.

"Down," he said. She obeyed. The strokes were firmer now, but not heavy. The sound was fascinating; the constant swish of the cane through the air, broken by a rapid succession of clicks as it flicked her skin, and the occasional little whimper.

"Stand up," he said. "Strip."

She took her dress and shorts off in a flash and resumed her position over the table. Marcus grabbed her left hand, and she offered her right, enabling him to cross them behind her back. He held them in place and swung the cane again. A stream of light strokes, causing Penny's breath to catch, her body to twitch and an occasional yelp. I watched the cane's contact with her bum, each stroke causing a slim depression in her skin before springing back as the cane rose again.

I was surprised there were no marks, no redness. But Penny's reaction showed the cane wasn't painless. Every so often, one of her legs would bend, the foot coming off the floor. He paused and pushed his fingers between her thighs, prompting an instant cry, and her legs spread apart, eager for more.

He went back to using the cane, a little harder now, and an occasional thin pink line appeared. Marcus still hadn't taken his shorts off, but it was clear this was exciting him.

Sally saw too, and knelt in front of him, slipping his shorts down, and taking his erection into her mouth, causing him to pause and moan. Penny looked back and let out a pleading groan when she saw what was happening.

The cane was biting her skin now, more thin lines were appearing, and Penny was whining as the barrage continued. Sally let Marcus's cock go and stood up. She whispered something in his ear, and came over to me, squatting beside my chair. Her hand trailed up my thigh, and I spread my legs as she sought my sex. When she found it, I grunted.

As my body reacted to Sally's touch, Marcus moved behind Penny and drove into her in one movement. She wailed as his cock filled her, instantly coming, her body shaking, both feet coming off the floor, her arms flailing, trying to find a grip on the table. My own body was enjoying Sally's fingers, and I saw she was using her other hand on herself.

Marcus slowed a little as Penny dropped from her peak. He bent over her and whispered something I couldn't hear. There was a breathless giggle, before he grabbed her hips and fucked her. They were both lost in pure animal lust, her urging him on as she twisted and bucked under the onslaught.

As she came again, I heard Sally do the same and she pulled me down to kiss her. When she subsided, she set to work on me, roughly fucking me with three fingers, as I tried to keep my balance on the chair.

As my orgasm built, I couldn't take my eyes off Penny, squirming on the table as Marcus fucked her, her legs now somehow crossed at the ankle behind him. I could see his cock sliding into her time and time again. I came. A short, heavy orgasm. A release of lust. Nothing loving or sensual.

As I slipped from the peak, Penny screamed as another orgasm overwhelmed her, closely followed by a loud cry from Marcus as he reached his climax. Several savage, deep thrusts followed, each accompanied by a grunt, as he emptied himself in her. She was trembling as he bent down, and her legs slowly returned to the floor.

He was quietly talking to her, but I still couldn't hear what he was saying. There was another quiet giggle, and he slipped out, before helping her to turn and sit on the edge of the table. Her face was flushed, but the expression was one of pure ecstasy, and Sal and I smiled at each other.

"Well, darling," Sal said. "I think I might like to try that cane if Penny will allow me."

"Of course," Penny said, still searching for air. "I'd like to see that."

The following days were a repeat of the previous year when Penny had been with us, including a memorable evening when Penny got her wish as Marcus used her cane on Sally as they played out a scene for our enjoyment.

We had a couple of girl's days out, including a return to the naturist reserve on the Île de Levant. We tried to persuade Marcus to join us, but he was adamant in his refusal. I couldn't work out why. He was happy enough walking around the fort naked in front of us, and I couldn't see the difference, but Sally didn't push it.

"Why don't you have a night out?" he asked one day. We liked the idea.

"Where shall we go?" Sal asked.

"Hyères, Toulon, St Tropez? Why not go over the top?"

"We could, couldn't we?" she replied.

"I haven't brought anything dressy," Penny said.

"Time for a shopping trip, I think."

The next day we went into Toulon and Sally led us around the most expensive shops she could find. By the time we finished, we were kitted out for a glamorous night. As I had been a year ago, Penny was embarrassed by Sally's largesse, but already knew only to make a token protest.

We spent a couple of hours getting ready. It was great fun, bathing, doing each other's hair, laying on the make-up. Sally had brought a lot of her serious jewellery with her, and after she'd picked the emerald set for herself, she let Penny and I choose from the rest. When we were ready, we looked in the mirror; we looked good. Marcus certainly thought so when we came downstairs.

We'd decided to go into St Tropez. Its glamourous air appealed, and Marcus had offered to be our chauffeur. We'd booked a restaurant for dinner, and he dropped us off just after seven. We had a relaxed meal and moved on to a casino. They were fascinating places. None of us were real gamblers, it was a bit of fun, and we were in the fortunate position that Sally was generous enough to allow us to play without real consequences.

But it was also a place to watch our fellow gamblers. Some were regulars, known to the staff and occupying the same chair all evening. Then there were the tourists, some unsure of the etiquette, looking nervous, others brash and throwing their money around.

We wandered from game to game, trying things as we went. My favourite was blackjack, and I spent half an hour winning and losing in equal measure. Penny had only been to a casino once before, with us the previous year.

She soon got into the swing and proved as objective as us. If you got onto a losing or winning streak, know when to pull out. We took a break at the bar and found some chairs to take the weight off our feet.

"I never imagined I'd be this dressed up and playing in a casino in the south of France," Penny said, as we looked out over the other customers. "It's like being in a film. Thank you."

"Penny," Sal said, "you don't need to-"

"I know, I know," Penny put in, with a big grin on her face. "But I can't help it. It's such fun."

"Another circuit, then on somewhere else?" Sal said. I knew she had every intention of making a night of this. An hour later, we left the casino and headed to a club recommended by one of the croupiers. It seemed to be buzzing, with cars lining up to drop people off. The guys on the door took one look at the three of us and waved us through.

Inside we weren't the only one's dressed to the nines. It was obviously the place to be, or at least, be seen. It was one of the strangest clubs I'd ever visited. It was fairly crowded, but everyone seemed to be on their best behaviour. People were wandering around, talking and drinking. But the music was quiet, and nobody was dancing. After an hour, we decided to move on. We weren't looking for the local dive, but this place was too staid.

We asked one of the guys on the door if there were other clubs with a bit more life. He pointed up the street to a neon-covered building, and we headed for it. It was a different world. Buzzing, lively, great music, even for us oldies, and a vibrant mix of people and ages.

"What time is it?" Sally asked.

"Half twelve," Penny replied.

Sally took her phone out.

"You calling Marcus already?" I asked.

"Hell, no," she replied. "Unless you want me to?"

Penny and I shook our heads.

"Remember our old safe routine?" Sal asked me, and it clicked. Penny gave me a puzzled look.

"She's texting Marcus to let him know we're okay," I told her.

"Come on," Sal said, putting her phone away. "Let's get a drink and see who we can wind up."

She wasn't joking. We sat at the bar, and I could see Sally was in her playful mood. We politely turned down approaches from a few guys, and cultural differences came into play. Those who appeared to be locals merely smiled and moved on. A couple of British guys were all smiles until we rebuffed them, at which they moved off, muttering a few choice insults.

"Why do they do it?" I asked.

"Because they're ignorant pigs," Penny replied, surprising us with the bitterness in her voice. "Sorry, but some men are."

"Sounds like someone's had a few bad experiences."

"Haven't we all?"

"Oh, God. Yes," Sal said. "But Lucy and I have had some fun over the years, haven't we?"

"Sure have."

"How do you mean?" Penny replied.

"Up for it?" Sal asked me.

We looked around and saw an empty booth. Leading Penny over to it, we made ourselves at home and waited. Sure enough, within a few minutes, the bees were attracted to the honey pot.

Two men wandered past a couple of times, obviously sussing us out, and doing a poor job of hiding it. They were at least our age but dressed like teenagers and finally stopped at our booth.

"Drink?" one of them asked, while his mate didn't hide his eyes wandering over each of us in turn, lingering on Penny.

"No, thank you," Sally replied sweetly. "We're fine."

"You're English," the second said, obviously relieved they wouldn't need the two or three French words they knew between them.

"We are."

"Thank God, we haven't had much luck with the locals."

Such gallantry.

"Speaking French might help with that," Sally said. Penny broke into a smile and had to look away.

"Can't be bothered," the first man said. "There's plenty of other fish in the sea."

"We're fish?" I replied, affecting offence.

"No, no, no," the second man said, giving his mate a cross look. "He didn't mean that. Just a figure of speech, ain't it?"

"I'm not surprised you're not having much luck."

The first man seemed to be confused already; this wasn't going the way he'd expected. The second guy, obviously the brainier of the two, which wasn't saying much, tried again.

"Ladies, I'm sorry. We didn't mean to offend you. Now, how about a drink?"

"Again, no, thank you," Sally said.

"Would you like some company, then?" he asked, still not hiding his wandering gaze.

"Thank you, but we have all the company we need." As she said it, she put her arms around my neck, placed her lips on mine, and gave me a long, lingering kiss. The facial expressions of the two men standing in front of us went from confusion to incomprehension, then slow realisation and finally, frustration. They turned away from us as Sal ended her kiss. The phrase 'bloody lezzers' drifted from their retreating figures.

Sally leaned back with a satisfied look on her face.

"I wouldn't have the nerve," Penny said.

"We used to do it a lot," Sal replied. "That was an easy let-down."

"How do you mean?"

"We've led them a lot further than that. Let them buy us drinks all evening."

"Didn't you have any trouble?"

"There were occasions when we went to the loos and did a runner."

"And a couple of times," I added, "when they found out, they asked if they could watch."

"Oh, yes," she replied. "I'd forgotten about that. Bloody cheek."

"But you weren't lovers then, were you?" Penny asked Sally.

"No, but we wanted to go out and have some fun. We weren't looking for anything. If we got pestered, it was our go-to response."

"And now," Penny said, a curious expression on her face, "you do have someone who watches."

"So we do. Talking of him …"

She sent him another text. We had another drink or two and danced. By three-thirty, we were too tired to dance any more.

"Let's see if we can find somewhere quieter," Sally said, and we headed out of the club. Shortly afterwards, we found ourselves sitting outside a small bar on the edge of an open square. It was still warm, and there were plenty of people about. We ordered a bottle of wine, coffee, and some water. We'd drunk too much but didn't want to stop.

"Won't Marcus be expecting to pick us up?" Penny asked, again allowing us to stare at her until she got embarrassed. "What I mean is …"

"Don't worry," Sally replied, "we can stay as long as we like. I told him we'll make it up to him."

Penny smiled at that.

"You like Marcus," I said, looking at her.

"Yes," she replied, a little hesitantly.

"Come on," Sal said. "Tell us why."

Penny shifted in her seat, embarrassed.

"I … I find him attractive," she replied. "Sorry."

Sally laid her hand on Penny's arm.

"Don't apologise," she replied, furtively looking around the square, before lowering her voice to a whisper. "To tell you the truth, so do I."

Penny laughed and it lightened the situation.

"What is it about him?" I asked. She thought for a few moments.

"If I was looking for a male dom, he'd almost be my perfect fit."

"Almost?"

"Except he's not twenty-four-seven," Sally said.

"Yes," Penny replied, before hastily adding, "and he's not available, either. But he's everything I've not found before in a master."

"Such as?"

"He doesn't try to be something he isn't. He does things his way but is always aware of his partner's needs. Whenever he teases or tops me, there's a glint in his eye or a smile on his face. He makes me feel special and I trust him."

"I do too," Sally said. "Completely."

"Exactly, you're very lucky."

"I know."

"And he's imaginative and thoughtful and caring." She was on a roll now. "And how many men would be comfortable with the relationship you two have?"

She was right. We knew it wouldn't be many.

"Anything else?" I asked.

"Well, he's got a nice cock, too."

Chapter 21 – Marcus

The fort was quiet the next day. I'd picked the girls up at six in the morning, and they'd all been sleepy on the journey home. Not much was said as they slowly climbed the stairs, although there were a few giggles as someone missed a step and the others tried to hold her up. I followed and kept an eye on them as they threw their clothes on the floor, before collapsing in a heap on the bed. I made sure the duvet was reachable and left them.

I'd gone to bed after dropping them off the evening before to get some rest. They'd rung later than I'd expected, and I'd had a full night's sleep, so I went downstairs and took some breakfast out onto the terrace as the sun was coming up. After a couple of hours, I took a jug of water and some glasses upstairs, along with some headache tablets. They were all sound asleep, so I left them on the side and quietly made my exit.

It was another four hours before the first one appeared. Penny came out onto the terrace, wearing a robe.

"Good morning," she said quietly.

"Good afternoon," I replied.

"Is it?" she asked.

"Can I get you anything?"

"It's fine, I'll find something."

"No, come and sit down."

She didn't argue. I went to the kitchen, and got some bread, cheese, and cured meats, along with some fruit, coffee, and water. After looking at it suspiciously for a minute or two, she tried some bread, gradually picking at the other things.

"Feeling rough?" I asked when she stopped eating.

"A little. My head's a bit … throbby."

"More paracetamol?"

"I took some before I came down. Thank you."

A little later, Sally and Lucy appeared, also robed, also looking somewhat the worse for wear. Not much was said as they gingerly picked their way through the food on offer and drank lots of water. I went and laid on a lounger, leaving them to their shared misery. Sal came over after a while.

"Sorry," she said," but we're all going back to bed."

I didn't see them until the evening. When they came down, they'd showered and were much brighter. They came and gave me a hug and a kiss, before going into the pool. As they joined me on loungers, they were still quiet.

"What do you fancy to eat?" I asked.

Someone groaned.

"Not hungry," Sal said.

I laid out a repeat of lunch with a few extra things, and as they slowly picked at the food, they perked up. Penny seemed back to normal.

"I don't know," I said. "Perhaps you're getting too old for these late nights."

Sally narrowed her eyes at me.

"If I felt better," she replied, "I'd think of some witty response. But I don't, so I can't."

"He may be right, Sal," Lucy said. "I felt shit when I woke up."

"Me too," Sal replied.

"Penny," I said. "You're a lot younger than these two." Frowns from Sal and Luce. "How are you feeling?"

"I'm fine now."

"See. That proves my point."

Sally threw an olive at me, but it missed by a long way, so she poked her tongue out instead.

We had a quiet evening lounging on the terrace. Penny and I chatted, while Sally and Lucy fell asleep. We had to wake them to go to bed.

***

We did get a little work done. While she was with us, Penny showed me the new website she was building for me. It was even better than we'd discussed, and after a couple of hours reviewing it and agreeing changes, I was happy it would fit the bill. Although Eva and her team would need to vet it, I didn't think there'd be any problems.

She also spent some time going through the site she was building for Lucy. After they'd reviewed progress, they showed it to Sally and me. Given the subject, Penny had been able to let her imagination run riot, and the result was spectacular.

They'd been working together closely for a few weeks, and Penny had spent hours filming Lucy drawing and painting several works. The result was some beautiful animated time-lapse films as each picture developed. They were spellbinding.

"Happy, Luce?" Sally asked.

"It's brilliant," she replied. "I'm not sure my work deserves it."

"Oh, come on," Sal said. "Look how the group loved it, and the commissions you've got. There's a real market for it."

"I'm not sure I've got the time."

"You set the pace," I said. "You can list your stock pieces for sale, and then take commissions. You only need to accept those you want to do."

"But how do I choose?"

"By price," I replied.

"Price?"

"Yea. Don't sell yourself short. Price the stock stuff reasonably, to allow as many people as possible to afford them. But make sure you price the commission work high enough to limit demand to what you can cope with."

"I guess I'll have to experiment."

"Yes. You can always pause commissions when you're busy. People will happily wait if they're keen enough."

"You can also put all the work you do in the gallery," Penny said.

"You'll need to get permission," Sal replied.

"As long as it's not identifiable, I can't imagine many people refusing."

"I don't know," Luce replied. "Faces are visible in some."

"But not all. The ones you've done of us are explicit, but I'd be happy for you to have them on the site. You wouldn't mind, would you, darling?"

"No, but perhaps not the one of your lips around my cock."

"Okay, there may be one or two exceptions."

"You're going to need some more models," I said. They looked at me, puzzled. "Well, most of your current work features the people round this table, and whilst we're all beautiful people, it would be good to find models of different shapes and sizes. People will be more inclined to buy stuff if they can identify with it."

"I'll need to think about it," Lucy said. "I know a few life models, but I doubt they'll want to be subjects for the more explicit stuff."

"You might ask the group. I suspect there are a few exhibitionists there and as long as they can't be recognised, I think some would pose for you. Or at least give you pictures of some of their more interesting activities."

"I hadn't thought of that."

"I'd wait a while and get the site up and running to gauge interest. Better to start too slow than find yourself unable to satisfy demand."

"True. Talking of models, how about I take some pictures tonight? I could do with some new inspiration."

"What of?"

"Anything we fancy doing."

It was a fun-filled night. Lucy acted as director, coming up with ideas she wanted to photograph. She spent a couple of hours getting us to do different things in various positions, moving legs or arms while we tried to keep control of our desire. There was a lot of giggling and posing before it all got too much. We grabbed the camera from Lucy's hands and jumped her, making her forget her art. By the time we finished, we made sure we had a lot of compromising pictures of her, too.

Penny's time with us was coming to an end. Two days before she flew home, she asked if she could spend the day looking after us. In practice, it meant she catered to our every need; keeping us topped up with food and drink, cooking, and satisfying any other whim we could think of. Strangely, through the course of the day, we thought of quite a few.

On the last evening, we dressed and went out for dinner. Penny was a little withdrawn to begin with.

"You're quiet," I said to her. She smiled, drawn from her reverie.

"Sorry," she replied. "I'm sad to be going."

"Perhaps we'll all come back next year."

"I hope so," she said, with real feeling.

"Anyway, Penny," Sally added. "I think you're going to have to talk to Helen about getting another male sub."

"I know. This reminds me how much I miss ... well, you know."

Our laughing made her blush and look away, grinning.

"Will she?" I asked.

"She would if we could find the right person, but our requirements are a bit unusual."

"Wanted; a guy with a big cock to sub to an ice queen and keep another horny little sub satisfied. Oh, and also switch for her once in a while. Only needed once a month."

"That's about it," she said, trying to suppress her laughter. "Plus, someone we can trust."

There was a pause while we all thought about Ben.

"That won't be easy, surely?" Lucy said.

"No, it won't," Penny replied. "I've never met anyone who ticks all those boxes." Another pause. "Still, we'll see. I didn't mean to bring the evening down. Sorry."

"Penny ..."

She gave me a brief confused look, then smiled.

"Sorry for saying sorry, Marcus," she said, with a wicked grin on her face.

"It's no good, darling," Sal said. "Penny's beginning to get the better of you."

The rest of the meal was more upbeat, and we went back to the fort, where the girls decided to get drunk. I was always amused by these sessions, as the few inhibitions they had melted away, and I could listen in to three women discussing their intimate thoughts. Whether they spiced it up for my benefit, I was never sure. But I always learnt a few things and stored away one or two for future use.

"Marcus," Penny said in a pause, "you haven't given me any marks to take back to Helen."

Unlike last year, we now knew what she wanted. She loved being used, being told what to do, being punished. A couple of sessions had concentrated on the task, and Sally and Lucy had joined in. Penny's reaction had amazed all of us. Pain and being controlled really was her thing. But I had prepared for this question.

"I will now, if you like." She sat up eagerly. "But you may be disappointed."

"I'm game."

"Can you get the heavier cane?"

She went to run upstairs, but the alcohol meant her path wasn't as straight as it should have been, and she had to slow down and hold the bannister.

"What have you got in mind?" Sally asked. "I know that look."

"Just a little idea I had before we came."

Penny returned with the cane and handed it to me.

"I'm not going to warm you up," I said. "I'm going to use this cold, but not for long." She looked puzzled. "Okay?"

"Yes."

"Good, strip."

She slowly undressed, a little wobbly, until she stood in front of us naked.

"Now," I said, looking around the room. "Sal, can you put some sofa cushions on the dining table?"

They were all wondering what I was up to but took the cushions to the table and laid them in a row.

"I want you lying on them, head at the end of the table," I said to Penny. "I need you to be stable and still because I need to be accurate."

Penny used a chair to climb onto the table and laid on her front on the cushions.

"I'm going to give you six strokes," I said. "They'll be firm."

"Ready," she replied, turning her head to give me a delicious smile.

I stood by her waist and made myself relax; if this was going to work, I couldn't afford mistakes. Sally and Lucy were standing on the other side of the table, curiosity etched on their faces. I lifted the cane and tapped it lightly a few times across her bum, then brought it down hard.

Her body tensed at the impact, and we heard a little bleat before she relaxed again. When her bum had settled, I repeated the stroke a few inches lower. She now had two horizontal lines across her cheeks about four inches apart.

I moved to stand in front of her head. She looked up at me with such an enticing smile, I nearly gave in, but I had work to do. I tapped the cane again, vertically, before lifting it and bringing it down hard on her right cheek. Then again four inches away. Her bleats had been replaced by whimpers, and her fingers reached out to undo my trousers.

I pushed them away, to laughter from Sally and Lucy.

"No," I said, and the pout she gave me was intoxicating. She held my eyes, a look that promised everything. "Later," I eventually added, at which a filthy chuckle echoed deep in her throat.

I repeated my actions on her other cheek. As the last stroke hit, her fingers had undone my button and zip, my trousers were on the floor, and my trunks joined them as she almost swallowed my cock, causing me to cry out.

"Well," Sally said, slowly running her hand over Penny's bum. "I was going to ask what this was about, but I think we'll leave it until the morning."

"Good idea," Lucy said.

They came over, and each gave me a kiss.

"Have fun," Sal whispered, bending to kiss Penny who came off my cock long enough to return it. Lucy and Sally helped each other up the stairs.

I leaned over Penny and stretched out to caress her bum, now clearly marked with a grid on each cheek. My fingers headed straight between her legs, which opened to allow me access, and she writhed as they found her wet slit.

Her mouth engulfed my cock, but I could hear her moans and knew she was near. As her hands went around my bum and pulled me closer, I pushed my fingers into her pussy, my thumb into her ass, and fucked her as best I could at full stretch, my cock jammed in her mouth.

As her climax came, she pulled me in until I could feel my cock touching the back of her throat. Her body jerked as wave after wave of orgasm washed over her. I gently removed my hand and pulled away. She coughed as my cock slipped out of her mouth and gasped for air, her face suffused with lust, her lips wet and shining. Still gripping my cock with one hand, she slid off the table and pushed herself against me, giving me a ferocious kiss.

"Take my ass," she hissed, before turning and bending over the table. I didn't need a second invitation. I moistened my fingers between her legs and pushed one into her ass, followed by another, causing her to grunt with each penetration. A few thrusts into her pussy coated my shaft.

"Now," she pleaded, her need evident.

I slid my finger out and moved the head of my cock against her tight hole. Gently pressing, I wriggled to ease my entrance, but she wasn't waiting, pushing backwards, and crying out as she impaled herself on the head. I eased forward, but her impatience took over again, and she slid back hard, growling as her ass swallowed the full length of my cock. I leaned over her.

"Okay?" I asked.

"Fuck me," was the only response I got, rasped through gritted teeth. She pulled a cushion under her and wrapped her arms around it, as I grabbed her hips, and did what she asked. No soft, gentle penetration, but a hard, rough assault on her tight ass. Long before I was going to come, another orgasm pulsed through her, my slowing down met with another demand to keep going.

Not long after, her body began to tremble and she hugged the cushion tighter and tighter before letting out a vibrating squeal, followed by a series of loud, hard bleats, her head rearing up with each one. I wasn't sure whether to carry on, but I was getting near now. If she needed me to stop, she'd tell me. I carried on, my groin slamming into her bum with each thrust.

Her orgasm seemed almost continuous now, her head rolling about, her throat emitting a range of whimpers and grunts. As she rose again, my time came, and I thrust deep, pulling her tight to me as the first shot came, long harsh strokes with each pulse. As my release washed over me, she subsided too, still making little bleats and giggles as she came down. I leaned over her.

"Okay?" I whispered, kissing her flushed cheek.

"I am now," she replied, before letting her head collapse onto the cushion.

Chapter 22 – Sally

We all went to the airport to see Penny onto her flight. As we were getting out of the car, Marcus took something out of the door pocket and handed it to Penny.

"Give this to Helen," he told her. It was a small, wrapped present, and she looked at him, puzzled. "When she opens it, you'll understand."

As we parted, Penny got quite emotional, hugging us, thanking us and a few tears were shed. We were quiet as we returned to the car.

"I hope we're not causing problems for her and Helen," Marcus said.

"I don't think so," Lucy replied.

"No?"

"No. Penny clearly loves Helen, and that's more than returned. But Penny is more sociable than Helen and I wonder if it's a bit stifling, particularly as she works from home as well. With Ben gone, I reckon Penny feels a bit isolated sometimes."

"Could be," I said. "That's why she likes the group events."

"Exactly, they allow her to meet people for fun. She has lots of work clients, but she keeps them separate from her private life."

"Except you two"

"Yes, well. That's true. And Ben's departure deprives her of something else she needs."

"How are they going to resolve that? I can't see them finding another male sub to meet their requirements."

"Nor me, but I guess they might get lucky. Helen seems to be more outgoing than she was when we first met her, too. Penny said so, didn't she?"

"Yes, she told me their relationship is changing."

"I just hope we're not the cause," Marcus said.

"What's the matter, darling? Feeling guilty?"

"Not exactly, but I still can't read Helen well."

"I think she'd tell us if she was unhappy with Penny spending time with us."

"More than that," Lucy said. "I don't think Penny would come if she thought Helen wasn't happy."

"You're probably right," Marcus replied. "There's a strong character under that soft, shy exterior."

"Quite demanding too," I said, looking at him. "Especially when she wants her ass fucked." He turned to me, frowning. "We enjoyed watching last night." He shook his head.

"Where were you?" he asked.

"At the top of the stairs. We couldn't resist."

"I didn't spot you."

"The way you two were, you wouldn't have noticed a herd of elephants stampeding through the room. We slipped away before you recovered. Looked like you enjoyed it."

"Me? Didn't you see her response?"

"Yes, her ass must be almost as sensitive as Lucy's." There was a chuckle in the back seat. "And she wasn't afraid to ask for what she wanted this time, was she?"

"No, she was almost as demanding as you."

"Come on. What was the present for Helen?"

"A noughts and crosses set."

I smiled as Lucy laughed.

"But how will they play if Penny's lying on her front?"

"I'm sure they'll find a way."

A thought hit me.

"Darling …" I said.

"Mmm."

"Did you buy more than one set?"

"As it happens, I did."

Sally

"So, you two will be needing a grid to play on ..."

The next evening, Helen sent us a picture of a naked Penny, lying on her front, with a couple of noughts and crosses on the grid on her bum. Her head was turned to the camera, a smile on her face. The only text was 'How about chess next time?'.
"I think that's a challenge, darling," I said.
"She can try that one," he replied. "That's at least seven lines each way. I don't think I could do that on one cheek."
"You could always practice."
"I might do that next time you're at my mercy."
"Promises, promises."

***

A week later, we went to pick Eva up at the airport. We'd eventually persuaded her to come over, but she was only staying for a long weekend. In a way, we were happy with that. She may now accompany us to the play parties, but her professional relationship with Marcus was the primary one. Anything else could be complicated. And that was even if any of us wanted it. Eva was comfortable in that world, but her interests were different from ours.

It was her turn to be fascinated by the fort, before I showed her to her room, and let her settle in.
"Eva," I said. "Just so you know, we stay covered while we have visitors; bikinis, at least."
"Marcus in a bikini; I can't wait to see that."
"Don't tempt him, he might surprise you. You're welcome to go with what's comfortable for you."
When she came down a little later, she was wearing a loose cotton shift. It was transparent enough to show a bikini underneath. I'd already seen at the play party I'd been wrong about her figure. She was thinner than Lucy or me, and was lean and muscular, but still had subtle curves. I guessed she was a regular at the gym.

Over lunch, we told her what we'd been up to – well, some of it – and asked if there was anything she wanted to do.

"No," she said. "I'm happy to chill for a couple of days, but if you're doing anything, I'm game."

We lazed around for the rest of the day. Eva went into the pool a couple of times but put her shift on after drying off for a few minutes.

"Do you have to keep the tattoos out of the sun?" Lucy asked.

"The ink fades over time and the sun accelerates it."

"Can they be re-done?"

"It's technically possible, but when it's intricate, it'll never look as good."

"You never lay in the sun?"

"I do sometimes but slap on the barrier cream."

Later in the afternoon, she joined Lucy and me on the loungers, taking the shift off and covering the designs in cream. They still fascinated me, and she caught me staring at them.

"Sorry," I said. "I can't get over the intricacy."

"It's fine, I'm used to it. You can't be shy if you uncover something like this."

"Does it mean anything? I mean, the designs?"

"No, not that I know of. We sat down and redrew them until we were happy."

"Pity you didn't keep those drawings," Lucy said.

"Why?" I asked.

"Because it would make painting them a lot easier."

"Difficult?"

"Challenging is a better word. I'm trying to paint them accurately rather than allude to them and getting them right on a flexed body is infuriating."

"Sorry," Eva said.

"Oh, I'm not complaining. I'm nearly there with the first one."

"How many are you doing?"

"I'm trying a couple of accurate ones, then I might do a couple of freer works, capturing the gist rather than every line."

"Are you including any piercings?" I asked.

"I haven't decided yet," Eva replied. "They're more … personal."

She wasn't wearing any today; at least, none I could see.

"Are they painful to do?" I asked.

"Some are."

"Can I ask how many you have?"

"God, uh …" She did some mental calculations. "Three in each ear, two in each nipple, eight on my tummy, and two … four … six … seven down below." She saw me wince and laughed. "Yes, those aren't for everyone. They do sting a bit."

"So apart from ears, they're all hidden."

"Yea. I'd like some more, but I need to balance them with my professional life. Besides, I like the idea they're only revealed to those I choose to show them to."

"Hidden treasures."

"Exactly."

I had another question but wasn't sure about asking Eva. I turned to her and saw she was expecting it.

"Yes," she said. "They can be fun, for both parties. They can also hurt if they get pulled the wrong way. Some people use weights on them or chain them together."

"A sort of chastity device."

"Yea, if you like. But you can also stretch them open."

The image of that floated around my brain, as I imagined the possibilities. "Of course," she continued, "you can achieve the same effect with clamps." She was challenging me.

"Yes," I replied, a little flushed. "I'm just wondering which gives more pain."

"Come on, you two," Lucy said. "Stop dancing around. Eva has the piercings, you've got the clamps, Sal. And you have them for different reasons."

She was right. The piercings weren't inherently sexual, they were an adornment, an artwork, a modification. If they were fun during sex, it was a nice coincidence. The clamps were purely sexual.

"It's funny, isn't it?" I said. "The idea of being pierced down there makes me shudder. But I'm more than happy for Marcus to use clamps in the same place."

"Each to their own," Eva said.

"Have you ever had a partner who had piercings?"

"On his cock?"

"Well, yes."

"Yea. Dizzie had a row along the underside, a couple through the head and a few in his scrotum. About twenty in all. It was heavily tattooed, as well."

"Wow. What … what was it like?"

"In a couple of positions, they had an effect. But generally, you knew they were there, but they didn't make much difference."

Lucy had been listening quietly, and I turned to her.

"What do you think, Luce? Interested?"

"I'm not sure. The idea has a certain appeal."

"Try it," Eva said. "If you don't like it, leave them empty. They usually close up."

Marcus appeared with a tray of drinks.

"We're talking piercings, darling," I said. "Fancy a ring or two through your cock?"

"Uh, I can think of better things to do with it."

Lucy chuckled.

"It doesn't appeal?"

"Not really."

"What about a tattoo?" Eva said.

"I have thought about it once or twice. But it would have to be something small and discreet."

"You're not going to have my name in big letters on your forearm?" I asked.

"On a scroll over a big heart," Lucy added.

"Not in a month of Sundays. Is there a hierarchy in the tattoo world?" he asked Eva. "You know, from the sort of work you have, down to 'Mum' or 'love' and 'hate' across the knuckles."

"There can be," she replied. "But the real divide is based around skill and creativity. There are lots of competent tattooists, but only a few real artists."

We spent ages suggesting different designs for each other. Some laughable, some silly, some grotesque.

Eva was good company. She'd left her work behind and joined in the banter. We spent a day showing her the local sites and took her into St Tropez one evening for dinner. Our usual trip to a casino followed and Eva proved lucky. She came home a winner, whereas we'd all lost money.

On her last day, as we all lounged around, she and Marcus had a relaxed chat about their next moves.

The launch of Shadows of Silver was booked, and it was already being printed. The two earlier works and Spewn Words were also at the printers and their soft launch scheduled. They light-heartedly argued about the next of his older books to launch.

"Perhaps we'd better wait and see how these do," he said.

"True, but if they sell, I want to re-publish some more."

"Okay, you can choose."

"I don't know them."

"You mean you haven't dedicated your free time to reading the work of your new phenomenally successful author?"

"Strangely enough, Marcus, no."

"I don't know what I pay you for."

"Unfortunately, I don't see much of our percentage."

He played an imaginary violin, humming a lament.

"Ignore him, Eva," I said. "He can be annoying at times."

He pointed to himself, an exaggerated look of hurt on his face.

"I've got his measure now," she replied, throwing a towel at him. "I have looked at your new website, though. Penny sent me a link. I'm impressed, she's done a good job."

"Yes, I'm happy," he said. "As long as it passes your censors, I thought we could launch it a month before Silver is published."

"Good idea. And they're not censors."

"Then why do we have to get their permission?"

"It's not permission, they just want to check it out."

"Censor it."

"No. They want to make sure … oh, I don't know. We're a big corporate, Marcus. You know what that means, guidelines for everything. Silly rules I have no say in."

"I know. But it's my site, not linked to you. I don't see why I can't publish what I want."

"Bear with me, please."

"It's not in my contract."

"I know," she replied, sighing.

"Your contracts are very leaky. I really think you need a new legal team."

She'd given up now and was taking his teasing with good grace.

After Eva returned home, we had the last week to ourselves. We didn't do much. Lucy and I finally persuaded Marcus to accompany us to the Île de Levant. He was cautious to begin with, but soon relaxed and we spent the day on the beach, except for a break for lunch in one of the restaurants.

"What do you think?" Lucy asked.

"Well," he replied, "I'll admit it's easier than I expected. But I'm not risking another accident." And he carefully laid a napkin over his lap before starting to eat.

As we drove the last leg of the journey home between Paris and the Channel Tunnel, we were quiet. Our holiday was over, and it was time to get back to normal. But normal was good; we were good. Life was nearly perfect. We had no inkling of the storm about to hit us.

Chapter 23 – Ensemble

Marcus

"Marcus? It's Eva. We've got a problem."

The call came late Saturday evening. It was an unusual time for Eva to call. As she explained the problem, I saw why. The next day, one of the tabloids was running a headline …

BESTSELLING AUTHOR IN KINKY BONDAGE GEAR AT FETISH CLUB

For once, the story seemed to be largely factual. I'd been seen attending a fetish party dressed in black along with 'a number of other people'. Women in revealing costumes were in attendance, along with men in rubber and a good time was had by all.

All fairly innocuous, but the article was illustrated with two or three slightly blurred pictures. I was clearly circled in red, but Sally and Lucy, although not named, were visible along with other members of the group. There was nothing in the pictures remotely scandalous, but that didn't matter. The papers always wanted a bit of scurrilous gossip.

Eva suggested trying to get an injunction to stop publication, but I refused. I knew immediately how I wanted to handle this. Or at least, how I would handle this if it wasn't for everyone else involved. Sally rang Lucy to warn her, and I spoke to Matt. He was furious.

"I don't know how it happened, Marcus," he said. "We're always careful about cameras, and I can't believe anyone in the group would do this."

"I know, and I don't get why it's newsworthy. But some of the people in the photos could be identified."

He promised to get a copy of the paper and contact any members who could be recognised. On Sunday morning, Eva rang again.

"I was asked for comment," she said, "but said nothing. Have they contacted you?"

"No, which seems strange."

"It's their usual tactic. They're supposed to warn people about coverage like this, but they only do it at the last moment. By ringing me, they've given notice, but without any chance of a response."

"I see."

"I think we need to get our PR people involved."

"Nope."

"Marcus, this could damage you."

"Your sales, you mean. Eva, I'm not bothered about myself. I'm a big boy now and can do what I want. But I want to protect those around me. I don't want your PR people – or any PR people, for that matter – speaking on my behalf."

"Somehow I thought you'd say that."

"I'll think about how I want to respond. In the meantime, I don't want anything said. No statements at all, agreed?"

"All right, agreed. But my management might not see it that way."

"If they decide to say anything, consider my contract cancelled."

"Marcus, I-"

"Eva, I'm serious. You know me well enough now. I'm not joking. I'll speak to you later."

As I put my phone down, Sally came over and put her arm around my shoulder.

"What do we do now?" she asked.

"I don't know. If we're lucky, it'll blow over. I'm not exactly a household name, and I can't imagine anyone being interested."

"But people love a bit of titillation."

"Yes, but hopefully something else will titillate them next week. Have you spoken to Lucy this morning?"

"Yes, she's looked at the article online. She's a bit upset."

"Right, do you want to go and see her?"
"What about you?"
"I'll be fine."

Lucy

I kept looking at the article. After Sally's call the previous evening, I hadn't slept. When it first appeared during the early morning, I read it and re-read it, zooming in on the pictures. There I was, in my underwear, in a national newspaper. The pictures weren't clear, but if I knew it was me, so would others.

I was surprised when Sally arrived.

"How are you?" she asked.

"I'm not sure. It's scary. It feels … dirty."

I made her some coffee and saw she was as nervous as me, just hiding it better.

"What happens now?" I asked.

"God knows," she replied. "Marcus has gone into logical mode. He's not worried for himself, but he's trying to control the collateral damage."

"At least he's the only one named in the story."

Sally

When I got home, Marcus was still in a strange mood. I'd never seen him like this. He was angry, I could see that. But he was also detached, thinking about the best way to deal with the situation.

"How was she?" he asked.

"She's scared and worried about being recognised."

"We have to accept that's going to happen. It's how we deal with it that matters."

"How do we deal with it?"

"I'm not sure. I'm concerned about you two."

"If it was just you?"

"I'd brazen it out. If anyone asks a question, I'll answer it as if it's all the most natural thing in the world."

"But it is."

"I know, but you know what the tabloids are like. They'll find prurience in the most mundane thing."

"We brazen it out?"

"I'm not sure. You've got family and workmates, as has Lucy. It's them we have to think of."

"Mary ..."

"Yes. You need to speak to her."

"I'll go now."

As I set out, I hoped Mary would be fine. She had a fairly good idea of our activities, anyway. I was proved right.

"Well," she said after I showed her the paper. "The photos could have been clearer. It looks interesting, perhaps I should come along next time."

"Mary! This is serious."

"Darling, are you ashamed of what you do?"

"No. But we're discreet about it. Not anymore, it seems."

"No, but it's not illegal, or even immoral. People will soon lose interest."

I slumped in the chair.

"I hope so, I really do, but I'm frightened."

Marcus

Matt rang in the afternoon.

"I've identified everyone in the photos and managed to speak to them," he said. "None of them are bothered, but they'd all like to know where the pictures came from. They all send their support, by the way."

"Thanks."

"And I've sent a group post out, letting everyone know what's happened, and asking if anyone has any ideas who took the pictures."

"Okay, Matt. I'll let you know if there's any news."

I rang Helen.

"Penny saw Matt's post," she said. "It's all rather amusing."

"I'm not sure about that, Helen. I don't want anyone outed because of me."

"Oh, Marcus, don't feel guilty. Everyone who goes to these things accepts there's the possibility of bumping into their boss. A few blurred photos in a sleaze rag aren't going to do too much harm."

"I hope you're right."

"It'll all blow over, you'll see."

Sally

On my way back from Mary's, I called into Lucy's again. She was still in shock. I got her something to eat and sat quietly while she picked at it.

"Are you going to talk to Annie?" I asked.

"What do I tell them?"

"The truth. Well, the basic truth. It's better than them finding out from someone else."

"I suppose so." She took a few more bites. "Oh, God. My mother."

"I didn't want to bring her up."

"She won't understand any of this."

"I know."

"How would I even begin to explain it?"

We spent half an hour going over the best way for Lucy to tell her family. I could see she was hurting. She'd spent the best part of eighteen months rebuilding her relationship with them. This could blow that apart in an instant. I offered to go with her to Annie's, but they didn't know about me and she thought it best to go alone.

As I left, I noticed a car parked on the otherwise empty street. It hadn't been there when I arrived, and someone was sitting in the driver's seat. It might have been my imagination, but they seemed to be acting a little too casually.

Marcus and I updated each other when I got home. We'd covered most of the bases we could. Now we had to wait. On a whim, I walked over to the window and peeked out. The car which had been outside Lucy's was now parked a few doors from our flat.

Lucy

I was shaking by the time I arrived at Annie's. I'd rung her in advance to let her know I needed to speak to her. She let me in and appeared concerned, but it was soon apparent she thought I had more revelations about Mum. I had to disabuse her.

She listened as I told her the bare bones of the story. My relationship with Sally, about Marcus, and a halting few basics about the play parties. She listened quietly, saying nothing. I couldn't read her expression. When I finished, there were a few seconds of silence.

Then she burst out laughing.

"What paper is this in?" she asked.

I passed her the copy I'd brought with me, and she carefully read the story, looking closely at the pictures.

"Well," she said finally. "My own sister in a sex scandal."

"It's hardly that," I replied, surprised by her reaction.

"I know, Lucy. I was joking. Sorry. These dirt rags blow everything out of proportion. I assume nothing you're doing is illegal?"

"God, no."

"Then hold your head up. What you do isn't for me, I don't even understand most of it. But if you enjoy it, what's the harm?"

I didn't know how to answer. I hadn't expected Annie to be supportive. I'd almost expected to be shown the door. I took a chance and told her almost everything. About my counselling, the start of my relationship with Sally, the fetish group. My doubts about the whole thing. Then about Marcus. All the time I was speaking, she had an amused look on her face.

"I can't say I approve of it all," she said when I'd finished. "Tim and I have tried a few things since we left Dad's church which they would have been shocked at. Nothing like you're trying, I hasten to add, but who am I to say what's right or wrong? If you need anything from me, from us, you only need to ask."

I burst into tears. The frustration, the fear and the surprise at the support Annie was offering. She came over and hugged me, the first really warm hug we'd shared in many years. Eventually, I drew myself together.

"Thanks, Annie. It means a lot. To be honest, I thought you might be … less understanding."

"A few years ago, I would have probably sent you packing. But not anymore. People's private lives are between them and who they're involved with."

"There is one problem, though."

"What's that?"

"How the hell am I going to explain this to Mum?"

Sally

"How long have they been there?" Marcus asked when I checked on the car again.

"About two hours now. They must have followed me home from Lucy's."

"Is it just one person?"

"Yes, I think so."

"Right. Are you happy to be seen with me?"

"Yes, of course. Why?"

He went to the kitchen and set the coffee machine going. Grabbing a plate, he put some biscuits on it and added a mug of coffee.

"Get your phone and follow me. As soon as we're out of the house, start filming and keep it going."

I followed him out of our front door and began filming. He walked to the car and tapped on the driver's window. A surprised face looked up at him, and slowly lowered it.

"Good afternoon," Marcus said, holding out his right hand. "I'm Marcus. And you are?"

The guy looked startled.

"Err, Chris," he replied, hesitantly raising his hand, which Marcus grasped and shook firmly.

"As it seems you're going to be following us around, we might as well get to know one another. I've brought you some coffee."

"Oh, thanks."

"And as you can see, we're filming you, as we're legally entitled to do in a public place. The film will be going on Social Media shortly. Every time we see you, we'll be happy to talk. And photograph or film you. Those will go on social media as well. But as you're so keen to publicise people's private lives, I'm sure that won't be a problem, Chris."

"I'm just doing my job." His voice was unconvincing.

"Just following orders, eh? That's a lame excuse, Chris. Still, you do what you want. We won't be going out again today, Chris, so you can hunker down and get bored. You can leave the crockery on the doorstep."

We walked back to the flat.

"Were you serious?" I asked.

"Yes. If you send me the video you've taken, I'll post it."

I wasn't sure about this approach, but within a few minutes, he'd posted the footage on all his social media accounts. We spent a little while going through these, as there were a lot of posts about the story. The vast majority were supportive but, as always, a few were slagging him off, and there were one or two obscene ones. All par for the course. When we went to bed that night, it seemed we had everything under control.

Chapter 24 – Ensemble

Marcus

Neither of us slept well that night. We ended up having sex at about three in the morning, but it was all a bit mechanical. The following morning, Sally went off to work and I sat down, wondering what the day would bring. It started early when Eva rang.

"Marcus, I'm not sure your video has exactly helped."

"What do you expect me to do? Simply sit here and take it?"

"My boss came to see me first thing. He wants to cancel the launch of Spewn Words and the two re-prints."

"Do that, and I'll rip up my contract."

"You can't do that, Marcus."

"Effectively, I can."

"How?"

"What is it with you and contracts, Eva? Peter and I were careful with this one. If you decide not to publish the older works, the full rights revert to me. I'll take them somewhere else or publish them myself."

"Did we really agree to that?"

"Yes."

"I'll speak to him again."

An hour later, my phone rang.

"Mr Foxton?"

"Yes."

"This is Mungo Carpenter, I'm-"

"I know who you are." I'd got his name from Eva.

"We appear to have a slight problem." His voice had the slippery tone of corporate speak.

"Do we?"

"In light of the revelations in the press this weekend, we feel it would be apposite to re-think the publication of your works scheduled in the next three weeks."

"No."

There were a few seconds of silence.

"Mr Foxton, I'm not sure you understand the intricacies of the publishing world."

"That's why I pay you."

His manner was irritating me, and I wasn't in the mood to be patient.

"Perhaps we can delay the publication, until-"

"No."

"If we decide not to publish, Mr Foxton, we don't publish."

"Threats don't work on me, Mr Carpenter. If you don't publish, I'll take them to someone who will."

Another moment of silence.

"Yes, I gather your contract allows that."

"Indeed it does, and you won't get Shadows of Silver, either."

"Ah, Mr Foxton, I think you may be wrong there. That is a separate contract, and you wouldn't want to break that."

"Why not? I haven't signed off the final version yet. Are you seriously saying you'd publish an unfinished edition, against my wishes, given how bad the publicity could be?"

"We'd sue you for breach of contract."

His mask had slipped, he was angry now.

"Go ahead. I'll counter sue you for breach of the second contract."

I could sense him trying to stay calm. He was in the right. If I didn't agree to publish Shadows of Silver, I would be in breach of my first contract.

"We have something of an impasse," he eventually said, back to his oily best.

"Not at all, Mr Carpenter. I expect a communication from you by the end of tomorrow telling me whether my three books are being published as scheduled. If they're not, I will consider you to be in breach of contract. I look forward to your mail."

I ended the call. I was shaking. I'd been assertive, but I wasn't used to dealing with the corporate world. That's what Peter, my agent, did. I called him and told him what had happened. He groaned as I recounted the details but agreed to support me if they contacted him.

"Have you heard from them?" Sally asked when I told her.

"No, not yet."

"Will you take them back?"

"Yes."

"And take them somewhere else?"

"I doubt anyone else will want them, but I could self-publish them again. How have you got on today?"

"Okay, I guess. I just feel numb. I did pluck up the courage to speak to David."

"And?"

"He thought it was funny."

"Ah."

"Which wasn't helpful."

"No, but it's not anything to do with them."

"I guess not. Have you seen our friend, Chris?"

"No, not today, but I haven't been looking. Did you speak to Lucy?"

"Yea. She got on okay with Annie, but she's got to speak to her mother."

I spent some of the following day monitoring social media and the comments on the tabloid site under our story. In general, the majority were neutral or supportive, with only a minority critical of us. There were plenty of replies under the article criticising the paper for running the story. It made me more determined not to allow it to affect us.

Sally came home earlier than usual.

"There's been someone asking questions," she said.

"Questions?"

"Yea, a couple of people told me a man had approached them asking about me. Who I was, what I did, about my private life."

My heart sank. I hoped the worst was over, but the paper was still on our case.

"Have you spoken to Lucy?"

"Yea, she's not doing well. She's sure people are whispering about her."

We sat in silence. This was all way over our heads. Perhaps we should have called in the PR people. I still didn't care what people thought of me, but it was Sally and Lucy who were bearing the brunt of it, and I didn't know how to help them.

Over the course of the week, both Sal and Luce were told people had been asking about them, and they were sure some of their colleagues and many of the students were aware of the story. Nothing had been said, but the looks and the smiles were obvious.

Peter called to tell me the launches had been pulled.

"Do you want me to formally notify them you're taking the rights back?" he asked.

"No, not yet."

I'd been doing something I didn't normally do, looking at the sales figures. Shadows of Gold had been selling in increasing numbers through the week, almost back to the figures at their height. I hadn't heard from Eva or Mr Carpenter. They'd gone silent; I'd remember that. By the end of the week, daily sales were the highest they'd ever been. I had a feeling I'd be hearing from them soon.

Sally came home at lunchtime on Friday; she looked shattered.

"I can't take any more," she said. "I heard snide remarks from two or three people this morning, and David let me come home. Someone was taking pictures when I left."

I held her tight, not knowing what else to do.

Sally

I was hurting. Everywhere I went during the week, I imagined people staring and sniggering. It probably wasn't happening, but I couldn't get it out of my thoughts. The photographer had been the last straw. By Saturday, I was exhausted, and there didn't seem to be an end in sight.

I couldn't sleep and lay awake, my mind filled with doubts. I'd laid the shadow to rest, but I felt the same darkness creeping back. This time, I wasn't trying to avoid a phantom, a figment of my imagination. Now I was trying to avoid real people; friends, colleagues, people from God knows where asking questions, taking photographs. It was worse than the shadow.

Marcus was still in logical mode. It seemed to work for him but wasn't working for me. He was concentrating on the practical things. For the first time in our relationship, I wasn't getting the emotional support I needed from him. And it hurt.

"Well," he said, "Shadows of Gold is heading to the top of the best sellers list again."

"And?"

"When it does, they'll come round and publish the others."

"Marcus, what's important to you here?"

"How do you mean?"

"You've spent all week sorting out your damn books, while I've been trying to stay afloat." He looked stunned, but I wasn't finished. "I've been to work every day where I don't know how many people have been gossiping behind my back about my sex life. This isn't a game. I can't stand it much longer."

I started crying. I was so tired, I couldn't be bothered to wipe my tears away. He came to sit by me.

"Sal, I don't know what to say. I don't know how to help. This is all beyond me."

"Then tell me. Tell me you're struggling as well."

He pulled me to him, and I snuggled in, feeling some of the old warmth. But it wasn't enough.

On Saturday afternoon, I got a text from Lucy. She'd been to see her mother, and it hadn't gone well. Her mum hadn't understood half the things Lucy had tried to explain and had told her to leave. Luce was now home and distraught. I wanted to go and help her, but we'd agreed we wouldn't visit anyone else's homes. We didn't know who was watching.

We got another call from Eva. The tabloid was printing a further story the following day with a couple more pictures, showing and naming both Lucy and me. When we saw the article the following day, I couldn't take any more. I couldn't face my work, my friends or anyone else. Not even Marcus. I needed to escape.

***

I watched as Genevieve read the two articles I'd given her. She was unchanged; immaculately turned out, but she always managed to look casual with it. She studied them carefully before putting them on the table in front of us.

"So," she said," the three of you have been having a lot of fun."

"It doesn't seem much fun now."

"I think this sort of thing sells papers in England."

"Not here?"

"In France, nobody bothers what you do. You never get this sort of thing in the press."

"I don't know what to do. I just needed to escape."

"And now you have."

"Yes."

"And what about Marcus and Lucy?"

"I ... I don't know."

After the second article came out, I'd told Marcus I couldn't stay there. He'd been stunned but was at a loss to come up with an alternative solution. I told him I was going to Paris. I'd already spoken to Genevieve and she'd agreed to my use of their guest flat.

"But what will you do?" he asked. I could see the anguish and fear in his eyes.

"I don't know, Marcus. I just need to hide."

He didn't argue, he knew me well enough to know he couldn't stop me. We had a brief hug before I left for the airport, taking the first available flight to Paris.

Now I was here, I felt safe. But Genevieve's question drilled into me. What of Marcus and Lucy? I'd escaped but left them in the lurch. I had some thinking to do. Sitting in the flat that evening, I called Lucy and told her where I was. She was astounded.

"What about Marcus?" she asked.

"I had to get out, Luce. I couldn't cope."

"I'm struggling too, you know."

"Come and join me."

191

"No, Sal. I've got things to sort out here."

The call ended icily. I lay on the bed in despair. I could see no way forward.

Marcus called me the next morning; the call was uncomfortably formal, and he was careful to avoid any mention of his books. I had to ask about them.

"I couldn't care less." There was a weary bitterness in his voice. "Have you spoken to Lucy?"

"Yes."

"Is she okay?"

"She's a bit upset about me ... running away."

There was a pause; I guessed he was struggling with it too and couldn't think of what to say.

"Oh, right. Maybe I'll give her a call."

"Yes."

"Can I call again tomorrow?"

"Yes, that'll be fine."

After putting my phone down, the changes hit me. Marcus thinking he needed to ask permission to call me. Lucy feeling I'd abandoned her. Me feeling shit because they were both right.

Lucy

I felt so alone. My lover had run off to Paris, my mother had disowned me for a second time. My colleagues said nothing openly, but it was a talking point and a few students had given me knowing looks. I took a few days off work and shut myself in my flat.

But I soon discovered I wasn't alone. Marcus rang me at least once a day. At first, our conversations were stilted, but his natural wry humour made me feel better. Annie came to see me, brushing off my warning my home might be being watched. Several people I'd done pictures for sent me supportive emails. Penny turned up with a box of chocolates and a bottle of wine from her and Helen.

"Don't get too down," Penny said. "This will all blow over, and you'll all get back together."

"I don't see that happening, Penny. I think things will be different. That's assuming this stuff in the press all dies down."

"Of course it will. They'll find the next story and forget all about you three."

She had more confidence than I did. Lying in bed at night, I couldn't switch my brain off. Even if I could believe the press would leave us alone, it brought back all my questions and doubts about the situation I'd got myself into. Perhaps it had all been too good to be true, after all.

I rang Jenny; she wasn't aware of the story, and I gave her a brief outline.

"That's an interesting situation," she said when I finished.

"Interesting? I don't know what to do, Jenny."

"Why don't you come and see me?"

"But I might be followed."

"I'm a counsellor. I see all sorts of people, and I don't care who knows it."

I found myself back in that familiar room, telling her the whole story and showing her the newspaper articles. She looked through them briefly, before passing them back.

"Typical sewer press," she said.

"I don't usually read them, but now I know how cruel they are."

"What are you going to do about it?"

"Me? I can't do anything."

"Not about the stories, no. But you can choose how you deal with them, both for yourself and your partners."

It was the first positive thing which penetrated my soggy brain since the whole sorry saga had begun. And Jenny came up trumps. She offered to see me every day, and I talked and talked at those meetings. A lot of it was going over old ground; reciting the doubts I'd had from the beginning which now resurfaced, almost proving their truth. If anything went wrong, I'd be the one who got hurt.

"But is that true?" Jenny asked.

"I'm hurting alright."

"But do you think Sally and Marcus aren't?"

"No, I guess they are too."

"Exactly."

"Perhaps it wouldn't have happened if I hadn't got involved."

"It was Marcus they were interested in, and he and Sally went to the parties before you did. You're collateral damage, unfortunately. This is nothing any of you have done."

That stuck in my head when I got home. We hadn't done anything wrong. We'd been plastered over the papers for doing something we all enjoyed which did nobody any harm.

Annie popped in to see me the following weekend. She brought me a homemade cake and I made some tea to go with it.

"What happens at these parties?" she asked hesitantly. I told her the basics without going into details. "Is it like Fifty Shades of Grey?" she said, before shyly admitting she and Tim had read it. I spent some time explaining why that particular book wasn't a great introduction to BDSM, although I knew I wasn't an expert on the subject.

"But it's not about doing anything," I said. "The events mean people with similar interests can meet others in a safe environment. It's like any other social event."

"Are there lots of these groups?"

"From what I understand, they happen all over the country, yes."

"Is there a website you can point me to which gives the basics?"

"Don't tell me you're interested? Not after all this?"

"No," she replied, looking embarrassed. "I wondered if I could look at something to try and explain it to Mum."

"Ah."

"I thought it might be worth a try."

"I doubt it, Annie. Let's be honest, she's never accepted my sexuality. Now, when she's got to the point where she could at least ignore it without being offensive, she finds it's even more complicated than she thought."

"I know, but I want to give it a go."

"I'll ask Marcus if he can recommend anything. I'm not an expert in all this, Annie. I was still a beginner."

Chapter 25 – Ensemble

Marcus

The flat seemed cold and empty. It was ten days since Sally had left. I'd spoken to her every day, but the calls were stilted and short. She was closed and I was struggling to understand why. I'd let her down when the whole thing kicked off. I'd concerned myself more with my problems than thinking about her. I'd apologised several times, but either it hadn't been accepted, or there was something else on her mind.

I spoke to Lucy every day as well. She'd been hit hard by this, and in truth, it had been her I was more worried about at the beginning. But she was seeing her counsellor every day, and it seemed to be working. It had caused another split with her mother, but her sister was being supportive.

She'd returned to work and had spoken in a staff meeting, apologising to her colleagues if the episode had caused any embarrassment, but not for her actions. She thought it had cleared the air, and most had been supportive. I admired her strength, which surprised me.

Penny had popped in a couple of times. I'd warned her someone might be watching the house, but it didn't faze her. She came around to get the final agreement to launch the website. As I was hardly speaking to my publisher at the time, I agreed, and it went live. She brought me a box of my favourite cakes, and after we finished work, I made some coffee and we sat and chatted.

"How's Sally?" she asked.

"Honestly, Penny, I don't know. We talk every day, but she's guarded. I don't know where she is mentally right now."

"She'll come back."

"I'm not confident. This is horrible, but I thought we'd come through it. Sally going off to Paris surprised me, and now I don't know what to think."

"Perhaps she just needs some time."

"But the longer she stays away, the harder it will be to come back."

She left shortly after to visit Lucy and discuss her site. Just before she opened the door, she turned and gave me a kiss. "Helen specifically told me not to tease you, but I'm sure a peck on the cheek won't hurt. You know we're here if you need us, don't you?"

"I do, thanks, Penny."

My three books all launched on Thursday that week. After the sales of Shadows of Gold soared on the back of our unwanted notoriety, someone on the corporate escalator decided they could make some money from our pain, and that they wanted the books after all.

There wasn't going to be any publicity, but that had changed, and a hurried re-print had been ordered to increase the initial offering. The day they launched, they sold out and the e-book editions did a roaring trade. Eva called me the next day. She was very formal.

"Marcus, I'm ringing with yesterday's figures."

"I saw them, thanks."

"We've ordered five thousand more copies."

"That'll keep Mungo happy."

"Marcus, will you please give me a break."

"Eva, our relationship has always been professional, for the very reason this episode has highlighted. Our goals are different. Yours is to make as much money out of me as possible; mine is to try and retain some integrity."

"That's harsh."

"But true."

There was a pause at the other end.

"I guess so."

"I like you; we all do. But when push comes to shove, you'll follow the corporate line. I won't because I don't have to. When the story was first printed, you were happy to drop me like a hot cake."

"Marcus, that's not-"

"It is true. I know it's not your decision. Slimy Mungo was calling the shots, but you're part of that process."

"Okay, Marcus." Her tone was formal again. "I'll keep in touch. We need to finalise plans for Shadows of Silver."

The release of my new book wasn't high on my agenda. I knew I'd have to attend the launch and repeat my performance of the year before, but I tried to put it to the back of my mind. Doing it was bad enough; doing it in front of an audience who would know the whole tabloid story was worse. But doing it without Sally, without Lucy and perhaps our friends was almost unimaginable.

I still didn't know what to do. I realised I'd been too focussed on myself when the story broke. I'd let others down. But I couldn't fathom Sally's reaction. She'd seemed confident at first, then something had changed. Changed so much she'd had to run away from the situation. That had only happened once before.

Sally

I spent a whole day with Genevieve, just talking. She listened. I told her the whole story of the shadow, how it had affected me, how I had overcome it. I'd told her a lot of it before, but she calmly heard it again. By the time I'd finished, I was empty. Even now, the story was hard, and although I'd been happier telling people recently, the current situation seemed to add a heaviness I thought had gone.

"Sally," she said after a long period of silence. "Why have you come to Paris?"

"To escape, I suppose."

"To escape what?"

What was I running from? Some gutter journalists looking for a cheap story. They could go to hell. But they'd got to me.

"To avoid having to constantly look over my shoulder, I guess. I want to be a private person again."

"But you still are. They've probably moved on to the next story already." I didn't have the answer to that, but Marcus had told me there hadn't been anything about us in the paper this weekend.

"But my friends, my colleagues. They all know about this now."

"And you think they don't have secrets as well?"

"Nothing like this."

"Don't be so sure. When I started as a working girl, I got used to all the stares and whispers as people got to know who I was. Most didn't care, treating me no differently to anyone else. But the ones who sneered, the ones who looked down on me were often the ones with their own peccadillos.

"It's amazing what men tell you after you've pleased them. I heard all the local gossip; who was sleeping with who, who had a lover in the next town. And they were always the people who treated me like dirt. I soon learned to ignore them."

"But I don't care what my colleagues do. I don't want to know."

"You don't need to. What I'm saying is you need to think about you, about how you deal with this. So, people now know something about your sex life."

"Quite a lot."

"Bien, quite a lot. There will be some who think it's sordid. You can't change their minds. Some will read it, shrug, and move on. But a lot will be jealous, envious of what you do. They'll look at their own lives and wonder where it all went wrong."

"Maybe, but that doesn't help me."

"Not immediately, no. But it can help you see that most people don't care what you do. Why has this upset you so much?"

As I sat alone in the guest flat that evening, I pondered the question. Marcus and I had gone into this world with our eyes open. We accepted we might meet people we knew. But meeting them at a munch would at least have meant we were both involved and would be discreet. This was too one-sided.

The next day, I decided to try and move forward, rather than sit in the flat all day. I spoke to David about work. He told me he'd seen the second story, but it wasn't a problem for him. Indeed, he was indignant the paper thought it was a legitimate thing to run. Several of my colleagues had asked after me and offered any help they could. I admitted to him it had brought back memories of the shadow, which he understood, and we agreed I would stay away for a while, and I'd keep him updated.

I put on a coat and stepped out to explore Paris.

Lucy

For a second weekend, we weren't in the papers. The rag which had run the story had latched onto a minor celebrity caught exposing himself at an awards ceremony. It appeared we were old news. I decided enough was enough.

Marcus was surprised when he answered the door.

"Oh, hello, Lucy."

"Hi, Marcus. Do I get to come in?"

"Err, yes, sorry."

I walked past him and took my coat off.

"I'm fed up with all the subterfuge," I said. "We've been outed; why are we still hiding?"

"I guess that's a good point."

"Besides, it seems we're yesterday's news."

"I sincerely hope so."

As we went through to the living room, I noticed he had changed. I hadn't seen him for nearly a month, only talked on the phone, but he looked drawn. He hadn't shaved for a few days and was lacking his usual sparkle.

"Are you okay?" I asked.

"Yea, fine. Coffee?"

I followed him into the kitchen and watched as he set the machine going.

"Are you still speaking to Sal?"

"Yes," he replied. "You?"

"Yea. It's ... hard work."

"I know what you mean."

It was. Our calls were brief and less than warm. Almost a duty rather than a pleasure. I had wondered if it was just me; that old worry about being the other woman again. But Marcus was having the same experience.

"She seems to have closed in," I said. "I can't get anything from her."

"Me neither. I've offered to go over and join her, but she made excuses."

"I did the same; same response."

"I'm baffled, Luce. I don't understand what's happening. I seem to have cocked this up."

"It's hardly your fault."

"The exposé isn't, but my reaction is. I didn't think enough about you and Sal."

"Marcus, this is about all our lives. Not just yours, ours. Sally and I have to take responsibility for ourselves. Yes, this has been a massive jolt for me, but I've got to deal with it. That's partly why I'm here. I'm fed up coping with it on my own without the people I … without those who mean something to me."

We took the coffee and sat down.

"How are you really doing?" he asked.

"At times, I sit there and laugh."

"Laugh?"

"Yes. My colleagues have discovered a side of me they didn't suspect. There were a few comments at first, but it's all back to normal now. Some of my students have given me a bit of stick, but it all seems to be light-hearted. I've even had one shyly ask me about the group."

"And your mum, and Annie and Tim?"

"Annie and Tim surprised me. They've been fine. Tim's made a few jokes about whips and chains, and Annie has been a brick. Mum is a different matter."

"Not speaking to you?"

"No, but Annie has been talking to her about it. She can't understand people do these things for fun."

"Because of your father?"

"Yes. All she sees is someone getting beaten as a punishment as he did to her."

"It's understandable, and I guess she's also confused about you getting involved with a man and a woman."

"Oh, that's blown her mind. It was difficult enough for her my being attracted to women. Now she's having to work out bisexuality, as well."

We looked at each other and burst out laughing.

"Don't look at me," he eventually said. "I can't explain it either."

"There's nothing to explain, though, is there? It is what it is."

"But for someone with her background, she's not going to get that."

"I know."

"What happens with her now?"

"Annie's trying to make light of it. Explain that Mum's sheltered life means she doesn't know what people do. Apparently, Mum isn't as aghast as she was at first."

"And in the meantime, you wait."

"That's about it."

"I'm sorry."

He looked genuinely deflated again.

"Marcus, please don't take this on yourself. It's not your fault, whatever you think. It's funny really."

"What is?"

"When Sally and I first started a physical relationship, the one worry I had was what would happen if things went wrong. I was convinced I'd be the one who got hurt. I never envisaged a situation like this, but it turns out we all got hurt."

"Yea. And Sally is the one who's gone missing."

"I never expected that."

"Me neither."

We sat with our thoughts for a few minutes.

"How's the book world getting on?" I asked.

He told me about the launch of the three new books. They'd all been more successful than anyone had predicted. The two older works were selling well and getting good reviews. But it was Spewn Words which had taken everyone by surprise. The critics had almost unanimously praised it.

"Are you pleased?" I asked.

"Pleased? Yes. But it's ridiculous."

"Why?"

"I'm happy with the book, but the way some critics have talked about it, you'd think I'd written a masterpiece."

I had, in truth, seen one or two reviews which had veered towards the pretentious end of the critical spectrum.

"I don't think they know what it is or where it fits," he continued. "But they don't want to be the first to say it's a pile of crap. A few of the reviews on consumer sites are somewhat more honest."

"But if it sells …"

"Oh, it's selling. Eva's already ordered a third re-print."

"I need to speak to her. I've finished the first two pictures."

"I hope you have better luck than me."

"Why?"

"We're hardly speaking."

"What happened?"

"We had a bit of a falling out when all this occurred. They wanted to pull all my books, cancel the launches, get a PR company involved."

"I suppose it wasn't necessarily her decision."

"No, but if you're part of a corporate structure, you take the flak. Our communications are somewhat formal at the moment."

"Don't be too hard on her, Marcus."

"I'm not sure who to trust at the moment."

We fell silent, drinking our coffee. I looked at him and saw a man I hadn't seen before. Deflated and vulnerable. Not self-pitying, but at a loss to know how to get things back to normal. From thinking I would be the loser if any problems hit our set-up, it appeared I was the one who needed to pull things back together.

As I watched him, it confirmed my thoughts of the last few days. Thoughts I'd discussed with Jenny at our counselling meetings. This was someone I had strong feelings for. I loved Sally; even in the current situation, she was my best friend, my lover, a soulmate. But Marcus … I couldn't imagine being without him now, either.

"What have you eaten today?" I asked.

"Oh," he replied, brought back from wherever he'd been. "I had a sandwich at lunchtime."

"And yesterday?"

"Err, I ate something last night, I think."

I went out to the kitchen and looked in the fridge. It was emptier than usual, but the freezers were full. I pulled a few things out and left them to thaw.

"I'll cook dinner in a bit," I said going back into the living room.

"Oh, you don't need to," he said half-heartedly. "I'll manage."

"No, Marcus. I'm cooking. We need to sort ourselves out. Then we can work out what to do about Sally."

Over dinner, we talked about anything and everything except Sally and what was happening. It was almost like normal times, except it was the first time I could remember spending time with him without Sally, and it reaffirmed what I knew she saw in him.

He was good company; it was almost as simple as that. As we ate, he softened and became something like his usual self; funny, warm, self-deprecating. Never talking over you, always listening. You were never bored when he was around.

After dinner, we moved to the living room, and I thought about leaving. But I didn't want to. I knew what I wanted and was battling with it. I wanted him. I wanted to spend the night here, sleep with him. I didn't want another night alone. I felt warm and comfortable in this familiar place and I wanted to enjoy this man I'd come to … what? Love? I didn't know. I'd given up trying to analyse our situation long ago.

But Marcus and I had never had sex without Sally knowing. It was normally the three of us, and when we'd been on holiday and Penny had been there, it had been a free-for-all. But Sally had always been around. Tonight, she wasn't, and wouldn't know.

When I returned from the loo, I went to his sofa and sat beside him.

"Marcus, can I stay the night?"

"Yes, of course. You know there's always a room here, Luce."

I could see he hadn't understood my intent.

"I didn't mean that," I replied.

His face changed as he grasped what I was saying.

"Oh, I … I'm not sure."

"I want to, Marcus. I want you."

"I don't know, Luce."

"You don't want me?"

"You know I do. I've shown you often enough."

"Then show me now."

His initial hesitancy wore off as I undressed us both, our urgency increasing as we took and gave pleasure in turn, finally driving out our frustrations in a frenzied, wanton fuck. Our almost simultaneous orgasms filled the room with cries and obscene shouts. It was glorious.

As we came down, we cuddled in and held each other close. His cum was oozing from me, but I was so comfortable, I didn't want to move.

Eventually, I went to kiss him and saw his eyes were wet; he'd been crying, silently.

"Are you okay?" I asked, slightly worried.

"Yes," he replied, smiling.

"Feeling guilty?"

"No, there'll be time for that." We silently acknowledged the truth of that. "I can't always explain why I cry, sometimes it's an overload of emotion."

"How about we go to bed?"

We turned out all the lights and went downstairs. As I lay in his arms, a variety of thoughts floated through my head. Guilt? Yes, there was some guilt. Had we been unfaithful? Technically, yes. Was it worth it? God, yes. But to make sure, before he fell asleep, I persuaded him to repeat the whole thing.

Chapter 26 – Sally

The nights were the worst. I couldn't sleep. I lay in bed, tossing and turning, my mind unable to settle. Conflicting thoughts doing battle while I was unable to do anything other than play host to these nightmares.

I'd run away from everything important to me. Marcus, Lucy, my job, my friends, Mary. The exposé in the press had affected me in a way I couldn't explain. It had hurt, yes. It had been embarrassing. But there had to be more to it than that. Images came and went. People laughing at me, Marcus looking confused, Lucy angry. But there was something else, always lingering in the background.

The dark phantom which had plagued me for years had returned. Or something like it. There seemed to be a host of them now, all laughing at me, watching me. But surely, I understood it now? I'd banished it. I knew what it was. For years, I thought it was some sort of memory of my father, watching and taunting me. But it wasn't. It was my own doubts and insecurities in ghostly form.

I spent hours thinking about how I'd overcome it. How Jenny and Marcus and Lucy had helped. Until that day when I'd seen its face. My face. Staring back at me. And I'd finally understood.

But now, every night, I sensed a presence in the bedroom, swirling around me. Gloating. I hadn't banished it after all, merely pushed it into the darkness, and now it seemed to have multiplied. Eventually, my tiredness and desperation got the better of me, and I cried myself to sleep.

I saw Genevieve every day, and she did what she could, suggesting various options, but I had painted myself into a corner and couldn't think of a way out. Jacques visited me most days, usually in the afternoon. We spent hours together, and I finally told him everything about the shadow, and how I'd overcome it, or so I thought. He listened intently, and even in my state, I knew he was looking for some guidance to help his own struggles.

"You carried a heavy weight," he said, "and you overcame it. You can't let it return."

"It already has, Jacques."

"Then we need to do something about it."

"I know, but I'm paralysed. I don't know where to begin."

"Why not go home?"

"I can't. I don't know why, but I can't."

"Are you not speaking to Marcus?"

"Yes. It's all a bit cold."

"Did you fall out over what happened?"

"Sort of. He seemed to think it was some sort of game. He was more worried about his books than me."

"Is that how you expected him to react?"

"No, that was the surprising thing. I think that was what tipped me over the edge."

"Perhaps he was struggling, too. It was his way of handling things."

"Maybe."

"You need to forget about this shadow for a while."

"Chance would be a fine thing."

"Get changed and come to the club with me tonight."

"Oh, I don't feel like it, Jacques."

"It wasn't an offer, Sally. You're coming with me."

Reluctantly, I showered and dressed, and accompanied Jacques when he went to work. It was the beginning of ten days of mayhem.

That first night, he took me to the cabaret club, installing me at his table and telling the staff to give me whatever I asked for. By the time he took me home, I was exhausted and very drunk. He got me safely into the bedroom, I flopped onto the bed, and the next thing I knew it was lunchtime.

I'd hardly moved, but I'd had a few hours good sleep with no nightmares, no shadows. I felt awful, but it didn't matter. Stripping off my clothes, I got into the shower and tried to sober up. I was still wobbly, my head throbbed, and I felt sick. But I'd slept.

I did the same thing the next night, but at the drag club. Again, returning in the small hours, exhausted, drunk, and tired. Night became day, day became night. Going to one of the clubs in the evening, staying until four or five in the morning, and sleeping most of the day. I felt physically awful, but my head was free of my problems. It was simply trying to keep up with my new schedule.

Jacques and Genevieve both tried to persuade me to take a day or two off. Jacques seemed to regret suggesting the whole thing. Genevieve fed me whenever I visited her, watching me with a concerned air. But I couldn't stop. This new routine was working. I was either drunk, asleep, or hungover. There was no room for shadows or darkness.

On Friday night, I went to the drag club alone. I knew some of the staff now, and they knew me. Even some of the regular clientele knew who I was. It was a relaxed place, and after I had one or two drinks, I mingled, talking to anyone and everyone. By the time the place had livened up, I noticed a couple I'd seen a few times before. They were both dressed in dark suits with skinny ties, slicked hair and more than a hint of make-up. Like Jacques, they were beautiful rather than handsome.

I bumped into them at the bar later, and we struck up a conversation. Leon and Noah proved interesting company. Flirting with each other and gradually with me. Before I knew it, our conversation had become surprisingly explicit. For the first time in a while, my libido appeared.

"You are Jacques's sister, yes?" Leon asked.

"Half-sister," I replied.

"He's a one," Noah added. "Well, he was. Before the Raoul thing."

They both fell silent for a moment, looking genuinely sad.

"Raoul tamed him," Leon said. "I think he's a bit lonely now."

I'd thought the same. After all, he ran these two clubs. If all he wanted was a good time, he could have had it easily enough. He was good looking, and one thing I had learnt, especially at the drag club, was it was a hive of hook-ups. People rarely went home alone unless they wanted to.

"Are you lonely, Sally?" Leon asked, his intent obvious.

"Aren't you two boys together?" I replied.

"We are," Noah added, looking lovingly at Leon. "But we like to add some spice occasionally."

I wasn't sure if they were being serious or not, but I couldn't get images out of my head. Images of Leon and Noah ... and me.

"Ever seen two guys together?"

"Er, no."

"Want to?"

"Perhaps some other time."

"Anytime you want," Noah replied, giving me a smile that made me shiver.

We spent more time together before they decided to leave, making their offer a second time. A second time, I politely declined but headed home and for the first time since I'd been in Paris, I gave myself pleasure, thinking about Noah and Leon ... and me.

On Saturday night, I returned to the drag club and found Noah and Leon sitting at a table in the bar area. They smiled when they saw me approach.

"Good evening, Sally," Leon said. "Join us."

We spent a couple of hours steadily drinking and talking about nothing. But the nothing got more and more sexual and explicit as time wore on. It may have been the alcohol, it may have been my state of mind, but when they repeated their offer of the previous night, I jumped at the chance.

That was how I found myself walking along a few streets with them to their flat. When we arrived, they offered me a drink and we chatted for a while. The candour continued. They asked me about my desires. I'd had a fair bit to drink, though was sober enough not to give too much away, particularly about my current difficulties. As we talked, they stroked each other; their hair, their faces, their arms.

At one point, the conversation paused, and Leon lent and kissed Noah full on the mouth. His response was instant, and they began undoing each other's clothes. It wasn't long before they were both naked, Noah lying on the couch, Leon on top of him. They seemed to ignore me, running their hands over each other, still kissing. I was drawn to their groins, mostly hidden by their position, but I couldn't take my eyes away, catching glimpses of two hard cocks nestling together.

Leon worked his way down Noah's chest, kissing and biting, eliciting brief gasps. He knelt between his legs and as he took Noah's cock in his hands, I had a chance to survey both men, taking in their erections. Noah's was nice enough, but Leon's was a sight to behold. Not that long, but as thick as I'd ever seen. It reminded me of a dildo we had ... at home.

My brief memory of home was ended by a moan as Leon took Noah's cock into his mouth. Slow strokes as his hands caressed Noah's balls, and a finger slid down to find his ass. When it did, Noah's back arched as it pushed straight in. My body was reacting to this, and I wasn't sure about that. This wasn't something on my list.

Noah muttered something, and Leon moved off the couch and knelt in front of it, allowing Noah to reach out and grab his cock. He took the head into his mouth and a hand came around and stroked his ass. Leon leaned down and I stared as they sucked each other in front of me.

My need had increased to the point where I didn't care. I removed my clothes, laying back on the chair and ran my hands over my pussy. It needed more, and I began to finger myself, still hypnotised by the sight in front of me.

To my surprise, I came almost immediately, letting out a loud groan. Noah and Leon paused and looked over, grinning.

"Like some help?" Noah asked, as my orgasm subsided. I wavered for a moment, before nodding. They moved off the sofa and came over to me, Leon getting down between my legs, and spreading them before going straight in to engulf my pussy with his lips. His touch was rough, but I wasn't complaining and reached out for Noah's cock. He moved nearer, and I couldn't resist the temptation, sitting up and taking him between my lips.

I closed my eyes as Leon licked me, enjoying Noah's heat in my mouth, then gasped in surprise as I felt Leon push into me. It was too late for regret, I wanted him. I stopped sucking Noah and concentrated on accommodating Leon, spreading my legs, and moving my bum to open myself as wide as I could. I gasped as the head split me, and the shaft slowly followed a little at a time. Each new stroke went deeper and made me grunt.

As he reached the full depth, I had to take a couple of deep breaths to let myself relax before he began to fuck me slowly. I returned to Noah's cock, and greedily took it between my lips. Leon was gentle and slow, and

I soon got used to his girth, though it made me wince a few times. He bent forward; he wanted to share Noah's cock. I pulled off him and he took it into his mouth.

This was surreal. One cock fucking me while its owner sucked a second. Occasional alarms rang in my head, but I silenced them. I needed this, no, I wanted this. Leon's hand dropped and squeezed my clit; it wasn't subtle, but it worked, and as he fucked me faster, another orgasm came.

As it passed, they swapped places, Noah kneeling between my legs and sliding into me. Leon stood by me, and I wondered how I was going to suck this cock. I began with the head, licking it, tasting myself all over it, slowly sliding my lips over the head until it was in my mouth. I knew I wasn't going to be able to take him very deep and he didn't push, aware of my difficulty. But I worked on the head with my lips and tongue as Noah continued to fuck me.

My whole body tensed as Noah's finger slid over my ass and pushed at it. Leon's hand went back to my clit and between them, they took me to another fierce orgasm. As I came down, I knew what I wanted. I let them both go, and pushed Noah onto the chair, kneeling between his legs and looking up at Leon. He knew what to do and got behind me. I concentrated as his thick cock pushed its way back inside me, stretching me painfully.

As I sucked Noah, Leon fucked me, his strokes going deeper, his pace quickening. My body was building again, and almost before I knew it, another harsh orgasm went through me. I paused, my body sagging, and they moved me to a sitting position on the floor.

Moving in front of me, Noah bent over, and in a practised move, Leon slid that thick cock straight into Noah's ass. Noah groaned before Leon started to fuck him hard, reaching around and grabbing his swinging cock. Gripping it between his fingers, he wanked it in time to his own cock sliding in and out of Noah's ass. Both were in their own world again, grunting, groaning, and building towards their climax.

Noah got there first. The combination of Leon's hand on his cock, and the thick shaft battering his prostate must have been something because Noah's orgasm certainly was. His cry filled the room as his body went into spasm, cum spurting onto the floor under him.

Leon didn't stop, wanting his pleasure and Noah held himself in place until Leon let out a long groan, thrusting into Noah's ass as his cum filled it. After a few more thrusts, they both collapsed onto the floor, panting.

As we recovered in silence, the reality of the situation began to dawn on me. I started to shiver, then tremble. What had I done?

I made my excuses as soon as I could and got a taxi back to the flat, sobering up all the way. When I arrived, I stripped off and got into the shower, frantically washing myself. I was now panicking. What had I done?

I finally turned the shower off and leaned against the wall, the water dripping from me. A month ago, I was happier than I'd ever been. Part of a love triangle which was the most fulfilling relationship of my life. I'd been so happy. What had I done?

I'd run away from them, fled to a different country. And tonight, without so much as a moment's thought, I'd fucked two guys I hardly knew. By the time I curled up on the bed, I was howling. Tears streaming down my face, my shoulders juddering as I struggled for breath. What had I done?

Chapter 27 – Ensemble

Lucy

Life had returned to something like normal. Our story was no longer of interest to the tabloids, they'd moved on to other things. Moved on to ruin other people's lives. Friends, students, and colleagues now made the occasional light-hearted remark, but I didn't detect malice in any of it. In fact, it was quite funny. Marcus and I were closer than we had ever been. We got over our guilt, talked it through, and now spent regular nights together.

But we missed Sally. The phone calls had diminished to two or three times a week, and neither of us could get her to open up. We'd suggested going to her but been rebuffed. We talked about going to Paris and turning up on her doorstep but ultimately decided against it. Marcus had spoken to Genevieve, who was keeping an eye on Sally and agreed with our decision for the time being.

Then there was my mother. We'd not spoken since she'd told me to leave. Annie had been working on her, and it bore fruit. I got an invitation to visit. As I arrived, I was more nervous than the first time I'd met her after our estrangement. It hadn't mattered if that meeting had failed. But now, when we'd both worked at rebuilding our relationship, there seemed more at stake.

"Come in, Lucy," she said, after opening the door.

I followed her into the living room, which was surprisingly light and welcoming, compared to the house she'd shared with my father. On the table was a pot of tea and a plate of cakes.

"Annie's been explaining things to me," she said. "I don't really understand, but I seem to have been unjust. I'm sorry."

"That's alright, Mum. You wouldn't be the only one."

"No, well. My knowledge of these things is limited. I've picked up a lot from some of the friends I've made. At first, it shocked me how open they were about ... those things." She poured two cups of tea and handed me one. "Your father and I never discussed it. Now, I realise we were the odd ones out."

"In a way, Mum. But everyone's different. Unfortunately, there are still far too many people – women especially – who don't feel confident enough to enjoy that part of their lives."

"Exactly. I didn't even know it was an option. And I certainly didn't know anything about ... well ... the things you and your friends get up to." I tried to hide a smile at the way she was carefully choosing her words. "But Annie has been educating me, well, I suppose we've been learning together, as she isn't familiar with half the things we talked about." Only half? I wondered what Annie and Tim had been up to. "And now I know there are things people do I hadn't even dreamed of, could never even have imagined."

"It's okay, Mum. I know something of how you were brought up and can only imagine what you were told about sex."

"Nothing."

"Exactly. And from what you've told me, that didn't change with Dad."

She looked out of the window for a moment, and I wondered if I'd touched a nerve.

"It didn't change at all," she finally replied. "I certainly didn't enjoy it." She paused again. "I'm not sure he did either." The air suddenly felt heavy, the weight of two wasted lives bearing down on us.

"He probably didn't know any more than you," I said softly. "You were both ... brainwashed."

"I guess so. But when I read in those papers about ... what went on. The - what is it called - BSM?"

"BDSM."

"Yes, well ..."

"It brought back bad memories."

"Yes," she replied, her gaze boring into me, "it did. Things I was trying to forget. And I feared you were somehow involved in the same thing."

"No, Mum. Anything I do is because I want to. I won't pretend my situation was planned; it certainly wasn't. It just happened. But I wouldn't change anything. Well, other than having it all appear in the press."

"And you're involved with a man?"

"Yes, don't ask me how, I can't explain that. That was a surprise, too."

"And a woman?"

"Yes."

"That sounds complicated."

"I know it sounds as if it should be. But it isn't. It just works."

Silence fell and I let her take it all in. God knows, it would be hard enough for any parent. But my mother? I was surprised we'd got this far. I poured us both some more tea and took a cake.

"Well," she said finally. "I'm never going to understand it. But as long as you're not getting hurt, or hurting anyone else, I guess it's not my place to interfere."

"We all have to live our own lives. All I've ever wanted to do was be me, and it's been hard at times."

"Because of me?"

"Not just you, Mum."

"Your father?"

"Let's say I don't remember him with any fondness."

She turned away again, lost in thought. But I knew it was more than that.

"Nor do I, Lucy," she finally said. "Nor do I."

"Can I ask you something, Mum?" She looked at me, an anxious look, but said nothing. "Why didn't Dad use corporal punishment on me or Annie?"

"Because you were girls, it was my job."

"But I don't remember you ever slapping me."

"No," she said. "I couldn't do it. My mother had slapped me regularly, and I'd hated it. I couldn't do it to you and Annie."

"How did you explain that to Dad?"

"He never asked. I think he assumed I did it when he wasn't around. When you told us you were ... well ... you liked women, it was one of the things he accused me of."

"What?"

"He told me I hadn't punished you enough growing up, that it was a result of ... your sins." That made sense; it was how his mind worked. "I didn't dare tell him the truth."

"That you hadn't punished us at all."

"Yes. And now, I'm glad I didn't."

For the first time, I felt a degree of warmth towards this woman. She may have been a less than perfect mother, but there had been a modicum of humanity in her, even before her enlightenment.

We moved to easier subjects and the atmosphere lightened. As I went to leave, she followed me to the door.

"Am I going to meet your friends?" she asked, catching me by surprise.

"Err, yes. I guess so. If you want to."

"I think I'd like to."

"I'll see. It might be a bit difficult at the moment."

Marcus

I didn't know how to get Sally back. Our phone calls had dwindled to one or two a week, and they were brief. One-word answers from her. I'd offered to go and see her or meet her somewhere, but the offers were declined. I'd spoken to Genevieve. She was her usual self. Things would sort themselves out, she said, but I couldn't see how. The longer Sally stayed away, the harder it would be to return to normality.

And things were normal. The excitement had died down. Lucy and I had resumed our usual lives, without anyone following us, or asking questions. There was still the odd occasion when I was recognised, but I ignored it as best I could. The launch date for Shadows of Silver was fast approaching and I wasn't looking forward to it.

Eva and I had been confirming the last-minute details, and our relationship had recovered some of its previous spark. It was essentially a re-run of the previous year's event, except this year, it seemed there would be no Sally.

I went to see Mary. Her relationship with Sally was close, and the oldest of any of us.

"She rings me occasionally," Mary said. "But I can't work out what's going on. I know she's scared."

"What of?"

"I'm not sure. At first, it was the people following you all. But that can't be it now."

"They're long gone."

"I wonder if the shadow has returned."

It was something I'd discussed with Lucy. We knew the hold it had had on her over the years, Lucy better than I did. Sal had banished it, but we both knew you could never guarantee these issues wouldn't return. But what could we do about it?

"Did Mary have any ideas?" Lucy asked when she came over that evening.

"She's as baffled as us."

Over dinner, we talked through the options again, as we had umpteen times. As we finished, my phone rang; it was Helen.

"Marcus, can you spare me half an hour?"

"Of course, Helen. When?"

"Now."

She and Penny arrived twenty minutes later. Both looked subdued as I led them from the front door to the living room.

"Ah," Helen said, seeing Lucy. "I'm glad you're here. It will save a second visit."

I looked at Lucy, but she shrugged, as mystified as me. Helen and Penny refused an offer of a drink, and Helen smoothed non-existent creases from her skirt. Penny sat rigid, looking at neither of us, and I thought she'd been crying. Lucy and I waited, wondering what was going on.

"I'm here to offer another apology," Helen said. Lucy and I shared a puzzled look. "I've discovered it was Ben who tipped off the press."

Silence descended on the room. It made sense, sort of.

"Why?" Lucy eventually asked.

"Cos he's a little shit," Penny said with real venom. Helen turned to her, surprised, and Penny dropped her eyes.

"I think that does sum it up on this occasion," Helen said. "He wanted revenge, I assume, for losing his comfortable life; or rather lives. He suddenly found himself looking for a new home, a new master, and a new mistress. All by his own actions, of course, but he evidently didn't see it like that."

"Why pick on us?" I asked.

"I assume he knew Penny and I wouldn't be of interest to a tabloid. But he knew of you, he knew you were our friends. He knew of your involvement in the group and he knew you'd suddenly become newsworthy."

"He set us up," Lucy said.

"I'm afraid so, yes. Probably made a few thousand out of it. I'm sorry."

"Helen," I said. "It's not your fault. He's responsible for what he did."

"He is, but yet again, I'm reminded of my error in trusting him."

"We all make mistakes, Helen. Even you."

"I do. But this time it's not hurt me or Penny, but our friends. That's something I vowed a long time ago to avoid at all costs."

There was a surprising amount of passion in her words, her voice almost breaking at the end of the sentence. We all noticed, even Penny looked at her mistress with a hint of concern.

"Helen," I said. "There is no need for an apology, as you haven't caused any of this. The little shit has got his money, the story's dead and over, and we're slowly picking up the pieces. Do you know how he got the pictures?"

"Ah, that was how we found it was him. He set up a couple of his acquaintances. He told them he wanted to play a joke on some friends and got them to come to our group and take the photos. When they saw them in the press, they were horrified and told Jason. They're really sorry; not that that counts for much. If I ever meet them, they'll wish they'd never been born."

"But at least we know there's no snooper in the group."

"True. I'll speak to Matt and apologise, just to clear that up."

"So, most things are back to normal," Lucy said.

"And Sally?" Penny asked.

"Still in Paris," I said. "Still keeping her distance." Lucy and I explained the current situation.

"Can you go over?" Helen asked.

"Yes, but Sally's told us not to."

"You could just turn up," Penny suggested.

"Yes, but ... well, Sally and I have been in this situation once before. My intuition then was not to do that, and it proved correct. Right, Luce?"

"Yes, I have to agree. Sally's best left to work things out when she's upset. Push too far, and it'll make things worse."

"I see," Helen said. "What are you going to do?"

We didn't have an answer.

***

I was back in Eva's office, laboriously signing copies of Shadows of Silver which her secretary was sliding expertly in front of me. By the end, my fingers were aching.

"Can't you make a stamp or something?" I asked Eva when she returned from a meeting. "Or print my signature?"

"That would be cheating, Marcus," she replied. "Finished?"

"I bloody well hope so."

"Good. Let's go for a drink."

"I don't feel like it."

"Please. A glass of something with a friend."

We walked to a bar near her office and found a table before ordering a couple of drinks.

"Sally still in Paris?" she asked.

"Yes."

"I'm sorry."

"I'd like to apologise, too."

"What for?"

"For some of the things I said to you."

"Oh, forget it. I get far worse from some of my other authors, believe me. And you were right, in a way. I am part of a system, and I have to follow the company line. It's difficult sometimes."

"Ever thought about going out on your own?"

"As a publisher?"

"Yes."

"God, in my dreams. That takes a lot of money. Indie publishers are risky businesses."

"True, but they exist."

218

"Yes, they do. They either go under or, if they're successful, they get taken over by one of the big boys."

"Pessimist."

"Just a realist, Marcus."

"Are we in the same place tonight?"

"Yes."

"Okay, let's get it over with."

Lucy

The train arrived at Paddington Station late, and I grabbed a taxi to get me to the bookshop where the launch was happening. I arrived in time and went upstairs to find Marcus standing with Peter, his agent. Eva was fussing around the stage on the opposite side of the room. Apart from one or two shop staff, no-one else had arrived.

I didn't know if anyone else was coming from home. I'd invited the usual suspects, but Helen was still feeling guilty about Ben and seemed to be avoiding us. Mary and Ken had promised to come but turned down my invitation to travel with me.

I gave Marcus a brief kiss on the cheek, and we made small talk with Peter while we waited. People began to arrive, the glasses of wine or juice were handed out, and one or two people approached Marcus to say hello or ask for autographs. This request always seemed to surprise him, but he was on his best behaviour and obliged with a smile.

Eva came over and greeted me. She was accompanied by a large man, who exuded self-importance. I smelt trouble, and Eva looked nervous.

"Mr Foxton," the man boomed, holding out his hand. "I'm Mungo Carpenter. I'm so pleased to meet you at last."

"Are you ...?" Marcus replied, keeping his hands by his side. Mungo's arm was left hanging in mid-air for a few seconds, before he smoothly withdrew it, smiling.

"Of course," he said. "One of our hopes for the future."

"I doubt that." Eva looked sharply at Marcus, Mungo looked puzzled and Peter, Marcus's agent, was frantically swinging his head between the combatants. "This book completes my current contract with you."

"I'm sure we can sort out a new one," Mungo said, an artificial smile on his face.

"I'm looking for another publisher for my next book."

"What? Has Ms Cassini not been looking after you?"

Eva had a resigned look. She knew Marcus well enough to know she couldn't rescue the situation.

"Oh," Marcus replied, "Eva has been fantastic. None of my success would have happened without her. But it seems those she reports to are missing something."

I cringed inwardly; he wasn't doing himself any favours.

"What's that?" Mungo asked.

"A backbone."

The silence was deafening. Mungo was lost for words, something I suspect rarely happened. Eva looked as if she didn't know whether to laugh or cry, and Peter was frozen to the spot, open-mouthed. Rescue came in the form of our support party. Mary, Ken, and Helen were heading towards us, with Penny in the lead, which surprised me.

"Hello," she said, giving Marcus and me a hug. "I've finally got them here."

The others greeted us, and Eva used the opportunity to quietly guide Mungo away.

"Thank you for coming," Marcus said. His tone of voice showed he meant it but before he could say any more, Eva returned, her face a picture of contained rage, and pulled him away to begin the evening. It followed the same pattern as the previous year. Eva made the introductions, and Marcus took over. He looked more confident this year, but there was a slightly melancholic air about him. It wasn't surprising.

"Good evening, everyone," he said, "and welcome. A year ago today, I stood on this spot and launched my first professionally published book. It appears to have been quite popular." Some laughter. "In that time, many people have come to know my work, and many more seem to have learnt rather more about me than I might have wished." Much more laughter this time, and a few whoops and cheers.

Looking around, there were far more people present than there had been the year before. Was this simply the popularity of his work, or the result of the tabloid stories? I hadn't thought to ask him what he was going to say and was surprised by how open he was about our recent troubles.

"If anyone has turned up tonight thinking my books might reflect what they read in the tabloids, I can tell them now, they're going to be sorely disappointed." More laughter, and cries of 'shame'. "But I do hope you'll enjoy this new work as much as its predecessor. I'd also like to thank everyone who bought the new editions of my older works. I've found that particularly gratifying, as it shows an author can produce good work without being mothered by a publisher."

I saw Eva roll her eyes as a few cheers came from the audience. He still loved winding her up, though it probably wasn't advisable in her current mood. He read three sections from the new book, and his voice was much more confident than the last time.

I spotted Penny near the front recording the whole thing on her phone attached to a monopod. I couldn't think why, but let it pass as Marcus came to the end of the readings. Polite applause followed.

"Thank you," he said. "I'd like, once again, to thank all those who have made this book possible. I'm not going to name you all, you know who you are, whether you're here tonight or only with us in spirit."

Eva led him to the signing table. This year, it took a lot longer. There were more people, most of whom wanted a dedication, and many asked for the obligatory selfie. I didn't remember one request the year before. Again, Penny was filming. Ken was talking to Helen in one corner, and Mary came to join me.

"You can thank Penny for us all being here tonight," she said.

"Penny?"

"Yes. She offered to bring us up with them."

"I didn't think she'd have your number."

"She didn't, but she remembered dropping us off after one of our birthday parties and came to see me."

I was confused.

"Why?"

"She told me about the whole Ben thing. Helen's upset about it - God knows why, it wasn't her fault - and she didn't feel it was right to come. Anyway, Penny offered to bring us up so she could use it as an excuse to persuade Helen to come as well."

I liked that; Penny was asserting herself. She'd been more fun on holiday this year when she'd made her needs known. Well, even more fun. I suspected Helen wasn't too unhappy about the change.

As the event drew to a close, Marcus signed the last few books, and our party and the shop staff were the only ones left.

"Why on earth did you film all that?" I asked Penny when she re-joined us.

"Oh, I thought I'd edit it and put it on Marcus's website."

We went to the same restaurant for a small buffet. I kept my eye on Marcus. He seemed to be holding up well and chatted for an hour before people started drifting away. Eventually Penny gathered the stragglers and took them home, leaving Eva, Marcus, and me.

"Well, Marcus," Eva said. "I appreciate it was hard today."

"Thanks, Eva. I think it went okay."

"Yes, it did, but did you have to make things so awkward with Mungo?"

She'd calmed down a little, though I'd noticed she'd avoided Marcus until now.

"He's a twat."

"I know that, and you know that. But he's my boss. And you could have told me you weren't re-signing with us. We haven't even discussed it yet."

"Who said I wasn't re-signing?"

"What?"

"Just think how pleased he'll be when, after tough and lengthy negotiations, you manage to sign me for another three books."

Her whole body drooped as she let out a heavy sigh.

"You're just a troublemaker, aren't you?" she said, finally smiling.

"Me? No. But the likes of Mr Mungo Bungo Carpenter can go hang, and if I can help someone get one up on him, I will."

As we left the restaurant, Eva gave us a kiss and a hug before setting off into the night.

"Going home?" Marcus asked. He looked tired, the mask had worn off and the grief returned.

"No, I'm staying."

"Thank you. The hotel's just around the corner."

Chapter 28 – Sally

I felt numb and dirty. The memories of the night before wouldn't leave me, and I was disgusted with myself. I tried to eat something but threw it up within minutes. Going back to bed, I curled up and found myself rocking gently, eyes wide open, staring at the wall.

Someone knocked on the door a couple of times, but I ignored it. I couldn't face anyone. I drifted into sleep a few times; a fitful, dark sleep. Images of my life filling my mind, fighting for attention. My parents, and Charlie and Mary. Shadows. Marcus and Lucy. Shadows. Friends and colleagues. Shadows. The newspaper stories, my flight, then last night.

"Sally …"

Always last night. Vivid images of what I'd done.

"Sally …"

Then a voice calling my name. It seemed so real.

"Sally …"

I woke with a jolt, my eyes bleary, my head still hurting. Then relaxed again, as I saw Genevieve standing by the bed.

"Sally, are you alright?"

I took a few deep breaths, trying to come to, and shake the fog from my brain.

"No," I managed to reply, before bursting into tears again.

Genevieve sat on the bed and waited for the emotion to pour out of me. In a rushed, manic outburst, I told her what had happened. Her expression didn't change. She listened without moving. When I finished, she studied me for a while, long enough for me to grow anxious about her response.

"Bien," she finally said. "And now you're lying here feeling sorry for yourself."

I hadn't expected the challenge and didn't know what to say.

"I ... I feel awful," I replied.

"I'm not surprised. Do you want my help?"

"Yes," I whispered, "please."

"Good. Have a shower, get dressed and come downstairs."

I didn't argue. I went into the bathroom, got into the shower, and stood under the running water. The images were still there. But now they were joined by thoughts of Marcus and Lucy. That made everything much worse.

I set about scrubbing myself again, trying to clean the memories of the previous night, but it didn't work. I dried off, put on a pair of jeans and a jumper, and went down to Genevieve's flat.

She was in the kitchen, a pot of coffee simmering on the stove and some brioche toast on the table.

"Sit," she said. "Eat."

"I can't—"

"Eat."

I took a cautious bite of the bread and almost gagged, but it stayed down, and I tried a little more. She pushed a bowl of coffee in front of me alongside a large glass of water, and sat on a stool the other side of the counter, watching me. Nothing was said for some time.

"You have a little too much of your father in you," she finally said.

"What?"

"Your father was a clever man. He had to be to get away with what he did. And for what we now know of his different lives. But he had a major weakness." I was interested now. "He didn't like it when life didn't follow his plan."

"In what way?"

"When the unexpected happened, he had a tendency to disappear."

"But surely when he wasn't with you ..."

"You think he was with his English family? With you?"

"Yes."

"Looking back, I think there were times when he simply ran away. He wasn't with me or your mother. He fled somewhere else, though given what we know now, it might be interesting to know where." I stopped eating as the truth sank in. "And you have a tendency to do the same."

"But I didn't—"

"You've run away from your problems. I gather it's happened before."

That hit me like a brick.

"What?"

"When your problems made you hurt someone you love."

"Marcus? He told you?"

I felt anger rising; how could he? Why would he?

"No, he didn't. Other people are concerned about you as well, you know."

"Who?"

She saw my fury.

"Sally, it doesn't matter. What matters is we sort this out."

She was right, I had run away. Even if it was Marcus who'd told her, I wouldn't blame him.

"How can we? Running away was bad enough, but last night I outdid myself."

"So it seems. Mistakes happen."

"What! Genevieve, I fucked two guys I hardly knew."

"Yes, you've told me."

"I've ruined everything now."

"How?"

I looked at her wondering why she was being so obtuse.

"How? How? I ran away for some reason I can't explain. Because I needed space, because I felt let down, because I could. I don't know. And now I've fucked the first two guys who asked."

She made a dismissive gesture.

"Oh, that's not important," she said.

"Not important? If that's not important, what is?"

"That you recognise the people who love you. Was your father faithful to me?"

"No."

"And do you think I was faithful to him?"

Her expression gave me the answer.

"No?" I ventured.

"Of course not. Even though I gave up my clients when I married him, he was always away. That wasn't enough for me. But I still loved him, even with all his faults."

"Did he know?"

"Of course."

"It didn't bother either of you?"

"Not me. I can't speak for him, but knowing what we know now, he wouldn't have been on very strong ground, would he?"

"I guess not. But Marcus and Lucy and I … Well, we were all about trust."

"And you will be again. Do you love them?"

I paused and thought about the question, although I knew the answer. "Yes."

"You need to reach out to them."

"But they're hardly speaking to me."

"Sally, listen to yourself. You're the one not talking."

"I'm hurting."

"So are they."

"You've spoken to them?"

"Yes, often. I gather they weren't getting much from you; no calls, no messages. Marcus and Lucy called me instead. We talk every day."

"What?"

"They're worried, Sally. More than worried." I couldn't believe it, and my feelings were mixed. "What you do is up to you. Our lives are different, and I can't decide for you. But I suggest you give up the nightlife for a while."

I stayed with Genevieve for the remainder of the afternoon. We didn't say much, but being with her comforted me, and she kept me watered and fed. By the time I returned to the flat, I felt physically better, but I knew the night wouldn't be as forgiving.

The next day, I tried to follow a routine. The night had seen little sleep, and what little I got was filled with sadness and nightmares. When I was awake, I felt the presence of my new shadows. Not mocking, not laughing, just hovering, reminding me of my predicament.

I got up early and went out to get some breakfast. It was all on autopilot. I wandered along a few streets, looking in shop windows, but nothing interested me. I returned to the flat, curled up on the sofa and fell asleep.

I was woken by my phone ringing … Genevieve, asking me to come down. Her door was open as usual, so I went in, along the long hallway and into her sitting room. She wasn't alone, and I froze as I recognised her visitor.

"Helen!"

"Good afternoon, Sally."

"Well," Genevieve said, rising. "I need one or two things, so I'll go and do some shopping."

With that, she came up to me, kissed me on the cheek and disappeared. I was still reeling from Helen's presence.

"Come and sit down," Helen said. She was her usual elegant self, but I couldn't comprehend her presence. She didn't know Genevieve; she knew of her, but how was she here? I walked to the sofa and sat opposite this unexpected visitor. Helen was wearing her inscrutable expression.

"Sally," she said. "I'm here to offer an apology and help if I can."

I was still speechless, trying to understand this turn of events. Helen told me Ben had been the person who sold our story to the press, and how bad that made her feel. It made sense and answered that hanging question, although I assured her I didn't blame her.

"Nevertheless," she said, "your friendship with me led to this horrible situation."

"But how did you find me?"

"I'm not here solely of my own volition, Sally." I must have looked puzzled. "We've been having councils of war about you."

"What?"

"We've been trying to work out how to bring you home."

"We? Who's we?"

"Why, Marcus, Lucy, Mary, Penny and me."

"I still don't understand."

"Sally, you ran away. You're not communicating with Marcus and Lucy and it's hard for them. They've offered to come and talk, but you refused. What could they do? When I found out about Ben, I told them immediately, and we also brought Mary into the discussions. In the end, we decided someone needed to come and talk to you. As you'd forbidden Marcus and Lucy, it had to be Mary or me."

"So, why you?"

"Because I feel a measure of guilt. Mary was more than willing to come, but we decided I'd try first."

"And she'd come if you failed."

"Something like that, but for some reason, it was thought I'd be better at knocking some sense into you."

"Am I seen as that much of a problem?"

"We don't know, Sally. That *is* the problem. We don't know what's going on."

My mind was racing. How many people knew I was here? How many people were trying to get me home? How could I go home?

"Nor do I, Helen. I'm lost and I don't know how to find my way out."

"Want to start at the beginning?"

I liked Helen. For all her perceived haughtiness, she was honest, warm, and loyal. She'd proved that by coming here. I thought for a few moments, drew everything together in my head and let it pour out. She sat still and listened as I tried to verbalise my reaction to the press stories and my anguish at Marcus's response.

I told her about the appearance of the shadows and darkness, and my growing fear of going home. I told her about my drunken nights and, after some hesitation, about my infidelity. When I finished, I sank back onto the sofa.

"As you see," I said. "I'm in a mess."

"Well, there was rather more there than I expected."

"I don't know what's happening. I don't know why I ran away, but once I did, I couldn't face going back. And now? When they find out what I've done, they won't want me back."

"Are you sure?"

"Helen, you of all people know what trust means. Marcus and Lucy and I trusted each other. I've put a bomb under that and set it off myself. They'll never trust me again."

"It may take time."

"Would you trust me after what I've done?"

She thought for a moment.

"It would depend on the circumstances."

"Would you trust Penny if she went off and fucked other people?"

"I seem to remember she has."

For the first time in a while, I couldn't hide my smile as the memories of Penny joining us on holiday came flooding back.

"True," I said. "But you knew about it beforehand."

"I did. But as to your question, the honest answer is, I might. I can forgive Penny most things."

"Because you love her?"

"Yes." She said it so softly, I hardly heard her answer and saw her looking wistfully into the distance. "But," she continued, a sinful smile on her face, "she'd pay for it."

That made me think of Marcus and the playroom. Of the play parties. All the intense experiences we had. Of submitting to him. And of Lucy becoming part of all that. I didn't want to lose it; I couldn't lose it. Helen stayed silent, allowing me to think. I don't know how long we sat there, but it was Genevieve who brought us out of our reverie, poking her head around the door.

"Would anyone like some tea and cakes?"

She brought tea in and were it not for the situation, it would have been fun. I didn't know how much Helen and Genevieve knew about each other, but they already seemed like old friends.

"So," Genevieve said eventually, "have you two resolved anything?"

"Not yet," Helen replied. "But we're working on it, aren't we Sally?"

"I hope so."

"We'll sort it out. But tonight, you're showing me the sights."

"The sights?"

"Yes," Helen said. "You're going to show me these clubs I've heard so much about."

I stared at her wide-eyed; Genevieve just laughed.

That was how I found myself back at Jacques's cabaret club, introducing him to Helen. He already seemed to know who she was. How was I the last to know what was going on? We stayed for the main show, Helen enjoying herself, and she wanted to go on to the drag club.

She fitted in straight away. She hadn't changed since the afternoon, but her day clothes were equal to most people's dressing up level. That, her height, and her red hair hanging loose over her shoulders and down her back, ensured she received a lot of appreciative looks.

She dealt with the attention in her usual way, by appearing largely ignorant of it. But I finally saw she wasn't. We grabbed some drinks and found a free table.

"You always appear confident in any situation," I said.

"Appearance is everything."

"Meaning you're not?"

"Oh, I am now, but I wasn't when I was younger. I stood out; my height and hair colour meant I couldn't hide anywhere."

"Do you like the attention?"

"Attention?"

"Yes, Helen. The fact everyone looks when you enter any room."

"Do they?" Her expression told me she was playing with me.

"You know they do, don't you?"

"Of course."

"Is that why you do it?"

"What?"

"The clothes and the hair always perfect, the distant manner."

"No, what you see is me. This is who I am now. I guess it was a bit of an act years ago, a defence mechanism. But I found I liked the persona I portrayed and adopted her."

"Wish I could do that."

"Do you not like yourself?"

"More than I used to. Marcus taught me that."

"Because that's who he loves."

"I guess."

"Sally, you're a beautiful, sensual woman and you're smart. An attractive package, believe me." She gave me a dazzling smile and I realised Marcus had been right about her interest in Lucy and me. "Be smart now and make the right decisions, because if you don't, you'll regret it for the rest of your life. So will Marcus and Lucy."

A few people who knew me dropped by to greet us and find out who my fascinating companion was. I saw Helen was conflicted. She genuinely was a private person, but also didn't hide her pleasure at being the centre of attention in the right environment. When the initial rush ended, she turned to me.

"I wonder how many of them thought I was a man?" she said.

"I hadn't even thought of that."

"Look around. There are plenty here in drag who look far better than I do. Some of them are gorgeous."

As I looked around, I saw she was right, then froze, as I saw Leon and Noah. Helen noticed.

"What's wrong?" she asked, as I turned towards her, trying to hide.

"The two guys … the two guys I … they're coming."

"Ah …"

I held my breath, praying they hadn't seen me. Too late.

"Sally," Noah said. "Good evening."

"Er, hi, Noah, Leon."

"Aren't you going to introduce us?"

"Oh, yes. Helen, this is Noah, and that's Leon."

They exchanged pleasantries, both men studying Helen closely.

"You left so quickly the other night," Leon said. "Did we do something wrong?"

"No. I needed to get home."

"That's alright then. It was fun. If you're ever interested again, let us know."

"Er, thank you. Perhaps another time."

"Sure."

I slumped in the chair as they walked away, Helen watching me, amused.

"You could have helped," I said.

"Why? You handled that perfectly well. Sometimes, we need to confront our mistakes and put them right. Besides, I wouldn't call those two a mistake."

"Helen!"

By the time we got back to the flat, I was happier than I'd been for days. Helen gave me a hug and a kiss, before going into Genevieve's flat, where she was staying. I'd have to watch out, those two together could be dangerous.

Chapter 29 – Ensemble

Lucy

After the book launch, Marcus and I spent a weekend together, trying to think of a way to bring Sally home, if she wanted to come back. In the end, we found ourselves going round in circles.

"We need help," Marcus said.

"But from who?"

"Well, Mary might have some ideas, for a start."

He rang her and she offered to come straight over. When she arrived, we swapped notes. We'd all been speaking to Sally since she'd fled, but she'd been as uncommunicative with Mary as she had with us.

"Has she done this before, Mary?" he asked.

"Not that I remember. She used to come to me if she had problems, and I guess to you, Lucy."

"Yes. I can't recall anything like this."

"There was one occasion," Marcus said. I knew about it, but he told Mary about the time Sally had accidentally hurt him.

"But we knew why she did it," he concluded. "She was going through counselling and it was difficult."

We found ourselves no further forward.

"What about Helen?" Mary asked.

"Helen?" I replied. "Why?"

"She has an air of authority, seems to take a no-nonsense approach, and she's neither partner nor family."

"I don't know," Marcus said. "She already feels guilty about Ben's part in all this."

"But that wasn't her fault," I replied.

"No, it wasn't. But she might feel obliged to help."

"Well, there's only one way to find out."

I rang Helen and explained our dilemma. Half an hour later, she and Penny joined us. We recounted our discussions and admitted our lack of solutions. At the end, Helen thought for a moment.

"Someone needs to go to her," she said, "and find out what's going on. Something has spooked her, and she doesn't seem comfortable telling any of you what it was."

"But she's already told us she doesn't want us to go," Marcus said.

"Yes. You and Lucy. She hasn't barred me."

"Or me," Mary said.

We spent some time discussing this option. I thought it a good idea, but Marcus wasn't sure.

"She might think Lucy and I don't care."

"No," Penny said, to our surprise. She'd been quiet during the discussion so far. "I think I understand some of what's happened. I don't know why Sally went away, but if she's anything like me, once she's run, coming back is hard."

She looked nervous, clearly battling something.

"I've been in a similar position," she said finally. "Years ago, I was with someone who … let me down. Badly and in public. The details aren't important. Anyway, I managed to find the courage to escape. It felt great at first, I was safe. But I soon realised I'd have to go back. In my case, not to the man who … not to him. But back to the same area, to my friends, to people who knew me.

"But the longer I stayed away, the harder it got. I imagined all sorts of things. That my friends and neighbours were laughing at me, that I'd never live it down. I'd be forever marked by this event. I couldn't get over it and pushed my closest friends away. Luckily, one of those friends found out where I was, and a friend of hers I hardly knew turned up on my doorstep, quietly took control and cajoled me into going back. Where nobody batted an eyelid; the incident had been forgotten.

"I'm not suggesting we use the same methods, but someone needs to talk to her, and help her come back. And that person may need to be strong with her."

"Volunteering, Penny?" Helen asked. She'd been watching Penny closely.

"No, Helen. I'm not the right person. And if you'll forgive me, Mary, I don't think you are, either. From what I know, you and Sally are close, and she may need you at some point. But Helen isn't emotionally involved with Sally and can stay objective and detached. And she can be quite … forceful."

I think every one of us stifled a laugh; we all knew it, but it seemed an inappropriate moment to giggle. Penny blushed and looked down.

"I think you're right, dear," Mary said. "If Helen is happy to go, that is."

"I am," Helen replied. "Will … is it Genevieve? Will Genevieve be okay with me turning up?"

Marcus went into the next room and gave her a call. When he came back, he confirmed that Genevieve was happy with the plan.

Marcus

After Mary left, we gave Helen Genevieve's address and contact details.

"Is she a typical French matron?" Helen asked. Lucy and I looked at one another.

"No," I replied. "Far from it. I think the two of you will get on well."

"You have a lot in common," Lucy added. "Though how much you'll want to tell each other is up to you."

Helen gave us a hard stare.

"We're not going to tell you Genevieve's story," I said. "That's hers to tell. But I will say you won't find her boring."

After they left, Lucy and I returned to the living room.

"Have we done the right thing?" I asked.

"We didn't have any other realistic options."

***

The first week's sales figures for Shadows of Silver came in and they were better than we'd hoped. Almost as good as Shadows of Gold. The early reviews were good, too. Under different circumstances, I'd have been ecstatic. Eva was pleased, and I even had a brief message from Mungo congratulating me. I didn't reply; he was someone I could easily ignore.

All we could do was wait. We'd agreed Helen would keep in touch, but not tell us everything that happened. We wouldn't necessarily know how things were going and it was going to be an anxious few days.

Lucy was effectively living at the flat now. We'd got over our doubts, although we knew it didn't look good to others. We both loved Sally and missed her; we wanted her back. But our relationship had changed in the last few weeks. Previously, we'd had fun as part of a threesome. We enjoyed each other's company, and her involvement had been good for all of us. But since Sally had left, and it had just been the two of us, we'd become emotionally closer.

Penny came around one afternoon to agree more changes to my website. She'd edited the launch event footage into shorter clips and wanted to publish them. I cringed when I watched myself. I hated having my photograph taken, let alone being filmed, but she assured me it looked good.

"You ought to do some clips of you reading," she said. "Or short video messages."

"Penny, you know I hate speaking in public. Why the hell would I put gawky clips of myself online?"

"Just an idea."

"I'm no vlogger."

"Perhaps not, but you read well at the launch. People might be interested in seeing you."

I gave her a hard stare, and she eventually broke into a giggle.

"Alright," she said. "But I'm not going to stop coming up with ideas."

"Expect a lot of refusals."

She gave me one of her mischievous pouting looks. A look that always put wicked thoughts in my head, and she knew it.

"Penny," I said, mimicking a shocked tone. "Your mistress is away on a mission of mercy, and you're here teasing an old man."

"Sorry, can't resist. And you're not old." She closed her laptop and began packing her things. "Right, I need to go and see Lucy. I've added some things to her site, too."

"You might as well hang around, then."

She turned to me, puzzled, before her face broke into a grin.

"Oh, I see."

"Watch it."

"Didn't say a word."

She was still grinning.

Lucy arrived a little later, and I cooked dinner while she and Penny went through the site changes. When they showed me, I was impressed. The subject matter allowed far greater scope for creativity and design, and Penny hadn't held back. It looked fabulous. There were many more pictures now, as well as the gorgeous animations of Lucy creating three works.

Penny stayed for dinner.

"How are you finding it without Helen?" Lucy asked.

"It's a bit strange. I haven't been there without her for more than one night before."

"I guess you don't know what to do," I said.

"I'm not helpless, as you well know, Marcus."

"Just teasing."

"I know. Don't stop."

But I did. I was hopeful Helen's intervention would bring results, but I wasn't in the mood to tease, even Penny. She understood.

"You two are good?" she asked. "If you don't mind me asking."

"Yes," Lucy replied, looking at me. "I know it looks bad."

"Oh, don't worry about it. It's good you've got each other to help you through this."

It was. Without Lucy, I'd have been moping around feeling helpless. She made me do things. After Penny left, we sat and watched a film. It turned out to be very emotional, and we both ended up in floods of tears.

Lucy

Helen sent us brief texts each day. Just a few lines. *Sally okay. Long chats. Genevieve great fun.* No details. It was a relief, but also a tease. What was happening? What were they doing? It was out of our hands. The calls with Sally had stopped and we weren't sure if that was a good sign or a bad one.

Marcus's book was selling well, and he was in the best seller's lists again. His prominence led to a few comments and online reminders of the tabloid stories, but this time, they were all light-hearted and positive and seemed to increase sales of all his books. From his publisher's point of view, the exposé had been great publicity.

I visited Mum again on Friday evening. We had dinner and the discussion was light. Her visits to friends, their visits to her. She'd made real progress building a network around her and seemed to be enjoying it. There was a wistfulness sometimes when she talked about things her friends were doing with their partners, but it soon disappeared. I was sure she was imagining an ideal partner, not my late father. He was rarely mentioned.

When I got back to the flat, I couldn't find Marcus. The lights were all on, and an open book and music playing indicated he was there somewhere. I went from room to room, looking for him. I found him in the playroom, sitting on the sofa, a look of pain on his face. I went to sit by him, and we held each other.

"Seems empty, doesn't it?" I said.

"Sally breathed life into this room."

"And plenty of screams."

"Screams, gasps, moans, giggles. And that intoxicating gaze."

"Her eyes are something else."

"Do they work for you too?"

"Yes. But not I think as much as they do for you."

"It was one of the first things I noticed about her."

We fell into maudlin silence, comforting each other. But I didn't want to drift into melancholy.

"Do you want to play?" I asked, without real enthusiasm.

"Not here. Sorry."

"I understand. It wouldn't be the same. Come on."

Ensemble

I led him out to the bedroom. We undressed and made love. Slowly, gently, without words, our bodies soothing each other. By the end, we were both sated and fell asleep in each other's arms.

Chapter 30 – Sally

Helen's presence in Paris brought me back to reality. After my initial surprise, I was pleased to see her. To have someone from home. After a couple of days of showing her around Paris, we were in Genevieve's sitting room having tea. Helen was telling her where we'd been that morning.

"You've packed a lot in," Genevieve said.

"Yes," Helen replied. "I need to go home soon, but I will definitely be back."

"When you do, please come and stay with me. You'll always be welcome."

"Thank you."

"Well, Sally," Genevieve said. "Will you be going home with Helen?"

We all knew the answer. I had to. If I wanted to try and retrieve something from my former life, I had to bite the bullet and go home. Since Helen had arrived, the shadows had been quiet; not vanished, but silent. I'd had three good night's sleep and felt refreshed.

"Yes," I replied. "It's time."

"You'll find things are easier than you fear."

"I'm not sure about that."

"Marcus and Lucy want you back."

"They don't know what I've done." I looked at each of them in turn. "Unless you've told them."

"No," Helen replied. "That's not my style nor, I think, Genevieve's. It's up to you how you deal with that."

"I'll have to tell them."

"I think it would be best," Genevieve said. "We all know how dangerous secrets can be."

I had toyed with the idea of keeping my infidelity a secret. I'd toyed with it for all of five seconds. It wouldn't be fair or right. Apart from the trust we'd built, other people knew about it, and I'd have to take at least one test for STIs. I'd stopped beating myself up about what I'd done, it didn't achieve anything. What's done is done. I had to deal with the consequences.

But I wasn't hopeful. In my head, I'd already started planning for a single life again. What would happen about the house, splitting things up. The heartache of losing one or even two people I loved.

As Helen and I sat on the Eurostar the following morning, every rhythmic clunk of the rails taking me closer to home, my mood dropped. Helen tried to take my mind off it.

"I like Genevieve," she said.

"She's lovely," I replied.

"You were right, we had a lot in common."

"Did you share stories?"

"A few. I left some bits out, and I guess she did as well. Jacques is nice too."

"He is."

"Is he anything like his … your father?"

"Nothing at all," I replied, smiling. "I suspect he's about as far from our father as it's possible to be."

We arrived at Waterloo Station around lunchtime.

"I suppose we ought to let Marcus or Lucy know we're on our way," I said as we made our way across London to Paddington.

"I suggest you come home with me first. Then we'll work out what to do."

Even though it was only putting off the inevitable, at least I'd have a bolthole if it all went wrong. When we arrived at Helen's house, Penny came and gave me a big hug.

"It's good to see you home," she said. "We've all missed you."

"Thanks, Penny."

"Penny," Helen said, "Sally might be staying with us."

"I've already prepared a bedroom; it's there if you need it. But I'm sure you won't."

Helen had assured me she'd told nobody about my indiscretion, and Penny's ignorance of it meant her confidence was misplaced.

She'd made us a late lunch, but I couldn't eat much. As they caught up, I stayed silent, and I saw Penny had picked up my unease. She tried to involve me, but I wasn't in the right frame of mind.

"Right," Helen said. "Do you want to wait until tomorrow?"

"No," I replied. "Let's get it over with."

She rang Marcus.

"He said to come on over," she told me, putting her phone down. "Lucy's there as well."

That answered one of my questions. I hadn't been sure whether to speak to them separately or together. Part of me wanted to see Marcus first. He was my primary partner; we lived together, shared everything. But as they were both there, I didn't have to make the decision. I'd only have to go through this once.

"Do you want me to come in?" Helen asked as she parked outside our flat.

"No, Helen. Thank you. If I have to leave afterwards, I'll get a taxi back to you. If that's alright."

"Of course. But if you need me, call."

"Thanks."

I leaned over and hugged her. She kissed me on the forehead.

"You'll be fine," she said. "But be realistic. Don't expect an instant return to normality."

I lifted my case up the steps and trundled it to our front door. Do I use my key, or ring the bell? The fact I had to ask the question was another indication of my doubts. In the end, I pulled my key out and opened the door.

That familiar scent of home hit me as I dumped my case in the hallway and slipped my coat off. I walked to the living room door and stopped as a wave of nausea hit me. I took a few deep breaths, called out a feeble 'hello' and walked into the room.

Sally

My heart missed a beat as I saw Marcus and Lucy for the first time in weeks. The relief at seeing them was countered by intense anxiety. They both stood and hovered uncertainly, none of us sure what to do next. After a moment, Lucy came over.

"Hi, Sal. It's so good to see you."

She put her arms around me and hugged me. My response was uncertain, and she picked up on it straight away, giving me a concerned look as we separated. Marcus held back.

"It is good to see you," he said. "How are you?"

"I'm okay. I …"

And I promptly burst into tears.

Lucy led me to an empty sofa, handed me some tissues and got me a coffee. They sat on the other sofas while I composed myself. It shouldn't have been like this. I should be here talking. Talking about why I ran, about my disappointment at Marcus's response to the tabloid stories. But I'd messed that up; completely messed that up. Now, I had confessions to make.

"I'm sorry," I finally said. "I don't know what to say. I feel such a fool."

"Sal," Marcus replied. "You're not a fool, and you know it. If you want to shout at me or curse me, please do. We need to try and work out what happened and what we can do about it."

"Are we still being watched?"

"God, no," Lucy said. "That stopped weeks ago."

"Are you back at work?"

"Yes, Sal. I told you in one of our calls."

"I'm sorry. The last few weeks have been a bit of a blur."

"Everything's back to normal here," Marcus said. "Except we've been missing you."

"And we don't understand why, Sal," Lucy said. "You wouldn't tell us."

"I know," I replied. "I couldn't. Not then."

"But now?" Marcus asked.

I began haltingly to explain how the tabloid stories had originally unnerved and embarrassed me. How I'd been frightened for myself and both of them. How it got worse when Lucy's mother had cut her off again. It had all gone wrong. Then become angry with Marcus when he'd concentrated on his books, and I felt left out, unsupported.

"I'm sorry, Sal," he said. "It was my way of dealing with what was going on."

"I know, but it hurt."

"I see that now. I'm sorry."

"Then it returned."

"The shadow?" Lucy asked.

"Sort of; lots of them. Shadows and darkness, and they got the better of me. I imagined people spying on me everywhere. I was constantly looking over my shoulder. At night they were circling me, laughing. I couldn't take it anymore. That was when I ran."

"Have Genevieve and Jacques been looking after you?"

"Yes. They've been brilliant," I replied. "I'm not sure what I'd have done without them."

"Gone to Mary's?" Lucy asked.

"No, it wouldn't have been far enough away. That was the problem. Is she okay?"

"Yes, but she's worried."

"I can imagine. God, I've cocked this up."

"No, Sal," Marcus said. "You've done what you had to do, and I'm sorry it was because of me. I don't know what else to say."

"No, Marcus, it wasn't because of you. Yes, I was angry with you for days. But I've had time to think, and you did what I should have expected you to do. Try and carry on and face things out. But I couldn't deal with it that way."

"I don't think any of us needs to take the blame," Lucy said. "We've never dealt with anything like this before."

"True."

"But we need to work out what happens now," Marcus said. "That's if we all want to."

I knew it was time.

"I do," I said. "I've missed you both so much." They both smiled, clearly of the same mind. "But there's something I need to tell you. And it might change your minds."

I told them what I'd done. As briefly and concisely as I could. About the clubs every evening, the drunken nights, and about Noah and Leon. When I finished there was silence.

"I'm sorry," I said, as my tears flowed again. "I'm so sorry."

They looked at each other.

"Let me get this straight," Lucy said, her voice level and cold. "You ran off to Paris because you couldn't take the heat here. The heat we had to put up with. People following us around and questioning our friends. I had to endure stares and nudges from my colleagues and students. My mother rejected me - again. Marcus had to stand up and face the public at his book launch. A launch which nearly didn't happen because some jerk at his publishers wanted to cancel it.

"Even when we told you the heat was off, you couldn't come back. You stopped calling us or answering our calls. We got so worried about you. Everyone did. Us, Helen, Penny, Mary. Some of your colleagues called me to find out if you were okay, and we had to make excuses, say you weren't well.

"Now we find what you were actually doing was getting pissed, spending your nights clubbing and fucking two men you hardly knew, while we dealt with the fallout here. Have I got all that right?"

"No," I replied, stunned by her bitter summing up. "Yes, partly. I … I … "

"Sal," Marcus said, his voice strained. "We were here for you. If we weren't doing what you needed, you only needed to tell us. Are we that unapproachable?"

"No, I … I couldn't. I can't explain why. It freaked me out."

"The shadow came back," Lucy said. "Yes, we know, we guessed. But why didn't you tell us? Why didn't you talk to us?"

It was a good question. Why didn't I share that with them? I still couldn't explain it, my first reaction had been to run.

"I don't know, okay? I don't know. I felt weighed down, I couldn't cope. I love you; I love you both. But for the first time, I didn't feel loved."

We fell silent, shocked by what I'd said, myself included. The silence hung in the air, all of us desperate to break it, all afraid to be the first.

"Do you still feel like that?" Lucy eventually asked.

"No," I replied. "I realised my mistake soon after I got to Paris."

"Then why didn't you come back? Or at least talk to us about it."

"I was too scared. I doubted everyone and everything."

"That's the shadows talking," Marcus said softly.

"Maybe," I replied.

"No maybe about it," he said. "That was how you lived for fifteen years, remember? Doubting yourself, doubting others, doubting everything."

He was right. I'd come to the same conclusion in Paris but had pushed it away.

"But I thought I'd dealt with it," I said.

"And you had, Sal. But something like that never dies. You're always vulnerable to its return."

"I hate it."

"No, don't go back to that. That was the problem in the first place."

"Then what do I do?"

"See Jenny," Lucy said. "Come on, Sal. You're not helpless. You sought help before, and you can do it again." I saw Marcus give her a worried frown. "No, Marcus, I won't be quiet. Sal, I know what the shadow did to you better than anyone. And the way you finally dealt with it was wonderful. Now you need to deal with these new shadows.

"But that doesn't solve the immediate problem. If your flight to Paris and the reasons behind it were the only issue, I could gladly welcome you back and help in any way I can. But this casual fuck takes it to a whole different plane for me. I don't know what you were thinking, but it clearly wasn't about me or Marcus."

Her bitterness hit me like a wave, I couldn't remember her speaking to me this coldly. Marcus was uncomfortable about her combative style, but that was him, he hated conflict.

"I'm sorry," I said.

"Saying sorry is easy," she sneered. "But I've been betrayed before and it fucking hurts."

I hadn't expected her reaction; it truly shocked me, and I burst into tears again.

"This isn't getting us anywhere," Marcus said. "The question is, what do we want to do now?"

"What do you want to do?" Lucy said to him.

"Honestly, I want to return to some semblance of normality. This has hurt all three of us, but I think – I hope – we're strong enough to overcome it."

"You're happy Sally was unfaithful?"

"No, of course I'm not happy. I'm not sure how I feel." His face was etched with the pain of my betrayal. "But let's not be too hasty. Do you still love Sal?"

Lucy looked at me, and her face softened.

"Of course I do," she finally said.

"So do I," he said. "Sally, how do you feel?"

I looked at them both, Marcus weary and deflated, Lucy detached and hurting.

"I love you both," I said. "You know I do. I just don't know how to put any of this right."

Another heavy silence fell.

"Okay," Lucy finally said. "Have you been tested?"

"Yes," I replied. "But I'll need another in a couple of weeks to be sure."

"Right, you're not sleeping with me or Marcus until those results are back." I had to agree, but it sounded so cold. "In the meantime, we try and do what we can to work things out. I suggest you make an appointment with Jenny."

I was surprised by Lucy taking control, speaking for both of them. Then something struck me; she was talking as if we were an established threesome. It seemed it wasn't me and Marcus with Lucy slightly apart anymore. Things cleared in my head.

"Have you two been together while I've been away?" I asked.

"Yes, Sal," Marcus replied. "We've supported one another."

"And slept together?"

"Yes," Lucy snapped. "At least we've only fucked someone you know about."

Her words were like a kick in the stomach and were meant to be. I couldn't argue; she was right. We had a quiet dinner, and little was said through the evening. I already knew I'd be sleeping alone that night in the spare room but when we went downstairs, we headed for three separate rooms. As I lay in bed, I wondered how we were going to heal this.

I was home but uncomfortable there. I'd dreamed of Marcus and Lucy being confident enough to play without me, but not in these circumstances. Circumstances mainly of my own making. I was envious of their time together, jealous even. I needed to think about those feelings and that was going to be difficult.

Chapter 31 – Ensemble

Marcus

I was first to surface; I showered, dressed, and went upstairs. I wasn't looking forward to the day. Three people, all upset, hurting, and confused, whose emotions were close to the surface. Lucy had been bitter and angry, something I hadn't witnessed before.

I wasn't angry, just hurt. Hurt that Sally would take her problems away without talking to me. If she had wanted something from me, why couldn't she ask? She always had before. And I was unsure what to make of her infidelity.

That was what had hurt Lucy, and her reaction had shocked Sally. My feelings were more mixed. Sally and I had been faithful to each other, it was important to us. When Lucy had become involved, that trust had extended to her. Now, Sally had seemingly broken that compact quite easily, without a moment's thought. But I could only guess how she'd been feeling at the time.

Lucy wandered into the kitchen, gave me a quick kiss, and leaned against the worktop.

"Good, morning," she said. "Is Sally up yet?"

"I haven't seen her."

"Is it best if I go home?"

"No, stay. If we're going to sort this out, we need to do it together. The three of us. This relationship is complicated, and we all need to be in the discussions."

"Okay." She poured a cup of coffee and took a couple of sips. "Was I a bitch last night?"

"You made your feelings known."

"Meaning I was."

"I didn't say that. You're free to say what you want."

"But did I make things worse?"

"No, Lucy," Sally said, coming into the kitchen. "You didn't."

"Good morning," I said. "Coffee?"

Sally came over and took the cup from me.

"Thank you. You told me some home truths, Lucy. I've messed up, and I don't know how to put it right."

She walked out into the dining room, clearly holding back the tears. I grabbed some brioche and croissants, Lucy picked up the accompaniments, and we followed. Sally was sitting at the dining table, holding her coffee in both hands, gently rocking. She looked in pain. We sat around the table and spread the food out. None of us felt much like eating.

"Sal," Lucy said. "I'm sorry I was angry last night. It probably didn't help."

"It's alright," Sally replied. "I deserved it. I didn't know what to expect. Penny had a spare room ready in case you kicked me out."

"Sal, this is your house, I can't kick you out. I thought I might need to go."

"I heard what you were saying, and Marcus is right. We can't talk about this as two couples, it's way beyond that. Please stay and help me. Help us."

I put a couple of things on each of their plates, and they toyed with them.

"Eat," I said, taking a bite, though my appetite was no greater than theirs. "Eat." They tore small pieces off and tried them, each struggling to force them down. My first mouthfuls stimulated my hunger and I tucked in. Both looked at me in distaste, so I pushed the plate away.

"Right," I said. "Back to basics. We need to work out how we're going to work this out. Plan a plan. Any suggestions?" Blank expressions. "Okay, then I have one. But we all need to answer a question first. Honestly. Do we all want to try and rescue this relationship, or do we want to walk out now?"

The silence was deafening, and Sally looked terrified. I didn't prompt, didn't say any more. I wanted us all to think carefully. I already knew my answer and picked at my roll again. Lucy stared at Sally, then at me, then out of the window. Sally stared at her coffee. For once, I was glad of my patience. The minutes ticked by and the tension rose.

"I don't want to walk away," Lucy said finally, focussing on Sally. "Right now, I feel … disappointed, let down. But I've known you for so long, I know who you really are, and it isn't this."

"Sal?" I said.

"I want to get back to how we were. I wish I could go back and change the last few weeks."

"You can't Sal," I replied. "But we can try and put it in perspective."

"What about you?" Lucy asked me.

"I'm not going anywhere right now. Life was too good to throw it away without trying."

Sally was looking at me with a strained expression, a mixture of relief and anguish.

"You had a suggestion," Lucy said to me.

"Yes. I suggest we split this into two issues. The first is trying to help Sal deal with the shadow coming back, work out why it happened and why we weren't able to provide the support she needed."

"But we were struggling too," Lucy said.

"I know but bear with me. The second is Sally's little orgy. I suggest we leave that to one side for a while. After all, sex isn't on the agenda, so there's no rush."

Lucy

I wasn't sure about Marcus's idea. I'd been happy to help her overcome her fears again but finding out about her infidelity had crushed me. I could see she regretted it, and it was totally out of character for her. In the fifteen years I'd known her, I wasn't aware of her ever being unfaithful when she was with someone. That made it hurt even more.

I was beginning to understand she'd done it when she was overwhelmed. But that was an excuse, not a valid reason. She wasn't a young naïve girl; she rarely did anything like this on impulse. Perhaps the drink muddled her thinking, but I knew of old she rarely let it get that bad.

"Okay," I said, "but I don't want to exclude it for too long. It's important to me."

"Sal?"

She nodded silently.

"Right. Luce, I think it would be good if you stayed here for a while, so any conversations we have don't have to be repeated."

"Fine."

"And Sal, I suggest you go and see Mary."

She left after lunch and I felt a weight lift; the atmosphere wasn't exactly healthy. Marcus and I sat on the sofas, mentally exhausted. Part of me wanted a good fuck, but it seemed inappropriate.

"She's miserable, isn't she?" I said.

"Yes. I've never seen her this flat. There's no emotion."

"I know what you mean. I feel bad about what I said last night."

"You were angry and had every right to be."

"I know. What can we do?"

We spent an hour talking it over. I had begun to feel sorry for Sally. She was obviously hurting too.

"Everyone makes mistakes," Marcus said at one point.

"Fucking one guy when you're pissed could be counted as a mistake. But two together?"

We looked at each other and burst out laughing, the first time I'd laughed for more than twenty-four hours.

"Wonder if it lived up to her fantasy?" I asked.

"Perhaps we should ask her."

"Oh, God, no."

"It might clear the air a bit."

"Are you serious?"

"We'll see."

After six hours, Sally returned.

"Okay?" Marcus asked. "We were getting worried."

"Yes."

"Is Mary okay?"

"She gave me a good bollocking."

"No!" I said.

"Yup. You haven't seen Mary in that mood. She doesn't get angry; just makes you feel like a child again. When I told her what happened she told me in no uncertain terms all the things I was risking and how stupid I'd been. Then she gave me a big hug and told me to sort things out."

"And?"

"I went for a walk by the river to clear my head." That explained the late return. "I've spoken to Jenny and she's fitted me in tomorrow, and I'm going back to work to face whatever happens there." This was better; this was more like the Sally we knew. "And I understand what you suggested this morning, but I don't think we can separate these things. We need to deal with them all together."

"If you prefer."

"Well, my running away was bad enough, even though I kind of understand why I did it. But the … the other thing. That's inexcusable and I feel so ashamed. I'm sorry."

"You don't need to apologise again," Marcus said.

"Yes, she does," I said. "I'm still far from over that."

He shrugged and I instantly regretted my outburst. It was true I was still angry about it, but I would have been better staying quiet for the moment. Even so, Sally's change of mood lightened the evening and we managed to chat about inconsequential things before retiring to our separate rooms.

Marcus

Shadows of Silver was still riding high in the sales lists. Eva was pushing me to work on another two books from my back catalogue, but my heart wasn't in it. She knew Sally was back, but not the issues we were dealing with. I promised to send a couple to Eleanor and look at her thoughts when she'd been through them. We were approaching the Christmas period and Eva wanted me to do a few signings and appearances. Lucy and Sally thought I should do them, one of the first things they were united about.

Sally was seeing Jenny every two or three days, and it seemed to be working. She slowly opened up. The shadows were already gone. They were discussing why they had appeared, why she had her week of debauchery. The three of us were getting on in the flat. It was nothing like we were used to, but there were no arguments, and even the occasional smile or laugh.

At the end of her second week home, Sally was much brighter, and the awkwardness between us had largely gone. On Saturday we had dinner and settled down for the evening.

"I want to say something," Sally said. "You two can sleep together if you want, I don't want to stop you."

"Sal," I said, "I-"

"Marcus, please. When you told me you'd been together while I was away, I felt my first pang of jealousy. And that's not right; I'm working through that, too."

"I don't think it's a good idea," I said. "Luce?"

"I agree," Lucy replied, "though I confess I'd like to. You've only got yourself to blame for my interest in Marcus, Sal." Sally had the grace to smile. "But at the moment, it's likely to cause more problems."

"Okay," Sally replied. "But I wanted to tell you."

On Sunday, I packed for a few days away doing some signings.

"Right," I said. "Are you two going to be alright, or am I going to come home to blood on the carpet?"

"We'll be fine," Lucy replied.

I hoped so.

Chapter 32 – Lucy

Marcus's departure meant Sally and I were alone for the first time since she'd run away. Thankfully, I'd calmed down in the weeks that followed, and we were able to talk normally. My feelings for her were returning. I still loved this woman, even though she'd hurt me and made me question my trust in her. That would take time to heal.

I wondered how we would deal with our issues while Marcus was away. I didn't want to talk behind his back. I was coming to accept my feelings for him were almost as strong as those for Sally. It scared me and excited me in equal measure. Luckily, Sally pre-empted me.

"I don't think we should talk too much about our problems while Marcus is away," she said.

"I'm happy with that, Sal."

She paused.

"Do you love him?" she asked tentatively.

What was my answer? Did I? If I did, could I tell her before I told him? Did he already know?

"I think so," I finally replied.

"Good," she said and didn't mention it again.

When Marcus returned at the end of the week, he was exhausted. He always was after these mini-tours. Sally and I cooked dinner and he told us about his week. It appeared his popularity was growing.

"Did anyone mention the press stories?" I asked.

"Oh, yes."

"Really?" Sal said.

"Yes, several times at each event."

"Was it bad?"

"Not at all. Everyone sees it as a bit of a joke. Some quietly tell me they're members of a similar group, others tell me they wish they were. It's become something of an ice breaker."

"Perhaps you should start writing about it," I said.

"It's not a bad idea, but I'd be terrible at it."

"Never know until you try."

"Was Eva with you?" Sally asked.

"No, but she joined me at two signings. She sends her love."

"Have you two made up?" I asked, prompting a puzzled look from Sally. "They had something of a frosty relationship for a while," I told her.

"Yes," he replied. "We're back to normal."

"Meaning you're back to winding each other up and pretending you hate one another."

"Something like that. She's fed up."

"Oh, why?"

"She wants a new challenge. I think this episode where she had to toe the party line was something of a final straw."

"What does she want to do?"

"Heaven knows. It'll be something unpredictable, knowing her. Anyway, how were your weeks?"

Sally and I briefly recounted what we'd been up to.

"And have you got any further with us?" he asked.

"No, we deliberately didn't talk about it too much."

"You could have."

"Yea, but we didn't want to."

"I have one thing to tell you," Sally said, looking a bit sheepish. She went over to her bag and pulled out an envelope from which she took a sheet of paper, unfolded it, and laid it on the table.

"I'm clear," she said simply, sitting down again. I was silently relieved as, I suspected, was Marcus. But it brought the question of sex to the forefront of our minds, and we fell silent. Until now, Sally had been waiting on these results and Marcus and I had refrained from sleeping together. But we were all aware of the physicality of our previous relationship.

"What happens now?" Sally finally said. It was a good question. My anger had gone, replaced perhaps by a desire to put things behind us. The previous three weeks had re-affirmed my love for these two people, whatever their faults. Did they feel the same way?

"What do you want to happen?" Marcus asked.

"I want to get back to how we were. I know you don't trust me; I know I need to prove to you again you can. But I … I miss you both. I want you."

"Luce?" Marcus asked.

"I think it's time to try," I replied. "I won't deny I've missed it, more than I imagined. What about you?"

"Yes, it's been difficult. Living with you two, knowing the fun we could have had, but with this hanging over us."

"Well," I said. "We all want to, but it's a bit awkward to know how to begin."

"Not at all," Marcus said. We both looked at him. "Sally, fancy telling us all about your little dalliance?"

Her face instantly flushed, and her look of horror was a picture.

"What?" she squeaked.

"Well, it was always a fantasy of yours. Why don't you tell us all about it?"

She was still flushed, but a nervous smile spread across her face.

"You want to hear about it?"

"Yup. Every explicit detail."

I wasn't sure, but the idea amused me. She picked up her wine glass and drank the remaining contents, then began to haltingly tell the story, right from meeting these two guys at the drag club. But her confidence grew and by the time the story had moved to their flat, she was giving us the vivid details.

There were things she hadn't told us, principally that Noah and Leon were bi. That came as a surprise, as did her detailed account of what they did together. She shifted in her seat, and I realised why when I did the same and felt the warmth between my thighs.

By the time she finished the story, her face was even more flushed, and her voice a little husky. She slumped back in her chair and gave us a nervous smile.

"Was it as good as your fantasy?" Marcus asked.

"No," she replied instantly. "It was all a bit mechanical. I didn't have any connection with them."

"Sounds like the three of you had a lot of connections," I said.

"You know what I mean."

"Want to do it again?" he asked.

"This one's caused enough trouble."

He looked at me and raised an eyebrow, I nodded.

"Stand up, Sal," he said. Surprised, she rose from her chair. "Strip." She briefly hesitated, before taking her jumper off, then her bra. She looked at him then at me as she pushed her jeans off, and slipped her briefs down her legs, before nervously standing straight again.

"What do you think, Luce?" Marcus said to me. "Fancy showing this gorgeous creature what two lovers can really do?"

I didn't need to think about it. I wanted her … and him. I didn't answer, just stood and removed my clothes in a flash, before walking over to Sally where we fell into each other's arms.

She began to cry, hugging me tight, and her emotion infected me, as tears ran down my face. After a few moments, we pulled apart and kissed, a gentle beginning followed by a savage, ferocious exploration of each other.

We separated, and I nodded my head in Marcus's direction. We turned and walked to him, holding out our hands and he got to his feet. Between us, we stripped him, and the three of us hugged and it all got quite emotional. As our tears dried, our hands began to explore each other, intimately rediscovering curves and crevices.

Our need took over, and the first twenty minutes turned into a sinuous melee of intertwined bodies on the floor, our mouths and fingers molesting anything within reach. The first orgasm, as usual, was Sally's, as my tongue roughly forced its way into her wet flesh while I massaged her clit.

Her cries were muffled by Marcus's cock deep in her mouth, and his lips were rolling my clit across his teeth. I let him take me to my climax, his hands squeezing my bum as he buried his face between my legs. As my orgasm subsided, I knelt up, pulled Sally off his cock, and pushed her over the sofa.

"Fuck her," I said. "Fuck the little slut."

Sally let out a deep chuckle as Marcus knelt behind her, and gasped as he plunged into her. I got up on the sofa, and positioned my groin under her head, pushing her face onto my pussy. She put her arms around my thighs and enclosed me with her lips, as Marcus began to slowly fuck her. He leaned towards me and we kissed, exchanging a look that sent shivers through me. I knew at that moment I loved this man. This man fucking the woman I loved.

He was watching Sally eating me while playing with her clit. I knew he was waiting for me. He didn't have to wait long; I felt my second orgasm coming. Sally beat me to it, her climax soaring through her, but I held her face on me, and her moans became warm blasts of air on my sensitive flesh.

She took me to the peak, holding me there until I began to feel numb, then stopping. Marcus took that as his cue and Sal shrieked as he gripped her hips and slammed into her, pushing her body against me with each thrust.

She looked up at me, her eyes wide and her mouth hanging open as she dealt with the onslaught. Her eyes rolled back as another orgasm swept through her before he cried out and emptied himself into her. After several final lunges, he leaned over her, and swept her hair to one side, kissing her cheek. He lifted and gave me a kiss.

"Well, Luce," he said. "What do you think?"

"She'll do," I said. "Needs more training, though."

A deep chuckle came from the face still buried between my thighs. Sally lifted her head, her chin and mouth glistening with my moisture.

"When do lessons start?"

After we cleaned up, we lay together on the sofa, enjoying each other's warmth again. My anger with Sally had gone, replaced by a need for her smile and her soft skin. As I lay, cuddled into Marcus, with Sally laying half over us, I knew we'd be fine. Our relationship had changed. Perhaps the initial stage was over; we knew there would be hurdles to overcome. Perhaps it had matured. But we were going to be okay.

Nothing was said for some time. The occasional hand stroked a face, a thigh, or brushed through hair. A brief smile when eyes met, a slow kiss on warm skin. I couldn't help wondering if things would be different.

"Are we good, then?" I finally asked.

"I think so," Marcus replied.

"I hope so," Sally said. "I really want us to be."

He looked down at her. "I think this little minx will be on probation for a while."

She pouted at us.

"And if you need a few more men," I said, "let us know."

"Yea," Marcus replied. "I'm sure there's a local rugby team who could use some entertainment."

She slapped his leg.

"I'm not that bad." There was a pause and a wicked grin appeared on her face. "Besides, a rugby team's a few too many. Even for me."

Marcus gave her bum a hard slap; all she did was stick it out further.

"Are we making any changes?" I asked.

"In what way?"

"I don't know. Do we need to rethink anything?"

"There are one or two decisions we need to make," he said. "Not necessarily now."

"Such as?" Sally asked.

"Are we still going to be so public? Stay involved in the fetish group, for example?"

"I don't see why not," I replied.

"I'd like to," Sally said. "And now we know there are no more amateur photographers, it should be safe."

"Doesn't matter, does it?" Marcus said. "Everyone knows about us now."

"True," she replied, and we all grinned.

"Okay," I said. "What else?"

"Only one more I can think of," Marcus replied.

"What?" Sally asked.

"It's the big one."

She looked at me, but I was as mystified as she was.

"What?" she repeated.

He looked at her, then me, then back at her.

"Would life be better if we all lived together?" I froze. The idea had crossed my mind a few times since we'd all been involved, but it never occurred to me it might happen. "I don't know if or how it would work. I need you two to be honest again."

Sally was smiling at me, that delicious, warm, inviting smile. I couldn't resist smiling back.

"Well," she said. "What do you think?"

"I don't know," I replied. "Can three people live together successfully?"

"Do you want to?"

I looked at them, their faces open and curious.

"I ... I like the idea, but this is your home, you're the couple and I'm ... well ..."

"Lucy," Marcus said. "Before all this, you were spending every weekend here, and Sally was staying with you at least one night during the week. Seems to me everything will be easier if we're under the same roof. We can work out the practicalities if it's what we all want to do."

I looked at Sally, her expression showing she was clearly in favour of the idea. I wanted to; my whole being wanted to do this. It was unusual, unconventional, and thrilling.

"Oh, by the way, Luce," Sal said. "Weren't you going to tell Marcus something?"

I scowled at her, knowing exactly what she meant, but I'd been unsure how to tell him or how it would be received. But the courage came.

"Well," I replied, "as it has some bearing on the subject under discussion, yes." I looked straight at him, seeing the warmth and peace behind his eyes but I found it difficult to say the words, even though I wanted to. "I love you."

His gaze held my own for a second or two before a smile slowly spread across his face. He leaned towards me and gently kissed my lips.

"And I love you, too," he said. It was my turn to cry, and the tears streamed down my face. Sally sat up and they held me, caressing and stroking me. The tension of the last few weeks poured out; the fear, the hurt, the bewilderment. All draining away, replaced by love. Love for these two wonderful, beautiful, flawed people. Love they freely returned.

As my tears ceased, Sally handed me a tissue and I wiped my eyes.

"Moving in, then?" she asked. "A trial period, if you like."

I nodded.

"Yes. Yes, please."

Marcus gently eased apart from us and wandered into the kitchen.

"What's he doing?" I asked.

"No idea," she said. "You know Marcus."

He returned with a bottle of champagne and three glasses, filled them, and handed us one each.

"To us," he said.

"To the future," Sally said.

"To love," I replied.

When we'd emptied our glasses, he turned to me, a look of pure mischief on his face.

"Right, Luce," he said. "Ready to start retraining this loose harlot?"

Epilogue – Sally

Nearly a year has passed since our lives were splashed all over the papers. It's an episode I'll never forget, though its lasting effects have been quite different than we'd feared. Marcus and Lucy still rib me about my adventures in Paris, but we've had plenty of adventures of our own since then.

We all knew within a few days that Lucy was staying. We had to make a few adjustments to our lives and to the flat to ensure everyone felt included. We invested in a huge custom-made bed, I gave up some wardrobe space and we found room for everything she wanted to bring from her old home. It turned out to be unnecessary, as everything has changed beyond recognition in the last nine months.

We sat down and reviewed our lives, deciding what we wanted for the future, and the result surprised us all. Lucy and I gave up our full-time jobs. I still work as a consultant to the library archive, but only work about seven hours a week during term time, and I do some freelance research if I feel like it.

Lucy quit completely. She now devotes her time to art; both her own, which is developing a strong niche market, and writing about art in various places.

Marcus's success continues, and he's even roped us in. He convinced us to try writing a book inspired by some of our adventures, with me contributing most of the words and Luce doing some provocative illustrations. It's proving great fun, but we don't know if anything will come of it.

When we mentioned it to Eva, she was intrigued and is going to try publishing it privately. We've had one or two conversations about investment to help her set up as an indie publisher. We're still talking, and Marcus hasn't agreed a new contract yet, in case he can become her first signed author.

And now, we're in the process of moving again. Marcus and I were always conscious the flat had been ours, and Lucy might never feel totally at home, although she always dismissed the idea. Then one day, Marcus came home with that gleam in his eye.

"I'm taking you to see a house," he said.

"A house?" Lucy said. "Why?"

"Trust me, come and see it."

He drove us up the hill to the north of the city and near the top, he turned into a driveway overgrown with hanging tree branches and much in need of maintenance. I thought he was mad. Until I saw the house.

A Victorian mansion on a grand scale, also in need of maintenance. Perfectly proportioned, sitting squarely in a large garden, with some outbuildings and a crumbling orangery. Marcus silently followed Lucy and me as we wandered from room to room.

The place was in a dilapidated state, but its potential shone through. It had originally been two houses, but they'd been amalgamated a long time ago. It needed a complete renovation, but it was beautiful.

"Well?" Marcus said as we arrived back in the entrance hall.

"It's in a state," Lucy replied.

"It's huge," I said.

"Yes, yes, yes, forget all that. What do you think?"

Lucy turned to me, grinning.

"It's magnificent."

"Sure is," I replied.

We drove home buzzing. We got a survey. We talked to the agent. We bought it. We contacted Clive, the project manager who'd worked on our current flat, and set him to work. Now, after six months, we're moving in. But there was to be one further major change of plan.

We saw Helen and Penny often. I will always be grateful to Helen for coming to rescue me, and we were close to them both. A couple of months later, they were having dinner with us and told us they'd given up the idea of finding any sort of replacement for the wretched Ben.

"We didn't expect to find anyone suitable," Helen said.

"How are you coping without one?" I replied.

"Oh, I'm fine. But this one here's missing a good seeing to from time to time." Penny blushed beautifully. "It's a shame about what happened because I had an idea I was going to run by you."

"What was that?" I asked, though I had a suspicion.

"Oh, I don't know it's appropriate any longer. It depends how the three of you are now."

"We're fine, Helen," Lucy said. "Even better than before."

Helen looked closely at each of us, then turned to Penny, who smiled and looked down.

"I had wondered," Helen said, studying the glass in her hand, "if you might be interested in keeping Penny happy once in a while."

"You mean Marcus," I said, already seeing a grin on Lucy's face.

"Specifically, yes," she replied. "But the suggestion includes all of you. Her experiences at the fort certainly seemed satisfying. However, I wouldn't want it to cause problems."

"Well, Penny?" I said. "Would that scratch an itch?"

"Yes," she replied quietly, looking deliciously embarrassed.

"Darling? What about it?"

"I don't know," he said. "It's a big change to *your* relationship, isn't it, Helen?"

She and Penny told us they'd ripped up their old contract, and had a new agreement which was more equal, with certain exceptions which were left to our imagination. It turned out it suited them both.

"Well, then," Marcus said. "I have a counter-proposal. There may be an opportunity for mutual benefit, Helen."

"Oh?" she replied.

"I'm happy to entertain Penny; we all are. But I wonder if you might like to take on these two."

I looked at Lucy, her mouth hanging open, staring back at me in amazement.

"What?" I said.

"Well, Sal," he replied. "Are you telling me you've never thought about Helen topping you?"

"Well … I …"

He knew damn well I had, as had Lucy. We'd talked about it several times.

"And," he continued, "I'm quite sure Helen's thought about it, too."

Penny was grinning and looking at her mistress, who had an amused expression on her face.

"It had crossed my mind," Helen conceded.

"And Lucy may be a bit of a switch," he added. "You might teach her some of your skills."

Lucy was moving her head between me, Marcus and Helen, the stunned look still on her face. Finally, she held my gaze.

"He's pimping us both, now," she said, and we burst out laughing.

But the idea was too good to ignore and we soon came to an arrangement. Penny joins the three of us every few weeks for some fun. And occasionally, she spends a night with Marcus, while Lucy and I go in the other direction and spend a night with Helen, who is introducing us to a different dynamic and new techniques. Lucy is indeed something of a switch and is becoming quite skilled; when she's not on the receiving end as well, that is.

Marcus is more than happy to watch us exhibiting our new skills when we get home. Before joining in, of course. He and Penny seem to enjoy their time together. They have a soft spot for each other but, thankfully, neither we nor Helen feel threatened by it.

After we bought the house, we soon found we'd given ourselves a problem. Even with three of us, it was huge with far too many rooms. We took Helen and Penny to see it, and they fell in love with it. Within a couple of weeks, it was agreed they'd live there as well. It surprised us all but seemed totally natural.

We re-designed it, splitting it in two again, though we made sure there were a couple of well-concealed connecting doors. The orangery has been re-built with a part of it re-modelled into two studios: one for Lucy, one for Helen. One of the outbuildings has been turned into office space, principally for Penny and her web design business.

We've also put Matt and Yas to work again, constructing a new playroom in the cellars like our existing one, only larger and more atmospheric, more like a dungeon. Helen and Penny are also having them build something to their requirements, altogether more chic and modern.

Today is our housewarming. Something none of us would have done years ago; we're all too private. But the last year has shown us what life is about: love, friends, and support. And we have all those things in droves, so we've invited everyone who's been there for us.

Helen and Penny, of course. They are a part of our family now, and one or two of their friends are here. Mary, who's been the one rock throughout my life, and Ken. They still claim to live separately, but I doubt they ever spent a night apart.

Ruth, who's accepted her daughter's relationship with Marcus and me in her own way. She still doesn't understand it but is revelling in her new life with her family and friends. And Annie and Tim, with Sarah and Nathan.

The other part of our family is also here. It brought a tear to my eyes when Genevieve and Jacques arrived yesterday. Quite what the response will be when someone asks who they are, I'm not sure. But I *am* sure Genevieve will have an appropriate answer.

Eva also arrived yesterday and has become another constant in our lives. She's with Anders, who she met at the fetish group. He's a lovely Dutch guy; handsome, funny, and rather shy. Their surprisingly tender relationship is sweet to watch.

Matt and Yas are here, along with Sophia and several others from the group where we've been able to spread our wings and learn so much about ourselves.

Some of our old colleagues from the university are also here, but we've been selective in who we invite today because it isn't just a housewarming.

As I wander around the garden, chatting and laughing with all these people, I can't help wondering how I could be so blessed. My life is like a dream, and I hope I never wake from it. I spent fifteen years denying part of myself, part of my story. Now, I can be open and accept it. And be open about other aspects of my life; aspects I didn't even know existed.

Sally

The sound of a soft bell drifts through the garden. A steady, insistent, rhythmic sound. People fall silent one by one and turn to the sound, puzzled. It's coming from a decorated wooden arbour in the centre of the lawn, where Penny is ringing the bell, with Helen standing by her. It's time for our little surprise.

The guests are wondering what is going on, as Marcus, Lucy and I head towards the arbour. When we arrive, he turns to them, and Penny puts the bell down.

"Friends," Marcus says. "We're truly delighted you're all here with us today. You're all so important to us, and we can't thank you enough for your friendship and support, particularly over the last year.

"We hope you'll all visit us in our new home for years to come, but we also want you to act as witnesses." A rustle of anticipation flows through the crowd, who slowly edge nearer. "Most, if not all of you, know of our relationship," he continues, taking Lucy and me by the hand on either side, "and we'd like you to share in a moment of love, as we three commit our lives to each other."

There's a murmur of excitement among the guests now, and they surround the arbour, smiling and whispering. Marcus, Lucy, and I turn to face each other in a circle and join our hands in the middle. Helen takes a long ribbon and wraps it around them. Penny passes her a second and she lays it over the first, followed by a third.

I look at my lovers, both beaming with joy, and know my own face is set in a similar expression. As Helen steps back, we are left tied together in the silence. Marcus is the first to speak.

"I take you as my companions in life. I will honour, respect, and support you throughout our lives together. I promise to stand by you and encourage your unique talents and abilities, so we may accomplish more than we could alone. I promise to be sensitive and respectful of your needs and wishes. I promise to make you the priorities in my life. I will love you always."

I feel myself welling up, but take a deep breath to steady my nerves, smile at my partners and repeat the vow. The words fill me with warmth, and my confidence grows as I say them. When I finish, Lucy repeats the vow for the third time. We're in our own world, our guests momentarily forgotten.

Helen gently undoes the outermost ribbon and ties it loosely around my wrist, then the second around Lucy's and the final one around

266

Marcus's. Penny holds a small cushion in front of us holding three identical rings. Lucy and I pick one up, and together slip it onto Marcus's finger as we speak in unison.

"This ring is a symbol of our commitment today."

Marcus and Lucy pick a second ring and repeat the phrase as they slip it onto my finger, and finally, Marcus and I repeat the vow to Lucy. There is a pause, as we look at each other, basking in the moment. We're brought back to the present by Helen's voice.

"I believe it's now traditional for the groom to kiss the bride," she says. "But in this situation, I'll leave you to work that one out for yourselves."

It relieves the tension, and the guests laugh and relax, as the three of us hug and kiss. Some applause breaks out, and soon all the guests are clapping and cheering, and we turn to look out at them. A few tears are being shed, and the love and warmth are almost overwhelming.

When Marcus and I first got together, he introduced me to the notion of quiet companionship. We *were* quiet companions. But as Lucy found out about our more interesting activities and began to share them, she suggested something more appropriate.

We're kinky companions.

And proud of it.

* * * * * *

The End.

Author's Note

I would like to thank all those involved in helping me bring this story to the page. You know who you are, and I will be eternally grateful.

If you've enjoyed this book, please think about leaving a review, either on the marketplace where you bought it or on one of the many book review sites, such as Goodreads. Reviews are helpful for other readers (and authors, as well!).

To keep in touch with my writing, you can visit my website, where you can subscribe to my bi-monthly newsletter and blog or follow me on social media.

Website: www.alexmarkson.com
Twitter: @amarksonerotica
Facebook: @amarksonerotica
Goodreads: Alex Markson

Alex Markson
December 2020

Printed in Great Britain
by Amazon